Death
Duties

Death Duties

A Rose Bennett Mystery

MARIAH KINGDOM

~ Perceda Press ~

First published in digital form 2017 by WL Fowler

Copyright © Mariah Kingdom 2020

This paperback edition Perceda Press 2020

ISBN 978-1-8380834-2-7

Cover design by www.ebooklaunch.com

Some people, eager for money, have wandered from the faith and pierced themselves with many griefs

Timothy 6:10

1

Alice Blacklaws took in a measured breath, and tried to calmly visualise the scene to come.

She could see the charming parish church of St Benedict on the Hill, nestled on the very outer perimeter of Kirkby, with its foreground of Norman architecture and its bucolic backdrop of rolling English countryside. She could imagine Nathan standing patiently at the altar, the congregation behind him chattering excitedly, anticipating the start of the ceremony. And she could see herself arriving on cue, fashionably a few minutes late, cameras snapping as she paused outside the kissing gate to smooth out the skirt of her dress. Somewhere behind her, bridesmaids were alighting from a vintage Rolls Royce and taking up their positions, ready to follow in her wake as she stepped forward to join Nathan at the altar.

So far so good.

The measured breath escaped her lips in an involuntary sigh, and she opened her eyes to glance down at the sheath of exquisite raw ivory silk wrapped around her body, the beaded strapless bodice tight against her lightly tanned skin. She lifted her left hand and looked at it. It looked like someone else's hand, the long fingers tapered into false talons, French-manicured claws to hide the evidence of weeks of nervous chewing at her fingernails. She lifted her gaze back to the mirror and took in the artfully-styled blonde chignon pinned at her neck, the faint blush in her cheeks, the unmistakable sadness in her eyes.

Once inside the church, in front of God, the Reverend James Griffin, and a congregation made up mostly of people she didn't know, she and Nathan would take their vows. They would take each other's right hand and promise, that from this day forward, for better for worse, for richer for poorer, in sickness and in health, they would love and cherish each other for the rest of their lives. The Reverend Griffin was going to turn to her and ask "will you, Alice Blacklaws, take Nathan Robert Kingsley to be your husband?" And Alice would smile, first at the Reverend Griffin, then at the photographer standing to the right of the altar, and only then – just as she had been coached – at Nathan, and she would say "yes".

Yes, she would.

She forced her lips into an upward curve to banish the sadness, and the mirror reflected an awkward, uncertain smile back at her. The knot in her stomach tightened again and she blew out a breath to ease the tension. She loved Nathan. Of course she loved him. And she wanted to marry him. They were two halves of the same whole.

She may have only known him for a little over eight months, but in those months he had changed her life beyond all recognition. She had moved from her damp, depressing council flat to Nathan's elegant Georgian townhouse, taken a role as his personal assistant, and swapped the lamentable unreliability of the local bus service for the leather-lined comfort of a convertible BMW. But the material comforts that he provided were nothing compared with the bond, that feeling of utter conviction that each wanted the same from life as the other, that each had the other's back, an instinctive kind of trust.

Why is there nothing in God's marriage vows about trust?

She turned her head away from the mirror and glanced through the dressing room's open door. In the bedroom

Vienna Fielding, uncharacteristically elegant in pale lilac silk, her wayward black curls almost tamed into a braid at the back of her head, was on her knees beside a small, rosy cherub of a child. The child, Olivia, pouted and tried to draw back as Vienna worked to pin a soft pink rosebud to the bodice of her dress, and Alice felt a less reluctant smile creep across her lips as she watched the stand-off between her only child and her oldest friend.

For Olivia, then.

Those were the words that Nathan always used to cajole her into choices she didn't really want to make. For Olivia she would put aside her doubts. For Olivia's benefit, for the warm, comfortable home that Nathan provided, she would trust in the outcome. For the money to send her to a good school, to give her a better start in life than her own, for this she would lay aside her fears, smile at the cameras, make her vows.

For God's sake Alice, stop being so bloody neurotic. Nathan loves you, and Olivia needs this. For God's sake, just get on with it.

Just get on with it? Easy to say, but not so easy to do. She had trusted once before, and knew where that had taken her. She cast another glance at Olivia, that beautiful, innocent result of misplaced trust. She had to keep Olivia safe. Nathan loved them both, deep in her heart she knew it to be true. And yet something had changed. Nathan had changed, and she didn't know why.

The familiar knot of tension began to build again in her stomach. Not much more than an hour now before the ceremony would start, an hour in which she and Nathan would make the final preparations for their wedding and take their own separate journeys to the church of St Benedict on the Hill, to be joined as man and wife. She wanted so much to believe that everything would be alright. It would be a blessing to know that her fears were unfounded, that she was wrong to mistrust. She closed her eyes once more and took in a deep, decisive breath.

In less than an hour, she was going to marry Nathan. And

everything was going to be alright.

'Oh Rose, why didn't you tell me sooner?' Lu Aylesbury's voice bristled at the end of the line, her tone an incongruent mix of sympathy for her niece, annoyance at being out of the loop, and just that added hint of triumph that she may have been right about the situation.

Rose inhaled a deep breath and sank back into the folds of the armchair. She tucked her mobile phone under her chin and folded her arms across her body, hugging herself in a small, subconscious act of self-defence against the barrage of questions to come. 'I don't know. Maybe because I didn't want to hear you say "I told you so". I know you didn't like him.'

'I have never said that I didn't like him. I said I didn't think he was right for you. There's a difference.'

Difference or not, it was a bit of a moot point now. It had been almost six weeks since Mike had reluctantly packed his bags and moved out of Rose's cottage. He hadn't had the grace to look hurt, only aggravated at the inconvenience of having to find somewhere else to live. She brushed the thought away. 'Well, whatever … you were right, and I was wrong.' She held back from adding the word "again".

'Is it safe for me to ask what happened, or is it still too raw to talk about?'

Was it raw? Rose was lonely, yes. And tired from working long hours to avoid sitting around moping in an empty house. But raw? That implied pain, grief, sorrow. 'I don't think it was ever raw. It was just miserable. I came home from work on the Friday evening and he had brought the girls to stay for the weekend without telling me. I found them in our bedroom, playing fashion shows with the contents of my wardrobe and jewellery box. Alexa was practicing her make-up artistry on Adriana with my collection of Chanel lipsticks.'

'What on earth was he thinking of?'

'Himself, as usual. He was holed up in the kitchen working on a brief that had to be finished before the weekend. He just left them to their own devices.' Rose closed her eyes and flinched at the memory. 'I can tell you now that it's impossible to get kohl eyeliner out of crepe de Chine.'

Lu's throaty laugh at the end of the line was less than sympathetic. 'And that was it? You asked him to move out because his daughters spoiled your blouse? Couldn't you just ask him to buy you another?'

'No, that wasn't it. It was the bit that came after that. The bit where I mentioned the words "boundaries" and "responsibilities". Swiftly followed by the bit where he told me that I was a useless stepmother and that I should learn to be more tolerant.' Rose sighed. 'He's right, of course. So what could I do but agree with him?' Despite her lingering anger she felt her lips begin to twitch with a smile. 'He didn't look quite so sure of himself when I said it wouldn't be a problem once he'd moved out.'

Lu gave a quiet whistle at the end of the line. 'You actually asked him to leave? What did he say?'

'Ah, that was probably his biggest mistake. He laughed. He thought I was joking. In fact, I don't really think it hit home at all until he came up to the bedroom to ask if I wanted a coffee, and found me packing his clothes into a suitcase.'

'Did he go quietly?'

'With the unmistakable aroma of burning martyr. He called the next day, of course, and frantically tried to back-pedal. But by then I'd realised that he was right. I *was* a useless stepmother. I'm just not cut out for it, Lu. Hell, I'm too self-contained even to let in the people I love. Bonding with another woman's children was never going to happen.'

'It might have done, if they'd been the right children.'

'And if he'd been the right man.' Rose let out a sigh. 'I

hope you're not going to start again with that whole "if you'd listened to me in the first place" thing.'

'No, of course not. But I always felt that he was using you.'

'Well, maybe he was. And maybe I was using him. People do use each other. But we weren't right together, Lu. You saw that long before I did. I think when I met Mike I was tired of being on my own, but perhaps for me being alone is better than being with the wrong person.'

Lu was silent for a moment. Then she said 'you don't have to be alone just because you're not in a relationship, Rose. Why didn't you accept Benny's invitation?'

'To Nathan Kingsley's wedding? That's today, isn't it?' Rose thought for a moment. The invitation had come out of the blue, and had carried with it a good deal of temptation. Benny Bradman was a turf accountant, an unlikely friend for her Aunt Lu, and he and Rose had crossed paths more than once in the last twelve months. He could be good company, and the opportunity to attend a summer wedding with him had been difficult to turn down. She knew it would have lifted her spirits. But Rose hadn't quite done with self-pity, and melancholy had won out. 'I know Benny just needed a plus-one, I just didn't think I'd be very good company for him. And the last thing a couple of newly-weds need at their wedding is a newly-single cynic. I might have decided to drown my sorrows on the toasting wine and made an exhibition of myself.'

'Benny would have enjoyed that. He's always saying that you're too uptight for your own good.' Lu laughed, and then her voice softened at the end of the line. 'Rose, would you like to come with us? To Naples? We don't fly until the morning. I could call the hotel and see if there's a room, and I'm sure we could get you a flight. Gerry won't mind, and the change will do you good. You shouldn't be on your own at a time like this.'

'Really, Lu, I'm fine. I've got an assignment to finish

for the ENB next week, down at the London office. Then I might take off for a few days on my own.'

'If you want the keys to my place, I can leave them with a neighbour. You know you can stay here any time.'

'At the risk of sounding ungracious, I was thinking of somewhere a bit more exotic than Market Melbourne. Maybe a spa break. Or a Greek island. Or better still, a spa break *on* a Greek island. I think it's time for some serious self-indulgence.'

'Well, I can't argue with that. This time tomorrow I will be languishing by a pool with nothing more taxing to think about than what flavour of gelato to try next.'

'If I know you, by this time tomorrow you'll be fretting by the pool and worrying that the dog will be alright while you're away.' Rose frowned to herself. 'Where are you leaving Mac, by the way? You're not putting him into kennels again? He hated it the last time.'

'Oh good heavens, no. Mac is going to be in safe hands, and he's probably going to be spoiled rotten. If anything, the challenge is going to be enticing him to come home again when I get back.'

The gravel was sharp beneath his knees, and he could feel it cutting through the fine woollen cloth of his trousers. Nathan was a dead weight in his arms, the body heavy in his grasp, the head lolling forward towards the ground. Blood was dripping steadily onto the path, staining the dusty white aggregate. Somewhere behind him, on the steps of the hotel entrance, a woman was screaming.

Luke Kingsley looked down at the silent, lifeless body of his older brother, and tried to work out where the blood was coming from. He couldn't see Nathan's face, couldn't know just then that the blood was oozing from a small, precise hole right between Nathan's eyes.

He felt numb, but the feeling didn't last more than a few seconds. A seething, burning mass of raw emotion was building in the pit of his stomach, fear and panic and blind rage all beginning to fight for supremacy. The weight of Nathan's body was dragging them both closer to the ground, and he fought to stay upright. *He mustn't let go, he mustn't let Nathan fall to the floor.* A sob began to rise in his chest and he swallowed it back, but he couldn't stop the tears from flooding down his cheeks. He squeezed his eyes tight shut and let the sob out silently, his body folding forward over his brother, his arms still frozen to the corpse, his muscles clenched in a spasm of shock.

A hint of something sweet and sickly, a cheap and cloying perfume, wafted into his nostrils and he felt the presence of another body behind him. A mature but manicured hand settled on his right shoulder, another followed to his left, a woman's head bent close to his. 'Put him down, lovey.' She whispered gently into his ear. 'Put him down, and let him lie still.'

He felt her hands work their way gently from his shoulders down across his chest, until her arms enveloped him in a firm, matronly grip. Her voice was mature and kind. 'Gently, lovey, let him slide to the floor. He can't feel it.' More quietly still, she said 'I've got you, sweetheart, it's alright. You can let him go now. The police are coming.'

He slowly turned a tearful face to look at her. 'He's my brother.' His vocal chords were tight with shock, and the words came out like a strangled squeak.

'I know he is, lovey.' Her eyes were warm and gentle. 'I know he's your brother. You're Luke. And he's Nathan.' She lifted a hand from his shoulder and stroked his cheek. 'Don't you remember me, Luke? I'm Patricia. I'm Patricia, from the hotel.' She lowered her body onto the ground beside him, resting her weight on her hip, her arms still wrapped around his chest. 'We're going to sit here and wait with him, Luke. We're going to wait until the police come.'

'The police? Why are the police coming?'

The woman paused, uncertain how to answer.

'Someone shot him, Luke. From over there in the garden.' She nodded across an immaculate flower bed to a row of tall yew trees that formed a tight hedge along the hotel's perimeter fence.

'Did you see?'

'No, I didn't see ... I saw ... the back of someone running away along the hedge.' She winced. She'd said too much. She stroked his face again. 'Never mind that now.'

Another surge of fear whipped through his body. 'Someone killed Nathan? Why would anyone want to kill Nathan?' His eyes dropped to the body in his arms.

She leaned into him and tightened her grasp around his chest. 'I don't know, sweetheart.' She jerked his body gently to get his attention. 'Look at me, Luke. Don't look at Nathan. Keep your eyes on me.'

He heard her words, and he knew why she'd spoken them, but somehow he just couldn't do as she asked. He loosened his grip on Nathan's body and let it slide to the ground, and then lowered his eyes to look down at the blood splattered face. 'It's Nathan's wedding day today. Nathan is marrying Alice.'

Patricia closed her eyes and took in a steadying breath. 'Not today, Luke. Nathan isn't marrying anyone today.'

2

Detective Inspector George Mulligan looked about him for something to sit on, a stool or a chair that he could place in front of Alice, so that he could look directly into her face. There was a small piano stool against the wall and he lifted it into the middle of the room, setting it down in front of her before lowering his bulk on to it.

She was a pretty thing, Alice Blacklaws. Beautiful really, he mused. Wisps of honey-blonde hair had escaped from a knot at the back of her head and they rested against her faintly tanned cheeks. Her eyes, blue and limpid, were watching him patiently, expectantly, waiting for answers. If she had been crying, then all trace of tears had been wiped from her face.

He was thankful that he didn't have to break the news to her. Another officer had already done that. But still, interviewing a bride on her wedding day, probing for information about who might have wanted to murder her groom just minutes before the ceremony ... well, it was up there, wasn't it? High up on the list of why he should have listened to Mrs Mulligan and taken early retirement when he had the opportunity.

Alice was sitting in the centre of a large, cream Chesterfield sofa. Her slim body, divested of the raw ivory silk, was now cocooned in a fluffy pink dressing gown, her gentle face oddly calm and composed amidst the unfolding horror of the afternoon. To her left, WPC Anna Hill, aware that her role was to comfort the grieving girl, appeared unsettled by Alice's unnatural composure, unsure of what comfort she could offer. Mulligan nodded at Anna and she responded with a shrug, and an expression of mild relief at the appearance of a senior officer.

To Alice's right another young woman was leaning in to the pink dressing gown, Alice's right hand clasped tightly in both of her own. She was dressed in lilac silk, a bridesmaid's dress, her raven curls pinned behind her head with a large, gold-coloured clasp, and she was watching him carefully through long, dark lashes. She looked familiar, but his head was full of the moment, no space to recall forgotten names or faces.

He cleared his throat and leaned forward on the piano stool, resting his forearms on his knees, and looked directly into Alice's eyes. 'I'm very sorry for your loss, Alice. There are no words to comfort at a time like this.' He looked at Anna Hill for encouragement and was rewarded with a faint smile. 'I understand that my colleague Anna has told you about Nathan?'

Alice gave a gentle nod. 'He's dead.'

'Yes, I'm afraid he's dead.' He sucked in a breath. 'I don't have the details yet, but I understand that it was all very quick.' He cast his eyes down to his knees, unsure how to proceed, and then looked back at her. 'I know this is very difficult, but I have to ask you if Nathan had any enemies, anyone who would want to hurt him?'

'Hurt him?' Her face expressed a mild confusion. 'Why would anyone want to hurt him?' The confusion developed into a frown. 'I thought it was an accident.'

Mulligan bit his lip. 'We're not sure yet, Alice. You see, Nathan was shot outside the Kirkby Manor Hotel. He was leaving the building with his brother, and someone in the hotel grounds fired a gun. The bullet hit Nathan. It was all very quick.'

The dark-haired girl beside Alice leaned forward and

fixed him with questioning, intelligent eyes. 'Are you saying that someone deliberately shot Nathan, shot to kill him?'

'We don't know. But we have to consider every possibility. The man who fired the shot escaped through the hotel grounds. We need to find him as quickly as we can. Anything you can tell us ...'

'No one would want to hurt Nathan, Inspector. He didn't have enemies, only friends.' Alice's voice was as gentle as her eyes. She thought for a moment, and then asked 'Where is Luke?'

'Luke? Nathan's brother? I believe he's still at the hotel. He's helping my colleagues to understand exactly what happened.'

'Was he hurt?'

'I don't believe so.'

'When you see him, please tell him that I'm sorry.' For a moment it looked as though Alice's composure would finally crack. 'Tell him I'm sorry that he's alone, and to come and see us when he can.'

Sorry that he's alone? Mulligan parked the phrase away for future consideration, and pushed himself up from the piano stool. 'If you think of anything, Alice, day or night, please call me. Anna has the number.' He nodded again at Anna Hill, and then turned to smile at the dark-haired girl. 'Would you mind showing me out?'

He sensed a momentary hesitation, and then she let go of Alice's hand and rose to her feet. She followed him out into the hallway and closed the door gently behind her. He waited until they had reached the front door, and then turned to speak. 'Have we met before?'

Despite the solemnity of the occasion a faint smile played across around her lips. 'You're not used to seeing me dressed like this, Inspector. You're used to seeing me behind a bar.'

He blinked at her for a moment, each flick of the eyelids recalling a memory, seeing her in jeans and a plain black t-shirt, mopping beer from a counter, leaning towards another customer, laughing and joking with him. The penny dropped and he returned her smile. 'It's Vienna, isn't it? Vienna Fielding?'

She bowed her head a little. 'That's right. I work at The Feathers, in Market Melbourne.'

'Of course you do. You're Michael Spivey's young woman.' He shot her a conspiratorial glance. 'I've heard on the grapevine that Mr Spivey has cleaned up his act since you came into his life.'

Her face softened, and the smile broke free. 'He's alright, Michael. He just needed someone to love him.'

Someone to love him? It took one hell of a woman, he thought, to love a hapless little weasel like Michael Spivey, an inveterate petty criminal whose only saving grace was the utter ineptitude he displayed in any criminal endeavour he undertook. He kept the thought to himself. 'And now he has you. Well, he's a lucky man, Vienna.' He put a hand up to the door latch, preparing to leave, and then turned again and said 'Alice needs someone to love her now. She's going to find this tough. Does she have any family?'

Vienna frowned. 'Only Olivia. That's her daughter. Michael's taken her to stay with my sister. We thought it best.' Her voice trailed off for a moment, and then she added 'She isn't Nathan's. Nathan's daughter, I mean.' As if it needed explaining.

'What about her parents, or a sibling? Someone to stay with her?'

'I'll stay with her. There isn't anyone else. She's an only child, and she hasn't seen her parents since Olivia was born.' She sighed. 'Nathan's parents are dead. And Luke ...' Her eyes met Mulligan's, and she fell silent.

'And Luke?'

'Nothing.' The dark eyes turned down towards the floor.

Mulligan knew better than to push. 'I'll be back to see her tomorrow. If there's anything I need to know before then, Anna Hill knows where to reach me.' He pulled on the latch and started to open the door.

'Inspector Mulligan? When will they let Alice see him? She needs to say goodbye.'

It was the question he'd been dreading. 'Not just yet. When the time is right?' He looked back at her face and could see that she understood. 'I know it's only words, Vienna, but tell her I'll do everything I can. Tell her that I'll get the bastard who did this.'

It was around five thirty when Jack Canning pulled the silver Ford Fiesta into a lay-by, parking it up about fifty yards from the entrance. The lay-by had originally formed part of the old Great North Road, an inconvenient bend on an otherwise straight stretch of trunk road. Now it was an unkempt diversion, the aging tarmac pot-holed and uneven, the verges littered with beer cans and empty burger boxes. A hedge of wild elder provided some useful screening from the main road, and Jack felt safe enough to pull a mobile phone from the glove compartment and dial a familiar number.

'Larry? It's Jack.'

'I heard the news. It's been on the radio.' The voice at the other end of the line sounded satisfied. 'Nice job, Jack.'

Jack Canning grunted. He'd heard the news reports himself on the car radio, regular bulletins announcing the brutal murder of Nathan Kingsley. His eyes narrowed. Not a good way to end your career, he thought, snuffing out a young bloke just minutes before his wedding vows.

He turned his attention to practicalities. 'When do I get the money?'

'It's on its way to your place now. I've sent it the usual way.'

'Thanks.' There was a long pause before Jack spoke again. 'Larry?'

'Yes?'

'Why *Nathan* Kingsley?'

The voice on the end of the line puffed out an impatient breath. 'No questions, Jack. That's the way we've always done business. I place the order, you deal with the delivery, I pay the bill. Best all round.' There was a loud click as Larry disconnected the call.

Jack looked long and hard at the phone, and tried not to think about Larry's brusque dismissal. Best all round for Larry, he thought, not to give him an answer. But then again, Larry's not the sort you argue with. Not if you value your own life, and the lives of those you love.

Back to the practicalities, then. The phone would have to go. He prised off the back and used a grubby fingernail to pull out the SIM card, and then got out of the car. There was a wooden litter bin a couple of yards away and he strolled over to it and lifted the lid, revealing a month's worth of putrid, rotting rubbish along with a healthy fly colony. He dropped the SIM card into the mouldering mess and closed the lid.

Back in the car he pulled a small thermos flask from a holdall on the passenger seat and poured himself a shot of strong coffee. By his reckoning, he needed three more lay-bys – one to dispose of the phone shell, one to change out of the suit he'd been wearing for the hit, and one to swap the plates on the Fiesta. After that he could head for home. It would be a long drive, criss-crossing the Home Counties, laying a false trail just in case. But it was always worth it for the peace of mind.

He opened the glove compartment again and pulled out an Ella Fitzgerald CD. He didn't want to listen to the radio anymore, didn't want to hear any more about Nathan Kingsley. Truth be told, he thought as he sipped on his coffee, he didn't want to hear Nathan Kingsley's name ever again.

Luke Kingsley stared into his whisky and soda, and then

slugged back a mouthful and swallowed it down. He was on his third since the police had arrived at the hotel, his fifth of the afternoon so far. None of them had steadied his nerves. He lifted his eyes from the glass and looked up across the room. In the opposite corner Detective Sergeant Ian Scott was furtively muttering into his mobile phone in the same irritating Welsh lilt that had sing-songed its way through an interview which had left Luke shaken and unnerved. He didn't much like Ian Scott, and not just because of his accent.

He shortened the focus of his eyes and took in the space between them, a vista of empty tables giving testament to the day's events. Crystal champagne flutes, destined to go unfilled, shimmered in the late afternoon sunlight and unused damask napkins lay neatly folded at each place setting. A tall sculpted candle stood to attention at the centre of each table, proud and unlit. To his left, the top table looked equally bereft, the place settings untouched, the blown roses chosen by Alice for the table dressings beginning to dry out in the day's heat.

Of all the rooms that could have been used by the police to conduct their interviews, did it have to be this one? He glanced again at DS Scott and wondered if the selection of this room had been deliberate. Was the policeman trying to unnerve him? Had he asked for this room on purpose?

He turned to look more closely at the place where Nathan should have been sitting. Here and there a mourning flower had dared to drop a dark pink petal onto the tablecloth, spotting the clean white damask in the way that Nathan's blood had spotted the clean white aggregate outside the hotel. He felt the contents of his stomach heave up towards his mouth and he forced them back down with another slug of whisky.

It occurred to him for a moment that he was completely alone in the world. No parents, thanks to the over-tired lorry driver whose juggernaut had slammed head-on in to their car on the A19 three years ago. No girlfriend, thanks to his Sagittarian reluctance to settle down with one woman. No real friends, due to his unenviable ability to attract only users and hangers on, those shallow individuals skilled in the art of targeting a minor celebrity and milking the acquaintance shamefully for their own benefit. Even his team mates, the other Kirkby FC players who would stand shoulder to shoulder with him in a game, were wont to give him a wide berth off the pitch.

The one exception to this landscape of human disconnection was Nathan, the brother that was always there for him. Nathan was the one constant in his life, the strategy before the game, the captain who set him straight when he played off-plan, the pragmatist who smoothed things over when a bad judgment call – and there had been plenty of those – resulted in injury or loss.

Until today. And now today, thanks to a stray bullet, there was no Nathan. What the hell was he going to do without Nathan? In any injury or loss he would turn to Nathan, but when losing Nathan *was* the injury, what then? He felt a knot of grief tighten in his throat and tears start to sting at the back of his eyes. Nathan was gone, and he was alone.

He stared back down into his glass, sombre now. His head was beginning to ache as the relaxing effect of the alcohol battled with the emotions fighting for supremacy in his gut. He felt suddenly tired, drained by the grief of his loss, and the need to surrender to it. He wanted to howl, to let out the pain, but he couldn't. He had to hold it together. The grief would have to come later. Right now, he had other things to think about.

He drained off what was left in the glass and placed it down on the table in front of him. His jacket was hanging on the back of his chair and he reached back with a hand to retrieve his mobile phone from the inside pocket, and then flicked at the keypad with tired fingers. The screen lit up with a scattering of familiar symbols. He had seven missed phone calls and thirty two unread text messages. He felt his face flush with a sudden surge of anxiety, and flicked his eyes up across the room to where DS Scott was still murmuring into his mobile phone, his face turned away from Luke towards the wall.

He looked back at the phone and tapped on an icon, displaying the list of missed calls. They were all from Vienna Fielding. He let out a spontaneous puff of breath, an exhalation of relief, not something he normally associated with Vienna. He tapped again to bring up a list of text messages and ran his eyes down the list. At least a dozen had come from Vienna, and a couple were from Alice. Others were from team-mates, Nathan's ushers at the church, still others were from numbers he didn't recognise, people he barely knew, guests of Nathan's at the wedding, people he didn't even know had his mobile phone number.

There was nothing there to worry about. He let out another breath, louder this time, and turned his eyes to the ceiling. Those messages from hangers on, from wedding guests, from Nathan's friends, they could all be deleted. And he didn't have to read the texts from Alice and Vienna to know what they would be about. At some point he was going to have to deal with Alice, but that would have to wait. Right now he needed a place to stay tonight, somewhere safe, somewhere other than his flat. When he'd sorted out a place to stay, then he could work out what to do about Alice.

He balked at the thought and pushed the phone into his trouser pocket. There was another four star hotel at the other side of Kirkby, a place called The Pavilion. There were still journalists hanging around outside the Kirkby Manor, it would be a reasonable excuse to say he was changing hotel and staying away from his own flat to avoid the press. He could go back into reception now and ask them to call for a taxi. He started to get to his feet, and as he did so the phone in his pocket vibrated with another incoming text. He pulled out the phone and tapped at the screen, and caught his breath at the sight of an all too familiar number. He tapped again and opened the message. It was brief and to the point.

I want my money.

His stomach contracted, a reflex of fear, forcing a stream of watery vomit up into his mouth. He put a hand over his mouth and swallowed it down, but the contents of his gut continued to churn. He stared at the message for a moment, and then tapped a reply with shaking, hesitant fingers.

You know I don't have it. And you know I can't get it.

His face was clammy now and his shirt was beginning to stick to his flesh with the perspiration of fear. He couldn't pay. The text was true. He didn't have it. And he couldn't get it. The thoughts had barely crossed his mind when the phone vibrated for a second time.

Nathan had it. And you can get it. Now Nathan's dead, it's yours.

3

Even a provincial bank like the East & Northern requires a presence in the City. The ENB's London office was tucked away in a courtyard off Gun Street, a modest suite of rooms in an old converted house, a surprisingly quiet spot in the eye of the banking district's noisy storm.

Rose usually enjoyed a visit to Gun Street, but today she wasn't really in the mood. Her latest assignment was threatening to overrun by several days, and her plans to escape for some down time had already been rescheduled twice. Now Clive Barden, the bank's Head of Risk, had asked for an urgent early morning meeting. It might pay dividends, she thought as she rounded the corner of Artillery Lane, to invest some time in educating Clive on the difference between his definition of "urgent" and everyone else's.

The building was too small to justify a reception desk, and she let herself in with her security pass, and shimmied up the narrow stairs to the second floor, where Clive's personal office space had somehow managed to expand into what almost passed for a suite. The floor was deserted, save for Clive himself. He looked relaxed, sprawled in a large leather chair, but as she stepped forward towards his desk he looked up at her and she saw that his thin, sallow face wore its customary worried look.

'Ah Rose, thank you for coming in so early.' He straightened in his seat and gesticulated to an empty chair with a flick of his fingers. 'I wonder,' he peered down at a sheaf of papers on his desk, 'does the name Nathan Kingsley mean anything to you?'

She thought for a moment as she sank into the chair. The murder of Nathan Kingsley had barely been out of the news since Saturday, and she shivered to think she might have been part of the congregation so brutally disbanded. 'It means a great deal. I was invited to the wedding, but I couldn't attend.'

He glanced up at her, concerned. 'You have a connection with the Kingsley family?'

'A friend of a friend.' She had considered calling Benny to offer her condolences, but stopped short of the deed, uncertain of how close he was to Nathan Kingsley, and not wishing to appear intrusive.

'I see.' He nodded. 'You are aware, then, that Nathan Kingsley was a footballer? In fact, he played for Kirkby FC.' He was watching her face, looking for a sign of understanding that was taking its time to appear. 'As our Head Office is situated in Kirkby we are, of course, the team's primary corporate sponsors.'

'You're worried about the nature of his death? Surely it won't reflect on the bank? I can't imagine his murder had anything to do with his professional life.'

'The death of a high profile customer may always carry a reputational risk for the bank, Rose, certainly until the nature of the death has been established. Sad and troubling though these events are for the family, we must ensure that the bank is mitigated against any risk.' He picked up the sheaf of papers and handed it to Rose. 'Nathan was also a personal customer of the ENB. These documents outline his banking business with us.'

'You've investigated his accounts?'

'Given the nature of his death, I considered it necessary to obtain a view of his financial affairs. It would appear that Nathan Kingsley recently made some banking transactions which, if not overtly suspicious, certainly raise questions.'

Rose looked down at the first piece of paper, her eyes quickly taking in the salient points. She nodded, and sighed her understanding. 'You think it was money laundering?'

'I can't be sure. There is nothing obviously dishonest in the transactions. The funds were transferred to a family member. But I do believe there is a risk, and I wouldn't want us to fail in our regulatory duties.'

'Have you informed the police?'

'I believe it's too early.' His brow furrowed. 'I don't wish to appear insensitive. There has been a tragic bereavement and a family are grieving. And in any case, there is nothing overtly criminal in what has taken place. But we have a duty to be vigilant.' He nodded to himself, and peered at her over the top of his spectacles. 'I don't want to make false accusations, Rose, but neither do I want to ignore something which may prove material in the investigation of a crime.' He was watching her closely. 'Could I ask you to put aside your current assignment and assist us with this?'

'Me?' Rose was nonplussed. 'In what way can I help?'

'In the same way that you always help us. By investigating the matter further and protecting our interests.'

'Has the bank been formally notified of the death by the next of kin?'

'No. That is the other curious feature of this case. Despite the death occurring three days ago, we have yet to receive any instructions regarding the estate. We have a dedicated bereavement officer in our Kirkby branch, a young lady by the name of Stacy Singleton. I have asked Stacy to monitor the situation, to prepare for a meeting with the next of kin, and to inform me as soon as that meeting is scheduled.' He pulled off his spectacles and laid them down on the desk, and regarded her again with unfocused eyes. 'Because the wedding didn't take place, Nathan Kingsley's fiancée remained just that. She is not his legal next of kin. But their financial affairs are interwoven, so we must speak to her in that capacity. I have written to ask her to attend an appointment with Stacy. I would be grateful, Rose, if you would attend that appointment. And the appointment which we hope to arrange with Mr Kingsley's next of kin, his brother Luke.'

'Have the police asked to be involved in meetings with the family?'

'The police?' Clive cleared his throat with an uneasy cough. 'The investigating officer is Detective Inspector George Mulligan. You are familiar with the Inspector, of course, from your previous work with us.'

'You know I am.' George Mulligan and the possibility of money laundering? No wonder, she thought, that Clive was looking so twitchy. It was barely a year since Rose had uncovered a fraud within the bank that had led George Mulligan to charge Clive's ex-wife Janis with money laundering offences, offences which should have been picked up by the bank's own processes. Clive always put on a good performance, but the shame of her betrayal still lingered just below the surface. 'What exactly would you like me to do, Clive?'

His relief at her decision was palpable. 'I would like you to be my eyes and ears in Kirkby, Rose. Stacy is a most diligent colleague, but I fear that she may be a little out of her depth with this one. And ... well, frankly I have been advised that many of our Kirkby colleagues are already a little star-struck by the sensationalism of the case, and the minor celebrity of the individuals involved. I would be grateful if you would support Stacy at all times, ensure that we get satisfactory instructions from the next of kin, and keep me appraised of anything I need to know. And I would appreciate an independent report which we could pass to the police, if we uncover anything that we believe to be material to their investigations.'

'OK, I can do that for you.' Rose placed an elbow on the desk and rested her chin on her upturned hand. 'And what about DI Mulligan? Any special instructions regarding him?'

Clive's face relaxed a little, and softened into an almost-whimsical half-smile. 'No special instructions that I can think of, Rose. But I'm sure I can rely on you to remember which of us, between myself and the Inspector, relies the most on your pragmatism and loyalty.'

Alice settled back into the armchair and pulled her long, tanned legs up under her, tucking them safely into the folds of the pink fluffy dressing gown. The chair was placed close to the French windows in the dining room, at just the right angle to permit an uninterrupted view of the garden, and she drank it in through child-like eyes. She had worked this garden for barely six months, and yet she knew every nook and cranny, every plant, every rockery stone. It had been a wasteland before she took control, a thankless patch of ground with a thatch of dying lawn and a sorry collection of long-suffering shrubs. She had wasted no time in cutting out the decay and filling the space with roses and lavender and lush, green foliage. The garden had become her sanctuary, the place where she could be herself, and she needed it now more than ever before. It wasn't going to be easy to give it up.

And there was no doubt in her mind that she *was* going to have to give it up.

Living in Nathan's house, making this garden her own, had been as much a dream to her as the misplaced belief that one day she would become Mrs Nathan Kingsley. Perhaps she had never truly believed that this house would be hers any more than she believed that the marriage would actually take place. She wasn't the sort of person for whom miracles occurred.

She'd fallen once before for the illusion that life could be good, made the mistake of investing everything in another human being, entrusted all her happiness to one man and blindly believed that nothing would ever go wrong. She had made that mistake with Olivia's father. She'd loved him, and trusted him, given of herself, turned her back on her family, brought Olivia into the world for him, and what had he done in return? Sent flowers to the maternity hospital with a message that he would always love her, and that he wished her well.

Wished her well? It had taken very little sleuthing on Vienna's part to discover the truth. That two days before Olivia's birth, supposedly away on a business trip to Edinburgh, he had married his childhood sweetheart in a pretty little church on the Suffolk coast, and flown off to Cancun on honeymoon without so much as a backward glance. Alice had been so sure of him, and Alice had been wrong.

And now she'd been wrong again.

She closed her eyes for a moment and rested her head against the wing of the armchair. It was barely nine o'clock and yet strong sunlight was already piercing the window and she felt its warmth against her cheek. She had been right not to trust wholly in Nathan, and right not to claim the house as her own. It occurred to her that nothing of her life with Nathan belonged to her now, any more than Nathan himself had belonged to her. They had made a promise to marry, and the promise had been broken. She wanted to say that it wasn't Nathan's fault, that no one expected to be murdered on their wedding day. But she couldn't.

Because Nathan had been keeping something from her.

It wasn't enough to try to blot out the past few days. She needed to blot out the last few weeks, to remember Nathan as he was, the open, honest, upright Nathan that she'd fallen in love with, not the unhappy, secretive creature that he'd become. A tiny sob caught at the back of her throat and her face began to crumple, the grief not just of days, but of weeks, beginning to break through the dam of self-control. She had no rights now, no claim on his body never mind his estate. Everything would go to Luke, even the right to bury him.

She wondered, for a moment, where Luke was. Almost three days had passed since Nathan's death, and still he hadn't been in touch. She wondered what he was planning to do, how he was feeling, whether he would ever speak to her again or whether he would take this moment to turn his back on her for good. She knew that Luke resented her, knew that he was jealous. And she knew that he would have done anything to stop the wedding from taking place. What a bitter-sweet outcome this must be for him, she thought, the triumph of seeing the wedding abandoned overshadowed by the horror of knowing that the price of victory was his brother's life.

She had promised Nathan in life that she wouldn't let Luke come between them, and she would keep that promise now in death. Luke was welcome to it all. She wasn't going to battle with him. The fight was over, and Nathan was lost to both of them. There was no doubt in her mind that Luke was going to lay claim to Nathan in death, just as he'd tried to lay claim to him in life. But that was OK. The Nathan who died on Saturday wasn't her Nathan. And squabbling with Luke wasn't going to give her the one thing she wanted more than anything.

It wasn't going to give her the truth.

'Maybe there was more to Nathan Kingsley than everyone thinks.' Ian Scott dropped a wad of papers onto George Mulligan's desk and pointed at it as he sank into a chair. 'I've been through every one of those witness statements and there's nothing at all to suggest why anyone would want him dead.'

Mulligan nodded towards the papers. 'What's in that lot?'

'Accounts from the hotel staff who were on duty the day of the wedding. Ditto the wedding guests who were waiting at the church. Ditto any non-wedding guests staying at the Kirkby Manor Hotel. And character statements from his team mates at Kirkby FC.' Scott paused to draw breath, and then added 'Statements from Luke Kingsley, Alice Blacklaws, Vienna Fielding. Photographs of Nathan Kingsley for identification. Photographs of the body. Photographs of the hole in the hotel's perimeter fence where the killer escaped, and of the tyre marks on the grass verge where his car must have been parked.'

'Description of the killer?'

'As per Patricia Hewitt's statement. Short, wiry, clean shaven, cropped grey hair. Dressed in a mid-grey suit and blue shirt, with a grey tie. She can't swear to it, but she thinks he was wearing a buttonhole.'

'A wedding guest?'

'Or someone trying to blend in by looking like a wedding guest. No one else reports seeing him. After the shot was fired, those few people who were outside the hotel either ran back indoors for safety or ran towards Nathan.'

'Well he's a cool bugger, I'll give him that.' Mulligan picked up a pen from his desk and twizzled it between chubby fingers. He'd seen Nathan Kingsley's body, and seen the bullet hole directly between the young man's eyes. He'd call it a lovely job, if such a job could be lovely. It was clean, professional, far beyond the capabilities of any of the kack-handed numpties who operated in Kirkby. 'If this *was* a contract killing – and it doesn't look to me like it could be anything else – he could be anywhere now. The other side of the country, for all we know. The only way we're going to track him down is by finding out who wanted Nathan Kingsley dead, and why.'

'Where do you want to start? With the brother or the fiancée?'

'With the brother. I can't get the measure of him.' Mulligan stared across the desk at his sergeant and tapped on the polished wood with the tip of his pen, thinking. 'And I can't get hold of him. I left four telephone messages for him yesterday, and he still hasn't come back to me.' He pulled a blank piece of paper from a tray on his desk and scribbled Luke Kingsley's name, then drew a ring around it. 'Anna Hill has been to spend time with Alice every day since Nathan died. She's reported back to me that Alice and Vienna have both tried to make contact with Luke, and he still hasn't responded. It's been nearly seventy two hours now, and someone needs to start arranging the funeral. The body's going to be released tomorrow, and we have no idea where to release it to.'

'Maybe he's still in shock, George. He was there when it happened. Nathan died in his arms. It's got to take its toll.'

Mulligan turned his face towards a window, thinking hard. 'If it had happened to you, Scottie, and someone reached out to you, someone who was also impacted by the death, wouldn't you respond? Wouldn't you be thankful that you weren't alone?'

'I dunno. Shock takes people in different ways.'

'When I left Alice on Saturday afternoon, I asked if she had a message for Luke. And she said "tell him I'm sorry that he's alone." Now what the hell does that mean? A young bloke like that, a successful career in soccer, you'd expect him to be surrounded by people, wouldn't you?'

'You can be surrounded by people and still be alone, George. Maybe he likes it that way.'

'So much of a loner that he wouldn't even want to speak to the girl his brother was about to marry?' Mulligan turned back to the paper on his desk and scribbled Alice's name beneath Luke's, ringing it with a flourish of the pen. 'Luke and Alice don't appear to get on. They don't get on to the extent that there's no dialogue between them about the loss of someone they both loved. No dialogue about the body, the estate, no words of comfort passing between them to salve the loss. No common memories shared.' He looked up at DS Scott.

Scott met his gaze with a shrug. 'There's no law that says a brother and prospective sister-in-law have to be friends. I've never been close to my brother's wife. We don't have anything in common.'

'Except for your brother.' Mulligan thought for a moment. 'Is she attractive, Scottie? Your sister-in-law, I mean?'

'I suppose that depends. You might think she was attractive if you had an eye for a prop-forward.'

'Not your type, then?' Mulligan's face creased momentarily into a wry grin, and then fell straight. 'Alice Blacklaws doesn't look like a prop-forward. She looks like a model. And she's a quiet thing, dignified. Well,' he gave a self-deprecating laugh, 'that's how she looks to me.' He dropped the pen onto the desk. 'On the day of the wedding Alice was at home with Vienna Fielding for company. But Luke Kingsley was alone. Alone at the hotel.'

'He wasn't alone, he was with Nathan.'

'No, I mean after that. After Nathan was shot. Why was he alone? Why did no one come looking for him?' Mulligan sat back in his chair and folded his arms across his paunch. 'OK, so he and Nathan lost their parents some years back. There's a paternal uncle overseas that they have no contact with, and no extended family on their mother's side. But there were friends at the wedding, surely? Team mates in the congregation? Yet no one came to the hotel to see if he needed support.' He put a thumb up to his mouth and chewed on the nail. 'And there's bad blood between him and Alice. When I told him that Alice had sent a message for him, that she'd invited him to go and see her, he barely acknowledged it.'

'He was still in shock.'

'Or maybe she just didn't figure in his view of the world. Maybe she was in the way. Maybe he was jealous. But jealous of who? Jealous of Nathan for finding someone to love, or jealous of Alice because she was taking his brother away from him?'

'I'm not sure where you're going with this, George?'

'Neither am I.' Mulligan's brown eyes narrowed and he fixed his gaze in the distance on some unseen vision. 'But the distance between those two – between Luke and Alice – is somewhere at the bottom of this. The distance between them, his refusal to talk to her about his brother's estate ... maybe even the estate itself.'

'Luke Kingsley didn't kill his brother.'

'Someone paid for Nathan Kingsley to be wiped out.'

'Luke was grieving, George. His grief was genuine.'

'His shock was genuine.' Mulligan picked up the pen again and idly scribbled Nathan's name on the paper in front of him, ringed it, thought for a moment, and then drew a larger ring around both the brothers' names. 'He wasn't just grieving. When I spoke to him on Saturday evening he was anxious, almost afraid. Now what would make him afraid, Scottie?' He turned his gaze towards the sergeant, and as he did so his eyes lit with a glint of possibility. He turned to the papers which Scott had dropped on his desk and put out a hand, gently flicking page after page to one side until he uncovered a photograph of Luke and Nathan Kingsley. He pulled it from the pile and held it up to his eyes. 'Where did this come from?'

'Alice gave it to us. It's of Nathan and Luke at Wetherby races last year.'

Mulligan nodded slowly, his eyes fixed on the picture. Luke Kingsley was a bit taller than his brother, but Nathan was the more handsome. Luke had the same square jaw, cheekbones, clear complexion, but his eyes were slightly hooded, his nose a shade sharper in contour. Where Nathan's face was open, his expression amiable, Luke's was hard, almost hawk-like. And yet they were so alike, two sides of the same coin. It would be easy, he thought, to mistake one for the other.

'I think,' he said slowly, 'it's time we paid another visit to Luke Kingsley.'

4

Hector Campling leaned his elbows gently on the highly polished desk and steepled his nicotine-stained fingers. 'We were most sorry to hear of your loss, Mr Kingsley. A very sad affair. We had the pleasure of conducting some business on behalf of your brother some months ago.' The solicitor was sharply dressed in an old-fashioned way, in an expensive grey pinstripe, and his appearance was incongruous with the rather shabby surroundings of a provincial office. 'Is there something in particular we can assist you with today?'

Luke thought for a moment, and tried to get the measure of him. Despite his dated appearance and thinning pate, Luke guessed that he was barely middle-aged. 'I need help to deal with my brother's affairs, Mr Campling. It's not something I've had to do before. Nathan took care of everything when our parents died.' He coughed to clear the nerves in his throat. 'Nathan mentioned to me some time ago that you did some legal work for him.'

'Indeed.' Campling's voice was unexpectedly soothing. 'We carried out the conveyancing work on two rental properties your brother purchased from us.' He licked his lips. 'May I ask if you have brought a copy of your brother's will?'

'He didn't make a will.'

'May I ask how you know?'

Luke frowned, puzzled by the question. 'He told me that he was planning to make a will after the wedding, but the wedding didn't take place, did it?'

'Ah, I see. You're making an assumption.' The solicitor's eyes narrowed, but glimmered with the hint of a smile. 'Perhaps his fiancée may know if a will was made?' He was watching Luke's face intently as he spoke.

Luke felt colour begin to rise in his cheeks. 'No. I mean, I don't think so. We haven't discussed it.'

'I see. May I enquire - forgive me, this is a little delicate – may I enquire as to the nature of your relationship with your brother's fiancée? Are you working together to deal with your brother's affairs?'

'No.' The flush in Luke's cheeks deepened. 'Alice isn't very good with money. She's not very streetwise. Nathan always looked after their financial affairs. And anyway, Alice isn't Nathan's next of kin. I am.'

'I see.' Campling raised an expressive eyebrow which indicated that he saw very well.

'What I mean is, I intend to sort out Nathan's affairs and make sure that Alice receives whatever is due to her. *If* anything is due to her. But as there isn't a will ...'

'With respect, Mr Kingsley, I have to say that at the moment we can only *assume* there isn't a will. We must take care to ensure that we establish the position.' Campling opened a drawer in his desk and pulled out an old-fashioned fountain pen. 'It is possible that a will may exist, and has simply not been located. I recommend that your brother's home be searched, and any office premises he used, in case a will has been stored with other personal or business papers. It may also be worth asking your brother's bank, in case a will has been lodged with them. It goes without saying that you have asked his usual solicitor? I am assuming here that he had a regular man of business. The only work I have carried out for him was in respect of the rental properties.'

'Nathan used Richard Fleming in Kirkby. We both did.'

He hoped that Campling wasn't going to ask why he wasn't using Richard Fleming now. 'I spoke to Richard first thing this morning, and he confirmed that he's never written a will for Nathan. As for the bank,' his right hand strayed subconsciously to the pocket where he had secreted a letter from the ENB, 'I'm going to make an appointment today to speak with them.'

'Good. Now, if a will cannot be located in any of the obvious places, our next step will be to place an advertisement in the press.' Campling began to make notes on a desk pad in front of him. 'In the meantime, we will need to ascertain the approximate value of his estate.' He looked up expectantly. 'Are you familiar enough with your brother's affairs to estimate its value?'

Luke swallowed hard. 'Not really. He owns … I mean, he owned a house in Haverland Street.'

'Mortgaged?'

'I believe so. There's his car, and a business. He runs a limited company to manage his soccer earnings and other business interests. He did modelling work and personal appearances, after dinner speaking, that sort of thing. And the rental properties you already know about.'

'Savings and investments?'

'I don't know.'

'Insurance policies?'

'I don't know.'

'Accountancy firm?'

'Marshall and Slaughter, in Kirkby. We both use them.'

The solicitor nodded. 'A long-established firm. I am acquainted with Mr Marshall.' He licked his lips again. 'It is likely we will need to wind up your brother's business interests.' He dotted his pen down the list. 'My firm would be most pleased to act on your behalf, Mr Kingsley. This is a list of our usual fees, should you wish to engage us.' He reached into the middle of an in-tray to his left and drew out a piece of paper, and passed it to Luke.

Luke took hold of the paper and ran his eyes down it

without taking in any of the numbers. 'I would like you to proceed. Fees won't be an issue, but time *is*. I need things tying up as quickly as possible.' His mouth felt suddenly dry. 'I need access to the money as soon as possible.'

Hector Campling gave a quiet laugh. 'I can understand your desire to have things processed in a timely fashion. However, I must advise you that to administer an estate without a will requires time and effort. There is property to be disposed of – assuming that you wish to dispose of it. There is a business to wind up, assuming you choose to wind it up. And that is only the beginning. Once we have a clear picture of the overall value of your brother's estate, we will be able to make an assessment for inheritance tax ...'

'Inheritance tax?' Luke had been staring unseeingly at the list of fees, and now he looked up into the solicitor's oily face. 'How much will that be?'

'Ah, always the burning question, Mr Kingsley. We cannot establish the extent of any tax until the value of the overall estate has been established. We will make best endeavours to complete the work as quickly as possible, but I cannot guarantee timescales which are outside of my control.'

Luke sat forward and leaned closer to the solicitor. 'How soon will I be able to access the money? If I make it worth your while, can you arrange for me to access his bank account?'

'If it's a question of personal cash flow, I may be able to advise on the best course of action for your needs. Funeral costs will have to be met, of course, and you will probably find that the bank will release funds from your brother's bank account to pay those, if you do not have the means. If there are other expenses, if – perhaps – an inheritance tax liability falls due before assets have been liquidated to pay that tax, then it may be possible to borrow against the property if you should choose to transfer it to your sole ownership. Providing, as we have already discussed, that the property passes to you as next of kin.' He forced an insincere smile. 'Which brings us back to the matter of a will.'

'It does?'

'I strongly recommend that you request access to your brother's property to search for a will, and make enquiries at the bank. In the meantime I will draft an advertisement for the Law Gazette and our local newspapers. If another firm has drawn up a will, the advertisement will bring them forward. In the meantime, I will need your brother's death certificate, or failing that an interim certificate issued by the coroner's office. When you speak to the bank, please obtain as much information from them as you can about your brother's financial position. I will need details of bank accounts, any outstanding debts, credit agreements, and so forth.' Campling smiled. 'I will need a written instruction from you to approach Marshall and Slaughter for information. If you would be good enough to wait a few moments I can have my secretary prepare one for you to sign now. If you are in agreement I will make it a generic instruction, so that we may act on your behalf in any respect of this matter.'

'And what about Alice?'

'Alice? Ah, the young lady who was due to marry your brother.' Campling put down his pen and stared into Luke Kingsley's face. 'She is, I presume, living in the house belonging to your brother? Is she there alone?'

'She's with Olivia.'

'Olivia?'

'Her daughter. She's only three.'

Campling arched an eyebrow. 'Is she your brother's child? That would complicate matters somewhat.'

'No. She's Alice's child. From another relationship.'

The solicitor leaned forward across his desk. 'Can I just be clear on one thing, Mr Kingsley? Should your brother's house in Haverland Street pass to you as next of kin, you will need to decide whether to keep the property or whether to sell it. Should you wish to sell, it will be necessary to ask Alice and her daughter to leave and find alternative accommodation. This may prove difficult, in some respects. Have you stopped for a moment to consider what your brother's wishes may have been?'

'Of course I have.' Luke drew back. 'If Nathan had wanted Alice to go on living in the house, he would have made it possible for her to stay there. If he'd wanted Alice to inherit, he would have done something about it. But he didn't. He wanted me to inherit. I'm his brother, I'm his only family. The money, the property, whatever he's left behind him, that belongs to me now. If Nathan had wanted it any other way he would have left a will. Wouldn't he?'

The 14.05 from Kings Cross was unsurprisingly quiet, given it was the middle of the working day. Rose boarded the train at Stevenage and was gratified to find herself in a deserted first class coach. She usually made her own travel arrangements but as the requirement to travel to Kirkby today was down to Clive's definition of "urgent", her tickets had been booked by his personal assistant Moira, a no-nonsense Scot with a mischievous nature that was wasted on the ENB. Rose could only smile at the short, handwritten note tucked inside the paper wallet containing her tickets. 'Don't tell Clive it's first class. We have to think of his blood pressure.'

As the train sped north, and fortified by a complimentary coffee, Rose sank back into her seat and began to trawl through the documented details of Nathan Kingsley's financial affairs. By Peterborough she had read through all of the paperwork provided by Clive that morning, and by Retford she had a pretty good grasp of how things stood.

Nathan Kingsley had owned a substantial house in the centre of Kirkby, easily worth close to a million pounds.

Mortgaged with the ENB in his own name, he'd paid a significant sum off the outstanding balance just three weeks ago, and then within days approached the bank with a request to make Alice Blacklaws a joint tenant of the property. That transfer was still not complete.

Of course there was nothing too unusual in a couple taking on a property together, especially in the run up to a marriage, and this couple already had other joint financial arrangements in place. Both were directors of Nathan Kingsley Holdings Ltd, the company through which all of Nathan's earnings were processed, and Alice appeared to draw her income from the company under the guise of being Nathan's personal assistant. In addition, a current account in joint names, its balance hovering around two thousand pounds, appeared to exist solely for the purpose of servicing their domestic expenses.

There were debts too, of course, but these were negligible compared with the couple's assets. Two car finance agreements in Nathan's name, one for an Audi coupe and one for a BMW convertible, gave Alice the right to drive either as a secondary driver. A credit card in Nathan's name had a modest outstanding balance of just over six hundred pounds. Rose smiled to herself. Looking back at his latest statements, Nathan hadn't been in the habit of lining the ENB's pocket by letting interest accrue on his debts. Each monthly statement had been paid in full.

It was the document outlining Nathan's sole accounts with the ENB which had given Rose most food for thought. Clive had provided her with two views of the situation, one outlining Nathan's savings accounts four weeks ago, and the other detailing the activity on those accounts from then until the present day. She could well understand why Clive was concerned. Three weeks ago Nathan Kingsley had begun to systematically divest himself of pretty much everything that he had on deposit with the ENB. By the date of his death the only liquid cash available to him was the balance in the joint current account he shared with Alice.

Rose wasn't a legal expert, but even with her scant knowledge of the law it was easy to see the confusion that was beginning to arise out of Nathan Kingsley's estate. He had begun to dispose of assets. There were insurances to claim, debts to be settled, a company to be dissolved, expenses to be met. He didn't hold a business account with the ENB, so there was at least one bank account of which Rose did not yet have visibility. There may be more. And as if all of that wasn't enough, his fiancée wasn't his next of kin, although her financial affairs appeared to be bound up with his, and there was so far no evidence of a will to make his intentions plain.

She leaned back in her seat and turned to gaze out of the window at the passing rural landscape, field after field of yellow, billowing rapeseed punctuated by an occasional livery stable. Thoughts were flitting through her mind at just about the same speed. Nathan Kingsley had been murdered just before his wedding. Rose herself had been invited to that wedding. Had she accepted the invitation, she might have learned more about Nathan and Alice. But then being a guest at the wedding might also have prejudiced her independence to investigate the case.

So near and yet ... maybe not so far. She hadn't attended the wedding, but she knew someone who had. If Benny Bradman had been invited to the wedding, then he must have known either Nathan Kingsley or Alice Blacklaws pretty well. And if he knew at least one of them pretty well, then it might be useful to pay him a visit before she started her investigation tomorrow. It was, she supposed, pretty shabby of her to turn up on his doorstep expecting information, given that she'd turned down his invitation to the wedding. But then, he didn't need to know that was why she wanted to speak to him.

After all, there was another reason why she might want to stop by and visit Benny, and it really didn't have anything to do with her assignment for the ENB.

Haverland Street was the only remaining example of a complete Georgian terrace left in Kirkby. Now forming a short cut-through from a main road into the town's Victorian park, it had survived a Zeppelin raid in 1915, a blitz of German bombing in 1941, and numerous attempts by town planners in the 1970s to replace it with a modern shopping centre.

As Benny Bradman arrived that afternoon, pulling his black Mercedes slowly to a halt outside the last house in the block, the place was under siege by a different kind of enemy. He took a moment to assess the blockade, noted two reporters chatting beside a silver BMW convertible and a photographer leaning on the railings outside number eight, and braced himself for the attack.

'Benny Bradman? It is Benny Bradman, isn't it?' A tall blonde with dark roots and a florid complexion broke away from the group as he opened his car door, and followed him to the foot of the short run of steps leading up to Alice's front door.

'How are you, Judy?' Benny recognised her from a previous encounter. 'Still workin' for the Kirkby Evenin' Press?'

She ignored the question. 'How's Alice Blacklaws?'

'How do you think?' He ran up the steps and rapped sharply on the front door. It opened immediately to admit him, and closed just as quickly behind him. 'Bloody vultures.' He muttered the words under his breath. More loudly he asked 'how long have they been outside, then?'

Vienna sighed. 'Since this morning. It's been three days now since Nathan died, and they still won't leave us alone. I called the police this morning and asked if they could do anything about it, but they said not at this stage. Apparently it's not illegal for them to stand around in a public place, however bad it's making Alice feel.' She led him down a long narrow hallway and into the light airy kitchen. 'Can I make you a coffee?'

'I'd love one.' He pulled a stool away from the kitchen counter and perched on the edge of it. 'How is Alice?'

'Weird.' Vienna shook her head as she filled the kettle. 'I want to say she's holding it together, but it's not that. She's so calm.' She glanced over her shoulder at him. 'I'm so glad you could come over, Benny. I just don't know what to do. There's so much to sort out, and I don't know where to start. And Alice is ...' She paused, searching for the right words. 'She's acting so strangely. It's like she hasn't registered what's happened.'

'Where is she?'

'Upstairs, in Nathan's office.'

'What's she doing in there?'

'Nothing. She's just sitting there. She said she wanted to be close to him. That the room smells of him.' She turned around and leaned against the kitchen counter. 'Do you think it's the shock?'

It would be the shock alright. He could still remember how it felt, a complete stranger telling him in a calm and measured tone that his wife had gone out water-skiing and wouldn't be coming back. One minute a husband, the next minute a widower. The light was on, then in an instant the light was off, and he was in darkness, alone with his grief, bringing up their son without her, never again to know the touch of her hand, the whisper of her lips.

'Benny, I'm sorry ...'

'It's alright, Vienna.' If her words had been careless he didn't blame her. It had been two years now, it wasn't unreasonable for people to think he'd be over it. He couldn't quite believe himself that the pain was still so raw. 'Any sign of Luke?'

'Not yet. He's still not returning my calls.' She poured boiling water into the mugs and stirred the frothy coffee around. 'Benny, he won't speak to her. And I'm at my wits end. Someone needs to deal with the practicalities, and I don't know what to do. Nathan made all the arrangements for the wedding. I've spoken to the travel agent about the honeymoon, and to the hotel about the reception. But the bills still need to be paid, even though the wedding didn't take place. And some woman called from the legal team at the magazine that Nathan had sold the press coverage to, she wanted to know who to talk to about the cancellation clauses in the contract. People are so bloody insensitive.'

She placed two mugs down on the kitchen counter and hoisted herself onto a stool next to him. 'The wedding gifts are still at the hotel. And what do we do about the funeral?' She let out a sigh that had been building for days. 'Alice hasn't even been able to say goodbye. The police have been really sympathetic, but they'll only release the body to Luke. Reverend Griffin has left messages for him, but his calls haven't been returned. Alice is grieving. And Luke – wherever he is – will be grieving. And there's no other family to take care of things.'

Benny stretched out a hand and laid it on her arm. 'We'll sort it, girl. I'll have a word with Alice, and then I'll drive over to Luke's place and see if I can find him. We need to get the two of them together, so they can discuss what happens next. Once they're agreed on that, we can do the runnin' around for them. You, me and Michael.'

'But only if they agree on what needs to be done.' Vienna frowned, a deep furrow across her brow that reflected the depth of her concern. 'What if Luke won't speak to her?'

'He'll have to speak to her.'

'Will he? He doesn't like her. And he doesn't really make any secret of it. But I don't know *why* he doesn't like her. How could anyone not like Alice, when she's so sweet?'

'Did Nathan know about this?'

Vienna laughed under her breath. 'Yes, of course. He was angry with Luke. And he told Luke that if he ever showed his feelings about her in public, he would wash his hands of him.'

'Well he made a good job of it. I never saw any animosity between them.'

'But Nathan isn't here now, is he? He's not here to make sure that Luke keeps his feelings to himself.' She blinked, and for a moment it looked as though she might begin to cry. 'I'm so worried about it, Benny. What if Luke won't be reasonable?'

'Reasonable ain't goin' to come into it, girl. Nathan's dead. They're goin' to have to patch up their differences and work together on this.'

'Yes, but what if they won't? Luke was only civil towards Alice because of Nathan. And now that Nathan's gone, he doesn't have to be civil any more, does he? He can do what he likes. He *is* doing what he likes.' A single tear of frustration escaped the lashes of her left eye and trickled down her cheek, leaving a trail of melted mascara in its wake. 'He isn't thinking of Alice at all. I mean … Nathan was murdered. Someone wanted him dead. And no one is giving Alice any answers. Is it too much to expect that Luke might at least be kind to her until the police are able to tell her why her whole life has been turned upside down?'

5

Luke Kingsley's apartment was on the top floor of a modern purpose-built block right in the heart of Kirkby's city centre. Fronting onto a picturesque riverbank, and fitted out with private underground parking and its own gymnasium and swimming pool, the building had gained a reputation as the most luxurious residential development in the area.

DI Mulligan and DS Scott navigated the concierge with ease, and found apartment 18 without difficulty. It took several bouts of loud knocking to encourage Luke Kingsley to open the door. He looked exhausted, his blond hair lank on his collar, his face unshaven, his hawkish eyes sunken into dark circles. He ushered them into a large, modern lounge and pointed to a vast, black leather sofa, before turning on his heel and heading back out into the hall. 'That's the phone.'

As they sank cautiously onto the sofa, Mulligan looked about him with an air of bewilderment. 'Who would want to live in a place like this? I've never seen anything so soulless.'

'Don't you like it, George? I fancied a place here myself after the wife told me I was surplus to requirements. I thought it might make me more attractive to the fairer sex, knowing that I rubbed shoulders with professional footballers and media types.'

'What stopped you, then?'

Scott's smile was non-committal. 'Well, I had to think about the kids coming to visit, didn't I? There are plenty of footballers living in here, but no garden for us to kick a ball about.' He could have added that a detective sergeant's salary wouldn't stretch far enough for even the smallest studio flat in the block, but the reappearance of Luke Kingsley saved him the embarrassment.

'That was the funeral director. He just wanted to let me know that he's spoken to the mortuary about collecting Nathan's body.' Luke sank into an oversized armchair opposite the sofa and leaned forward, elbows resting on his knees. 'Have you made any progress?' He directed the question at Mulligan.

'We believe we know how the gunman managed to escape out of the hotel grounds without being seen. We're waiting for the hotel to provide CCTV footage from their security cameras. We're hoping that will help with identification.' The policeman paused, and then asked 'do you remember a slight, middle-aged man in a grey suit? He was in the hotel grounds as you and Nathan left the building.'

Luke's face folded into a frown. 'I can't really remember anything, Inspector, other than holding Nathan after he was shot.'

'So you haven't been able to recall anything that might help us? Nothing about any enemies Nathan may have had, any grudges which might have been borne against him?'

'My brother was a good man, Inspector Mulligan. I can't imagine why anyone would wish him harm, let alone want to kill him.'

Ian Scott leaned forward to mirror Luke's posture, and tilted his head to one side. 'How's Alice bearing up, Luke?'

The unexpected question appeared to touch a nerve. A flush of colour made its way into Luke's cheeks, and he looked down at his fingers. 'Very well, under the circumstances. It's hard for her. It's hard for both of us.' He glanced up and focused his eyes to the right of Scott's head, avoiding eye contact. 'I'm going to see her again this afternoon. I've appointed a solicitor now, to deal with Nathan's affairs. I want to let her know what he recommends.'

Mulligan adopted his best avuncular tone. 'Well, it's good to know that at least the two of you have each other for support. It doesn't do to be on your own at a difficult time like this.' He watched Luke's face, trying to read his reaction. 'I understand that you don't have any close family?'

'Nathan and I only had each other. We lost our parents in a car accident three years ago. Our mother was an only child, and our father's brother emigrated to Canada in the seventies after an argument with the family. We have no contact with him.'

The policeman nodded with a sympathetic smile. 'I believe Alice is in a very similar situation?'

'I don't really know anything about her family. I think there was a falling out. Something to do with Olivia.' He rubbed a hand across his forehead. 'Nathan adored Olivia.' He appeared to be struggling to keep his emotions in check, the enormity of his loss perhaps finally beginning to register. 'Alice has Vienna, of course. They've been friends since their schooldays.'

'Yes, I know Vienna. I've met her before.' Mulligan gave a disarming smile. 'I'm ashamed to say I mistook her boyfriend for a murderer last year.' He shook his head with a laugh. 'It's a funny thing, mistaken identity. You can be so sure sometimes, that you've got the right person.' He leaned a little further forward towards Luke. 'I suppose there have been times when people have mistaken you for Nathan? You were very alike.'

Luke blinked, an almost imperceptible flinch at the policeman's words. 'I was taller than Nathan.'

'But you were the same colouring, and the same build?

You even had the same hairstyle. You must have looked almost identical in your wedding suits.' Mulligan paused, and then quietly asked 'do you have any enemies Luke? Anyone who may have wanted to hurt you?'

This time the reaction was clear for both policemen to see. What little colour was evident in Luke Kingsley's face drained away, leaving his cheeks pallid, and a mist of perspiration began to show across his upper lip. For a moment he appeared to sway in the large leather armchair, and then he forced a smile and lifted his eyes directly up to George Mulligan's face. 'You think the bullet was meant for me, and not for Nathan.' It was a statement, not a question. 'I'm a second league soccer player for a provincial team, Inspector Mulligan. What possible reason could anyone have for wanting to hurt me?'

Jack Canning picked up the remote control and flicked it at the TV screen. It didn't seem to matter these days how many channels you paid for, there was never anything decent to watch. The screen went blank and he dropped the remote onto the coffee table with a clatter. Somewhere behind him a woman's voice puffed out a sigh of reproach. He turned his head and grumbled at her over his shoulder. 'What's up now?'

'You ought to be outside enjoying the sunshine, not sitting in here in front of the telly.' Her words were critical but her tone was soft.

'I'm alright where I am.' He caught a glimpse of her, warm and curvaceous, out of the corner of his eye and smiled to himself. She was rolling out pastry on an old wooden board, her hands and wrists covered in dusty white flour. 'Steak and kidney, or chicken and leek?'

'Apple and blackberry.'

He chuckled to himself. She was a woman of few words, Lucy, just how he liked a woman to be. She knew how to cook, how to keep a comfortable house, and best of all, in all the years they'd been together, she'd never had too much to say for herself.

That had been the trouble with the first Mrs Canning. Too much to say for herself by half. The first Mrs Canning only had one skill, and that was nagging. She could have turned it into an Olympic sport. Lucy wouldn't know how to nag if she tried. One up to the second Mrs Canning.

He permitted himself a wry smile. Neither of them were ever legally Mrs Canning, of course. He'd contemplated marrying the first Mrs Canning after she'd casually announced an unexpected pregnancy over a five course Mandarin dinner at the Peking Garden one Friday evening. But she'd badgered him in that "you'll have to marry me now" way that some women do, and it just made him all the more determined not to comply.

He'd stood by her to begin with, in his way. He'd provided for her, and for the boy, when he came. But he hadn't been much of a husband or a father. He'd be the first to admit that. Perhaps if Lucy had been the boy's mother it might have been different.

If Lucy had come into his life sooner a lot of things might have been different. His hadn't been a life to be proud of. Banged up for more of his life than he'd spent in society, he'd been a disinterested father to the son he hadn't wanted, and a violent partner to the boy's mother. Lucy was a diamond, loving and loyal, and he'd been lucky the day she came into his life. But then Lucy didn't know everything there was to know about him. It was a rare skill, he thought, to spend six years of your life with a woman and not give anything away.

His eyes wandered to a small old-fashioned desk in the corner of the open-plan living room, and to the drawer where Larry's pay off was hidden in the long, slim box normally reserved for his snooker cue. Lucy disliked that box, and the snooker cue that went with it. They took him away from her at times when she wanted him at home, although she never would have asked him not to play. He always used that box for a pay-off, because he knew how much she disliked it. It was the one place he could be sure she wouldn't go poking around. And anyway, it had a key. He'd never worked out why the hell anyone would want to lock up their snooker cue, but he couldn't deny it had been handy.

The contents of that box were something he had to keep from her. He doubted very much that she would stay with him if she knew where the money had come from. In fact, he was sure of it. She wouldn't stay with him. And he needed her now, in a way he'd never needed anyone before.

He turned round to look at her properly, her round cheeks glowing with the exertion of pastry rolling and the reflected heat from the oven, and he watched as she opened the oven door and slid the pie onto a shelf. She wiped her hands on her apron, smearing flour and bits of lard into the fabric, and looked up at him. 'What time's your appointment?'

'Half past four.'

She turned and glanced at a clock on the kitchen wall. 'The pie will only take a half hour. There's time for a cuppa before we go.' She turned to the sink and filled the kettle, busying herself with the making of a pot of tea. 'We don't want to be too late, you know how difficult it is to get parked.' The words that might have ended that sentence were left unspoken. She didn't like talking about the bad stuff.

There had been a lot of bad stuff in Jack's life, bad stuff that Lucy didn't know about. He felt a sudden chill, a surge of guilt and shame seeping through his body, an anxiety that when he was gone some of the bad stuff might come out. That it would change the way she felt about him. He'd never cared before what people may or may not feel about him. But he cared what Lucy thought, what Lucy felt, and for the first time in his miserable life Jack Canning knew what it was to feel afraid.

The main building of the Kirkby Manor Hotel had once been a private house, a substantial Edwardian villa grotesquely built in a castellated style. The artificial appearance of its exterior was matched inside by muted colour schemes and reproduction furniture, and a faint smell of camphor. But the staff were friendly, and the air conditioning worked, and its close proximity to the ENB's head office building made it a natural choice of accommodation for Rose's stay in town.

A bright young receptionist by the name of Jo, a nice-looking girl with flawless skin and a fine set of braces on her teeth, showed Rose to her room. It was an old-fashioned courtesy, delivered with a hint of a lisp. 'I do hope you'll be comfortable in this room, Miss Bennett. It's one of our best.' She crossed the room and drew the curtain back slightly. 'We're in the east wing, so you get a lovely view across the front of the hotel and the south gardens.' She let the curtain go and smiled shyly at Rose. 'Can I make you a reservation for dinner?'

'I'm going out this evening to visit a friend. But a table for tomorrow evening would be good, say around 7.30?'

'Of course.' The girl nodded her agreement. 'I'll leave you to settle in, then. Please just call reception if there's anything we can do for you.'

As the door closed Rose crossed the room to the window and took in the view for herself. A classical portico doorway was set into the centre of the hotel's front wall, its Greco-Roman pillars tastelessly incongruent with the red brick of the building. Four deep, curving steps led down onto a gravel drive, and where the lower step met the gravel a small display of white roses rested unobtrusively against the wall, and Rose realised with a shiver that what she had was a lovely view across the exact spot where Nathan Kingsley had been murdered.

She stepped back from the window and turned towards the bed, and pulled her suitcase up onto it, ready to unpack. She had barely unzipped the case when her mobile phone began to ring, competing noisily for her attention, and she fished it out of her handbag and answered it. 'Rose Bennett.'

A familiar voice at the other end greeted her heartily with an unseen smile. 'Hello Rose Bennett, George Mulligan here.'

'Inspector Mulligan? Am I under surveillance?' Her tone was teasing. 'I've just arrived in Kirkby. The bank has booked me into the Kirkby Manor.' She sensed him thinking about it and added 'it's just a coincidence. The ENB has a corporate account here.' She glanced in the direction of the window and decided not to tell him about the view.

'Well I won't deny that's a handy place to put you. You're only a ten minute walk from the police station.'

'Why would I need to be close to that?'

A deep laugh echoed down the phone line. 'I've just appraised Clive Barden that we intend to apply for a warrant to obtain all of Nathan Kingsley's banking records. Clive told me that he'd sent you up here to look into Kingsley's financial affairs, and that he'd get back to me when you'd pulled everything together.'

'And you decided to just cut to the chase and call me direct?'

'I'll be honest with you, Rose.' Mulligan's tone softened and took on a sober edge. 'We're struggling with this one. You'll have seen the news coverage on the case. We have what appears to be a contract killing, with no obvious line of enquiry. We're looking at a number of theories at this stage, and one of the theories we want to test is financial gain. If someone has been willing to pay for Nathan Kingsley to be murdered, there has to be a reason. An idea of his financial profile, and the people he was linked to financially, would be useful to us.' He clicked his teeth.

'How soon will you be able to give me a view of who benefits financially from his death?'

Rose puffed out a sigh. 'Inspector Mulligan, I'm a banking consultant. I specialise in banking operations and risk. I'm not an expert in probate law. You really need a solicitor to assess the estate, and look at the terms of his will.'

'We're not sure that there is a will.'

'Then you need a solicitor to look at how the estate will fall under the rules of intestacy.' She thought for a moment. 'And in any case, I can only see the ENB view of things. I can access details of Nathan's accounts with the ENB, and we have what we call a "customer profile" – a listing of key details such as his occupation, his sources of income, and so on – but I don't have any visibility of any assets or liabilities he might have with other banks. People with substantial assets often spread their money around, you know. It's a sensible thing to do.'

'I understand that. But you have one very crucial advantage at the moment that I lack in this investigation. If a middle-aged plod like me starts asking awkward questions about a bereaved fiancée and a grieving brother, people are apt to clam up. Now if a representative of the bank has reason to talk to them, for what seems to be purely business purposes, well …'

'You're asking me to do that "eyes and ears" thing again, aren't you?'

'Am I that obvious?' There was a moment's silence and then he said 'look Rose, you can tread where I haven't a cat in hell's chance of going. You're well placed to talk to Alice Blacklaws, and to Luke Kingsley, and see and hear things that they would never reveal to me.

'Does Clive know you're making this call?'

'No. You've got me there. He still hasn't forgiven me for putting you at risk the last time you helped me.'

'I won't compromise the bank.'

'I'm not asking you to.'

Rose considered for a moment. Her brief from Clive was clear. He suspected Nathan Kingsley of money laundering, and he wanted Rose to establish the veracity of that suspicion before he reported his misgivings to George Mulligan. Mulligan had made no mention of money laundering. He wanted to know whether the crime he was investigating had been motivated by the prospect of financial gain. She smiled to herself. She wasn't sure she could be eyes and ears for both of them, but then again they were both barking up different trees. 'All I can tell you at the moment is that it's a complicated situation. Alice isn't Nathan's next of kin, but they do have joint financial business with the ENB. That's going to reflect on how the estate is assessed. Whoever is assigned by the next of kin to deal with probate would be able to give you a more accurate position on who will benefit and by how much. But ... I can take a look at the initial position on Nathan's accounts and let you have a view tomorrow. I'm meeting the bank's bereavement officer at eight thirty, and Alice Blacklaws is coming into the branch at eleven. We're still waiting for Luke Kingsley to set up an appointment.'

'I'd appreciate that view, Rose. Would you be able to meet me for lunch to discuss it?'

'Only lunch? Doesn't a generous offer like that qualify me for dinner?'

'Dinner? On my pathetic expense account?' At the other end of the line Mulligan chuckled. 'Dinner would have to be on me, and there's no way I can face explaining that charge on the credit card to Mrs Mulligan.'

6

Luke Kingsley swore under his breath as the Jaguar's front nearside wheel scraped along the kerb, the coarse concrete ripping tiny scratches into the highly polished alloy. He turned the steering wheel anti-clockwise with the heel of his hand, straightening the car up, and yanked up the handbrake. He had parked up in Haverland Street some five or six houses short of number twelve, close enough to see the front door, far enough away not to be readily noticed by anyone looking out of the window. Nathan's Audi was still parked outside the house, and the sight of it brought an unbidden lump to his throat.

He turned off the engine and pushed back the seat, stretching out his legs, and leaned his body against the door's cool leather interior. His eyes scanned the street in search of Alice's BMW, and found it a few yards beyond Nathan's car. She was probably at home, then. He hoped she was there alone, or at least with only Olivia for company. There was a risk that Vienna Fielding would be there, and that would complicate things. The last thing he needed was that nosy bitch poking her nose into things that were nothing to do with her.

He put a hand out to the passenger seat and retrieved his mobile phone, and flicked at it with his fingers, searching for the last text he'd received from Alice. *Still thinking of you, Luke. We're here whenever you need us.* No demands, no drama, just an offer of support. She'd lost everything, and yet she was still ready to give before taking. How the hell could she be this strong? He blew out a breath. He had to pull himself together, stick to his plan.

Which particular plan he was going to stick to, well … that was a bit more problematic. Fortunately at this stage the starting point for any possibility was to access Nathan's money as soon as he could. He closed his eyes and thought for a moment. He had to find a way to access Nathan's office, to get his hands on the documents that Hector Campling needed to settle the estate, and on the bank cards that would give him access Nathan's readily-available cash.

The only way to access the office, of course, was to visit Alice and persuade her to let him in. He hadn't seen her since Friday evening, since he'd stopped off at the house to pick Nathan up on his way to the Kirkby Manor Hotel. He'd driven away with her fiancé, and left her a widow in all but name, and so far he hadn't even picked up the phone to ask how she was. How the hell was he going to explain himself?

Easy, he thought. He would tell her that he'd gone to pieces, that the shock of seeing Nathan murdered, of holding his dying brother in his arms, had caused a kind of breakdown. That she hadn't heard from him because he hadn't been thinking straight, that he'd been holed up in a hotel room trying to grieve. It sounded plausible, he reckoned, and not least because it wasn't a million miles away from the truth. If he wanted to, he could lay it on thick, tell her that he couldn't face her, that he felt responsible in some way for Nathan's death. That he couldn't face adding her grief to his own, that it was all too much to bear. He rubbed at his forehead with his hand to ease a growing tension. That story wasn't a million miles away from the truth either.

After that, all he had to do was get her on side. Ask her to deal with the funeral. Tell her that Nathan would have wanted it that way. That it was her right to choose the flowers, the reading, the order of service. Ask her if she would deal with Reverend Griffin, make her feel involved, important. Lead her to believe that as Nathan's fiancée she had a right to take responsibility for the celebration of his life, and the mourning of his loss.

And then, when she was busy with all the funeral arrangements, he could quietly deal with the financial matters. She must know already that everything was going to pass to him as next of kin, it should be plain sailing. Unless there was a will, of course. There may be a will hidden somewhere in Nathan's office, and if there was it was bound to be in his own favour. That would make things a whole lot easier.

He leaned over to the glove compartment and pulled out a small spiral notebook, and flipped it open to a page of scribbled notes, a list written in his scrawling, untidy hand. His eyes scanned down the list. *The will. Bank cards. Credit cards. Bank statements.* He would need all of these for his meeting at the bank tomorrow. Alice was bound to understand. *Savings accounts?* He knew Nathan had cash savings with the bank, there must be a passbook. Maybe more than one passbook. His attention wandered from the list for a moment, and he wondered how quickly he could get his hands on the cash, and then it wandered some more, to how much cash there was going to be.

He hadn't really thought about how much he would inherit until Hector Campling had asked him. He hadn't stopped to think about just how wealthy his brother was. And that it was all going to be his. He hadn't thought of it as his, just thought of it as blood money, atonement passing through his hands on its way to someone with a stronger claim. But now? It occurred to him that perhaps there was a different possibility. Would there be enough to go under cover, somewhere hot, Spain maybe? He could skip his debts, skip the country, lose himself in a beach resort, live quietly for a while. He'd lose his place in the Kirkby team, but he'd never been a passionate player.

Football had been an easy choice, a sport for which he had an aptitude rather than a hunger, a desirable alternative to a desk in an office or a place at a workshop bench. Anyway, he couldn't bear to be on the pitch again, to run across the turf knowing that Nathan wasn't on there with him.

If he lost himself abroad, he reasoned, maybe he could hang on to the money. There must be enough liquid cash to pay for a flight and a hotel, and then when the estate had been settled Hector Campling could transfer the money to him. He looked up out of the car's windscreen towards Alice and Nathan's house. Time enough to think about that tomorrow, after he'd been to the bank. Right now, he needed to focus on getting as much information out of Alice as he could. Nathan would have understood. Nathan had loved him, had always loved him. And until Alice came along, Nathan had always put him first. Nathan would want him to take the money, to run, to be secure, to be safe. *To hell with Alice.*

He let out a sigh and lowered his head, resting his forehead on the steering wheel. Who was he trying to fool? Nathan loved Alice. He loved Alice, and he loved Olivia, as much if not more than he'd ever loved his brother. *What the hell was he doing?*

He could feel his courage beginning to wane. He couldn't do this now, he needed more time to think. He lifted his head and slipped the key back into the car's ignition and turned it, firing the engine into action. As he did so the mobile phone beside him on the passenger seat jumped with a persistent buzz. His heart sank. Maybe Alice had seen the car parked in the street after all.

He picked up the phone and jabbed at it with his finger, and the screen lit up with the incoming text.

Tick tock, tick tock, you're running out of time …

'You're on a cushy number here, aren't you? I hope you're

not forgetting your roots.' Rose pulled the West Highland terrier up onto her lap and he circled once or twice, digging his claws into her legs, before curling up and settling down in a comfortable position. He turned his head and eyed her with his one good eye, and she ran a hand around his head and lifted his chin so that she could look directly into his face. 'Don't you be getting your paws under the table. You know Lu will expect you to show some loyalty when she gets back.'

He twisted his head free and gave her fingers an artful lick, before settling down for a snooze. Rose sighed. She knew Benny Bradman had a soft spot for the dog, and Lu's decision to leave Mac with him while she and Gerry were in Naples was a dangerous decision. Benny was obviously enjoying his role as dog-sitter, and Mac wasn't going to be in a hurry to leave someone who spoiled him every evening with a long walk to the pub and half a packet of pork scratchings.

She turned her attention towards the bar, where Benny was paying for a pint of Guinness and a large glass of Pinot Grigio. She liked Benny almost as much as Mac did. He had that sort of easy-going manner that didn't make a drama out of an unforeseen turn of events, and if he suspected that she had an ulterior motive for travelling out from Kirkby to see him, then he was too polite to say so. He'd taken her unexpected call with his usual good humour and suggested that they meet at The Boar, an unprepossessing pub a couple of miles outside of Market Melbourne. The décor was bland, and the food not much better, but the landlord was a dog-lover and Benny knew that Mac would be welcome.

'A glass of wine for Rose.' Benny placed the drink down on the table in front of her and took a gulp from his own glass before sitting down in the seat opposite. 'And a very welcome pint for me.' He leaned his forearms on the table and regarded her with undisguised amusement. 'Well, this is a pleasure I weren't expectin' at the start of the day.'

Rose offered him a coy smile. 'I wasn't expecting to be here myself, to be honest. Something came up at the ENB and they asked me to come up to Kirkby. I thought it was a good opportunity to kill two birds with one stone, treat you to supper as an apology for not being able to make it to Nathan Kingsley's wedding, and see my favourite terrier into the bargain.'

'There's no need to apologise about the weddin', Rose. You were better off out of it.' He took another swig from his glass. 'A whole church full of us sittin' there at St Benedict's, waitin' for the service to start. And everyone starts whisperin', you know ... where's the groom, he's a bit late, has a done a runner, little jokes to cover up the embarrassment because somethin' don't feel right. And then the vicar appears at the front of the church and tells us it's off. He can't tell us any more than that, and please will we just make our way home. I won't deny it, it turned my stomach when I heard what had happened.'

'Did you know Nathan well?'

'Pretty well. We were involved in the same charity, a boys club in Kirkby that encourages youngsters to play football. Nathan used his media profile to get them publicity, and we were both involved in the fund-raising. You know, charity auctions, sponsored golf tournaments, that sort of thing. He was a strange lad at times. To see him in public you'd think he was surrounded by people, but he'd lost his parents and didn't have any extended family. Just his brother, Luke. And then Alice, of course.' He sipped again on the pint, his brow creased with some private thought.

'Was he a good player?'

'Very good. Too good for Kirkby FC, but he had local loyalties so we won't condemn him for that.' He frowned. 'He had a good business head on him. He knew how to play the system. He used his sportin' profile to generate other opportunities – modellin', personal appearances, that sort of thing. He'd even sold the coverage of the weddin' to a magazine in return for a fee and a luxury honeymoon.'

'And his brother?'

Benny shook his head. 'Adequate. Average. He can play the game – football, I mean. But there's no brilliance. He puts in a pretty pedestrian performance. But then,' he mused, 'it wouldn't be a good thing to have a team full of brilliance, you need a few workmanlike players in there to give it all structure.'

'He doesn't seem to be average off the pitch. I've heard on the grapevine that Luke Kingsley might be the lesser player, but he's certainly the most notorious.'

'Nathan was the sensible one. Luke drinks too much, gambles too much, and womanises too much. But he adored Nathan. And Nathan always looked out for him. Well, he did until Alice came on the scene.' His face lit up. 'She's a lovely girl, Alice. A gentle soul, kind hearted. One of those rare sorts that always asks about you, and never talks about herself. Nathan was a lucky bloke, and he knew it.'

'And Luke?'

'I heard he was jealous.'

'Jealous of Nathan for finding Alice?'

'Jealous of Alice, for takin' Nathan away from him. Nathan used to fight Luke's battles for him. But that all changed after he met Alice.'

'Isn't that a little strange? A thirty-something professional footballer being jealous of his brother's fiancée?' Rose stared into her glass and jerked her wrist to swirl its contents around, releasing a soft, citrusy aroma. 'Has he always been like that?'

'I've only known them for a couple of years. Since just after their parents died. He and Nathan were very close, and that tragedy brought them closer together. But I've heard people sayin' that Luke's always been a bit on the immature side. I think he's always lived in Nathan's shadow, and he's played up a bit just to get the attention. The trouble is, Nathan's always been there to bail him out when he goes a bit too far. But that ain't goin' to happen now.'

'Does he often go a bit too far?'

Benny shrugged. 'I suppose it depends on your definition of "too far". I'm an easy goin' sort of bloke, Rose. I know we've all got a hidden vice or two. But Luke? It seems to have passed him by that livin' an excessive lifestyle went out with the nineties. The Kirkby team are a conservative lot. Most of them have wives and kids, and they're happy just to have a bit of local adoration.'

'Did it bother Nathan?'

'Bother him? I don't know about that. But he never shirked sortin' out the mess. I suppose that was another sort of attention, Luke knowin' that if he made a mess his brother would mop it all up for him. I've known Nathan settle his debts, sober him up, even pay off his one night stands to keep them quiet.'

Rose gave a whistle. 'Was that really necessary?'

Benny shrugged. 'Sport's all about reputation these days. There's too much reliance on sponsorship. You ought to know a bit about that. The ENB sponsor Kirkby FC. Can you imagine Clive Barden's face if one of the players was splashed all over the Sunday papers cavortin' in clubs in his underwear and fighting dodgy paternity suits? That wouldn't do the ENB's reputation much good, would it?'

She broke into a spontaneous laugh. 'Unfortunately I *can* imagine it. Clive's worried enough about the bank being associated with a murder.' She thought for a moment, and then asked 'so if Nathan was always having to bail Luke out, Luke's own financial position can't be that solid?'

'I don't know. I've known Nathan settle his gamblin' debts. Not with me, you understand?' He shot her a warning glance. 'I wouldn't take bets from Luke. He's too much of a liability. But it went deeper than the money. If Luke started a fight in a nightclub, Nathan would host a party for the staff. When Luke threw a drink over a girl who turned him down, Nathan bought her a new outfit and booked her into a health spa for the weekend. He was like Luke's own personal fixer.'

'And when Alice came along, that all changed?'

'I never saw any evidence of it myself. But I've been told that Luke didn't like havin' to play second fiddle. Some folks think Luke blames Alice for turnin' Nathan against him. But I don't think she did. I think that Nathan just found somethin' – someone – that he loved more than his brother. And he grew up. And maybe that opened his eyes to the fact that he was enablin' Luke's behaviour.' He sipped again on his drink. 'Luke was always civil to Alice in public, but when I think back, I think maybe there was a sort of undercurrent.'

'That he didn't like her?'

'I can remember seein' Nathan and Alice together, and I can remember seein' Nathan and Luke together. But Luke and Alice?' He shook his head. 'I only ever remember seein' Luke with his back to her. What conclusion would you draw?'

Michael Spivey cast a glance around The Feathers lounge bar. The Market Melbourne pub was never busy in the early evening but today it seemed quieter even than usual. Apart from himself, perched at the bar on a tall stool, there were only a scattering of other customers. At the far end of the room, an elderly couple were complaining to each other about the poor quality of the steak pie. A little closer, in a table mid-floor, a middle aged man was leaning back in his seat, hidden behind a copy of the Kirkby Evening Press. For the third day in a row the paper's headline screamed about Nathan Kingsley's murder. Spivey scowled, and turned back to the bar.

He leaned his elbow on the counter with a heavy sigh, and pulled a crumpled envelope from the pocket of his jacket. He looked at the postmark again, and then laid it down on the bar, unwittingly placing it in a wet ring of beer. He snatched it up again and rubbed it against the hip of his trousers to dry it off.

The envelope was addressed to him in a familiar if long-forgotten hand, an untidy black scrawl across the paper. He hadn't set eyes on that writing since long before his mother had passed away. He wished he wasn't looking at it now.

'Are you going to open that letter? Or just let it go on dragging you down?' Vienna, on duty at the other side of the bar, leaned her elbows on the counter and peered at him through the dark curls of her fringe. 'You've had it for three days now, and all you've done is carry it about with you.'

Three days. The letter had arrived on Saturday lunchtime, just as he was leaving the house to head for the church. He hadn't paid much attention to it then, just stuffed it into the pocket of his wedding suit and forgotten about it. It was only later, in the evening, that he remembered. When the television coverage of Nathan Kingsley's murder had stirred up a memory of something that he'd worked so long and so very, very hard to forget.

He licked his lips and turned a doleful eye towards her. 'I fink it's from my Dad.'

'Your Dad? You told me your Dad was dead.'

He ducked his head a little, a tiny shrug of contrition. 'I know.' He wanted more words, but the right ones wouldn't come. 'He is dead. To me. He has been for years. I didn't fink I'd ever hear from him again.' He cast his eyes down at the envelope.

Vienna pulled a clean glass from the rack behind the bar and shoved it up against an optic, jamming it not once but twice against the lever. She placed a double Scotch down on the bar and he picked it up without a word and drank it down in one thirsty, grateful gulp.

'He's a bad lot, my Dad. In and out of prison when I

was a kid. Knocking my Mum about. He broke her teeth once. I was there. I saw it.' Worse still, he heard it. He felt a lump begin to form in his throat. 'She took me away from him in the end. Got us a council flat.'

Vienna put out a hand and stroked the side of his thin face. 'Why didn't you tell me before?'

'I dunno. I suppose ...' He supposed, correctly, that it was the shame that had kept him quiet, but he couldn't quite put that into words. 'We was alright after she got us away.'

She squeezed his cheek with her fingers and then drew back her hand. 'I'm on my break in twenty minutes, we can open it together.' She turned her head away, to the other side of the bar where the middle aged man was waiting patiently to be served. 'Yes, love, what can I get you?'

He watched her go, and waited until she was fully absorbed in pulling a pint for the customer before picking up the letter, and slipping off the bar stool. Out in the car park the evening was cooling. His cigarette lighter was in his pocket, and he pulled it out with his right hand and clicked it until a long flame shot up and met the corner of the envelope dangling from his left. It was well alight in seconds and he dropped it onto the tarmac, watching only as long as it took to be sure that nothing would be left but charred scraps of paper.

7

'It still doesn't seem real to me, Alice. I just can't believe that he's gone.' Luke looked down at his hands, and twisted his fingers in what he hoped was a subtle display of sorrow and torment. 'I couldn't bear to speak to anyone, not even the police.' He cast his eyes up to her face. 'Inspector Mulligan says it's the grief, it takes people differently.' He gave a self-pitying sniff. 'But I'm here now. To apologise, and … and … to … make things right. If I can.'

Alice was sitting opposite him on the sofa, with Olivia on her lap. Her hands were around the child's waist, and he saw her slender fingers gently pull the small body closer to her. She bent her head to the girl's ear and whispered something that he couldn't hear. All the time her eyes were on his face. There was no malice in them, no hint of blame or denunciation. Perhaps he might have preferred it if there were.

'I can't quite believe it, either.' Her voice, when she finally spoke, was clear and calm. 'There's no need to apologise, Luke. You've lost your brother. You were there when he died. I can't imagine …' Her words trailed away and her eyes misted. She gave a gentle cough and cleared her throat. 'They say I need your permission to see him.'

'To see him?' Luke was momentarily thrown.

'There are things I need to say to him. He's been gone three days now, and I haven't had the chance to say goodbye.'

'Of course. I didn't think.' His heart began to beat a little faster. 'Of course you must see him.' He pulled his wallet from the inside pocket of his jacket and took out a business card. 'This is the funeral director I've arranged. Inspector Mulligan says the body will be released to them tomorrow.'

She stretched out a hand and took the card from him. 'You've begun the arrangements, then? For the funeral?'

He knew where this was leading. 'Inspector Mulligan made it clear that it was my responsibility as next of kin. But you need to be involved, Alice. It's only right. The flowers, and the readings, and stuff … would you ..?'

'I'd like Reverend Griffin to be involved.'

'Of course.' He put up his hands in a gesture of surrender. 'He knew you both. We could speak to him tomorrow.' The funeral, the flowers, the readings, the vicar, all covered in one short exchange. This was going better than he could have hoped. He leaned forward in his seat. 'There's something else, Alice, that we need to speak about.'

Her face softened and her eyes closed as her lips curled up into the gentlest of smiles. She gave a barely imperceptible shake of the head. 'I know, Luke. We need to speak about the house. And the rest of Nathan's estate.' She lifted her hand and pulled a strand of wispy blonde hair away from the side of Olivia's face, and bent her head to whisper again into the child's ear. The child slid down off her mother's lap and without a backward glance at Luke toddled across the room to a blanket and a pile of toys.

Luke could feel his mouth becoming dry, and the beat of his heart begin to gather pace. He knew what he had to ask now, but guilt was beginning to get the better of him. He needed to keep it together. The easy bit was done. He'd broken the ice, he'd apologised, and he'd offered up the body. If you could call that the easy bit.

He licked his lips again in a vain attempt to moisten them, but his tongue was dry and it didn't help. 'I've been to see a solicitor today.'

'Richard Fleming?'

'No. Hector Campling.' He saw her eyes narrow just a fraction, the first sign of discord since he'd arrived. 'He's based in Market Melbourne.'

She nodded. 'I've heard of him.' Her pretty face formed the nearest thing it could manage to a scowl.

He felt his shoulders stiffen with a new tension. Did it matter, that she knew of Hector Campling? He couldn't see any reason why it would. Hell, this was tough. He had to get it over with. 'Alice, there's no easy way to ask this. Did Nathan ever speak to you about leaving a will?'

'Of course he did.'

'You mean there's a will?' His voice rose, the words coming out a little too quickly.

'No. At least I don't believe so. But that's not what you asked me. Nathan wanted us to make mutual wills after the wedding. It would have been pointless making them before the wedding, because our marriage would have rendered them invalid.' She sounded far more knowledgeable on the subject than he had expected. 'There's no need to worry, Luke. I don't intend to challenge you over Nathan's estate.'

For a moment he thought he had misheard. 'Challenge me? Alice, I never …'

She put up a hand to stop him. 'You are Nathan's next of kin. You're entitled to Nathan's estate. If you could just give me a few more days, I'm trying to sort out somewhere else to live.'

A wave of sudden and unexpected guilt swept over him, and he impulsively stretched out a hand towards her. 'There's no rush, Alice. I know Nathan would want you to stay here for as long as you need to.'

'It's very sweet of you Luke, but I can't. I can't afford to. Nathan paid all the bills, and he isn't here to do that now. I have some savings put by, but not enough to afford the running costs on this place. Not if we want to eat. Olivia and I will have to find somewhere a lot smaller than this if we're going to keep our heads above water.'

'Look, I can pick up the bills until you find somewhere. And I could arrange for you to have some cash. There must be cash in Nathan's accounts.'

'Nathan would have understood, Luke.' An involuntary sigh escaped her lips. 'Look, I know that you have to do what has to be done. I know I'll have to move out of the house. And there is other stuff to be sorted out.' She stood up from the sofa and crossed the room to a small walnut desk. She drew a large manila envelope out of the top drawer, turned, and handed it to him.

He took it from her without a word, and stared down at it. This wasn't panning out how he expected it to. It was almost too easy. 'I don't know what to say.'

'You don't have to say anything.' She was back on the sofa now, and smiling at him. 'There's no battle to fight here, Luke. Nathan's estate is yours. I've put most of the documents I think you need into that envelope. You can check it now, if you wish.'

He tried to raise his eyes to look at her, but his head was heavy now with unexpected shame. Perhaps he was beginning to see what Nathan saw in Alice. She wasn't just beautiful. She was dignified. She didn't want anything that didn't belong to her. He felt suddenly humbled. 'Alice, I …'

'Please don't. I think we should change the subject now.' She was still smiling at him, but the light in her eyes was beginning to fade. 'I'm so pleased that you came to see me. Why don't I make us a coffee, and then maybe we can talk some more about Nathan. I've been clearing his office out and I found some old photo albums. I thought we might sit and look through them.' She didn't wait for him to reply.

He watched as she left the room, and then turned to

look at Olivia. The child was sitting on the floor, playing happily with a threadbare donkey, her tiny hands working feverishly to dress him in a small straw hat that refused to sit straight atop his head.

What a bloody mess. He sank back into his chair and put up his hands to cover his face. He needed the money, and now he hated himself. He needed Nathan to tell him what to do, needed him more than ever now that he was gone. Needed him *because* he was gone. He uncovered his face and looked towards the mantelpiece. Nathan looked back at him, his smiling, open face staring out from a large, framed photograph. Luke looked away, but his eyes were drawn back.

And it seemed to him that Nathan's eyes were staring straight at him, willing him to do the right thing. Willing him to look after Alice and Olivia, to open up and tell Alice the truth. Willing him to do something that was so far beyond him that he wouldn't know where to start.

'Is Michael Spivey still working for you?' Rose had always found Benny's choice of lieutenant a strange one.

'Don't sound so surprised. You know I made a promise to look out for him.' Benny looked disappointed that she might have forgotten. 'You'd hardly recognise him now, Rose. He's still hooked up to Vienna Fieldin'.'

'The barmaid at The Feathers?' Rose remembered raven-coloured curls and wise eyes framed by long, dark lashes. No one could believe it when she showed a soft spot for the hapless Michael, least of all Michael himself. 'Benny, that's wonderful. She must be good for him.'

'She's good for all of us. A contented Michael is a well-behaved Michael. Even I've seen a side of him that I didn't know existed.' Benny stared into his glass. 'She was meant to be Alice's bridesmaid. She was *the* bridesmaid. Well, apart from Alice's daughter. But she's only a little tot.'

'So how does Vienna come to know Alice so well?'

'They grew up together. They lived on the same street, and they're the same age, so they were in the same class at school.'

'Vienna grew up on the Barnfield Estate, didn't she?'

His face lit up into a smile. 'Blimey, what is this? Twenty questions?'

'I'm just interested.'

'No you're not. You're diggin' for dirt, girl.' He nudged her with his elbow. 'What you really want to know is how a single mother from the Barnfield Estate managed to hook a professional footballer as a husband.'

'Am I that transparent?'

'Yes.' He leaned back in his seat and eyed her with a cynical amusement. 'I hate to disappoint, but Alice ain't your typical gold digger, if that's where this line of questions is headin'.' He shook his head with a knowing smile. 'They met in a club in Kirkby, but Alice ain't really the partyin' sort. She's too gentle for that.'

'And Nathan?'

'He was too middle-aged for his own good. He would go out to the pubs and clubs with Luke, but I heard that he spent most of his time sittin' alone at the bar. That's how he met Alice. She was out with Vienna, celebratin' a mate's birthday. I think they were kindred spirits, quiet souls not wantin' to spoil the party but both wishin' they were somewhere else.' He looked wistful for a moment, remembering a kindred spirit of his own. 'You'll see what I mean when you meet Alice.'

'When I meet her?' Rose tried to look bemused.

'Come on, Rose. I ain't that dense. Of course you'll meet her. That's what you're up here for, ain't it? To watch the ENB's back while George Mulligan finds out who murdered Nathan?'

'Oh hell, I really *am* that transparent.' She had, at least, the grace to look abashed.

'It don't matter, Rose. I'm pleased to see you all the same. And so is Mac. Ain't we, fella?' He put a hand down to the side of his chair where Mac was diligently licking at a paw, and he ruffled the fur behind the terrier's ear. 'To be honest, I feel better for Alice knowin' that you're goin' to be up here. There's a storm brewin', and it ain't goin' to be pretty.'

'I don't understand.'

Benny scowled. 'Luke hasn't spoken to Alice since before Nathan died. And I don't trust him as far as I could throw him. They need to work together to sort out Nathan's affairs, and I don't just mean the funeral. Alice ain't exactly streetwise, and I can see Luke takin' advantage of her. Nathan would have wanted Alice to be safe, and that little tot of hers. But Luke?' He shook his head. 'It wouldn't surprise me to hear he plans to turn the two of them out on the street. But if you're here ...'

'Benny, I'm sorry. I can't talk about this. Their financial affairs are confidential.'

He paused, awkward now. 'I weren't askin' you to break a confidence, Rose. I was married to a criminal barrister for over twenty years, I know when to ask a question and when to keep my mouth shut. I'm just tryin' to tell you where I stand. Me and Vienna, we're tryin' to help Alice get through this. And we're afraid that Luke is goin' to take her for a ride. All I'm tryin' to say is that I'll sleep a bit easier tonight knowin' that you might be involved. At least I know she'll be dealt with honestly.'

It was an unexpected compliment, and Rose felt a guilty blush warm in her cheeks. 'I'll do my best. You know my brief is to protect the bank, but that doesn't mean that Alice won't be protected too. Everything will be done by the book, and the ENB will be sympathetic to her situation. But we can't bend the rules.'

'I weren't askin' you to do that, either.' His face darkened. 'Blimey Rose, you don't have a very good opinion of me, do you?'

She let the words hang in the air for a moment. The directness of the question discomforted her, its simple honesty jarring against her own manipulations. She had invited Benny to meet for supper so that she could learn a little more about Nathan Kingsley, about his brother and his fiancée, and the unhappy set of circumstances that had brought them all to this unexpected place. She'd underestimated Benny's ability to put two and two together and come up with seven. He'd seen her shallow motivations for what they were and met with her anyway, if only to let her know that Alice was gentle and Luke was jealous and that someone needed to keep an eye on the situation. 'Can I get us another drink?' She knew it didn't answer his question, but it was the only olive branch she could offer.

His brow puckered, and he fixed her with a stern gaze over the top of his glass. 'You don't deserve the opportunity. But on this occasion I'm feelin' magnanimous.'

'Another Guinness?'

'They've a decent bottle of Lagavulin behind the bar. I'll have a double.' He waited until she was on her feet. 'And bring a packet of pork scratchin's for Mac. And we don't want any of that earache about them not bein' good for him.'

Rose looked down at the terrier. He'd shuffled closer to Benny's leg and was eyeing her with a reproachful stare and a slightly curled lip. She opened her mouth to speak and thought better of it. Dealing with Benny was one thing, but dealing with both of them at the same time? She turned on her heel and made for the bar without another word.

Hector Campling clasped his hands behind his head and stared up at the ceiling. It was clean, a pristine white, far removed from the grubby, cracked ceiling he stared at during office hours. Mrs Campling wouldn't condone a grubby, cracked ceiling anywhere in their home, not even in the purpose-built den above the garage, the almost-private space which Hector had claimed as a home office.

It had been an interesting day, he had to admit. The visit from Luke Kingsley had been quite unexpected. He laughed softly to himself. The brains in that particular generation of the Kingsley family had obvious gone to Nathan. The boy Luke was an idiot. He had a natural ability as a soccer player, a skill which could leverage great wealth in today's skewed marketplace where young people were dazzled by Z-list celebrity, good looks and the ability to kick a small piece of inflated leather around a field. Hector had never understood the appeal of football himself, a tedious game with its origins firmly rooted in the Establishment's desire to find a harmless distraction for the masses on a Saturday afternoon. But he understood its power.

Nathan Kingsley, he thought, had been far more astute when it came to understanding his worth in today's foolish world. The older brother had cashed in on both his skill and his celebrity. He had sold his looks to the media, and used his name and his social currency to endorse a number of products, using the proceeds to invest in property. If Campling had heard correctly, he'd even sold the rights to cover his wedding to Alice Blacklaws, not to the local press but to the highest bidder, one of those trashy periodicals that permitted the general public a glimpse into another world. It wouldn't have been a difficult sell. Alice Blacklaws, he thought, had been a very shrewd addition to the Nathan Kingsley portfolio. The public loved a rags-to-riches story.

He lowered his gaze away from the ceiling and stared at the small pile of folders on his desk, the contents of the Kingsley file brought home with him this evening. It was a shame about Alice Blacklaws, he thought. The girl had been lifted from the Barnfield Estate by her love affair with Nathan Kingsley, and introduced to a different kind of life. But her tenure in that life required more than sweet words and soft caresses to endure. All that promise, all that expectation hinged on a legal document. A marriage certificate at the very least, and failing that a will. It was probably the least romantic concept anyone could conceive, Campling thought, declaring your intentions for your worldly goods after your own demise.

Possibly the least romantic concept, and possibly one of the most powerful motivations of human behaviour known to man – the simple piece of paper that answers that one question that everyone wants to ask after a bereavement, and which no-one dares to utter – *who inherits the estate?*

That was what Hector Campling loved about the law. It's role in intention. The simple way in which a few words committed to paper and signed in front of witnesses could bear testament to a man's intentions. The way in which even the very existence of such a piece of paper could show that a man cared enough to make provision for those he left behind.

If Nathan Kingsley had truly loved Alice Blacklaws he would have declared his feelings by making a will to keep her safe. He wasn't a feckless fool like his brother. He had brains, business brains, and he would have made a will to protect the woman he loved. And what a protection it would have been.

He pulled a blank piece of paper from a tray on his desk and picked up his pen. Based on what he already knew, information received so far from Luke Kingsley, and an early communication from Marshall and Slaughter regarding Nathan's holding company, he could pretty much guess at the value of the estate. Almost four hundred thousand pounds in the holding company account, and around nine hundred thousand for the house in Haverland Street, assuming that the insurance policy assigned to the mortgage paid out. Another two hundred thousand for the two rental properties in Scarborough, with their sitting tenants. And sundry liquid cash assets on top of that, with minimal outstanding debts to settle. He tapped the pen down the numbers as he totted up the total, and scribbled one point five million at the bottom of the list, ringing it with a flourish of his pen.

He sucked in his cheeks and considered the numbers. Assuming his usual rule of thumb of targeting twenty percent of the estate before inheritance tax in return for his efforts, he would be looking at approximately three hundred thousand pounds in fees. It wouldn't be easy to justify such a large figure with a client who had any brains, but with Luke Kingsley it wasn't going to be a problem. He knew that. All he had to do was drag out the case over many months, and keep issuing inflated invoices. In fact, dealing with an estate like this under the intestacy rules provided him with plenty of opportunity to drag things out and blame the system.

He put the pen up to his mouth and chewed on the end. Luke Kingsley was a special case. There was an inherent anxiety in his manner today, desperation in his eyes when he asked how quickly he would gain control of the money. Luke Kingsley was scared. Campling guessed that Luke Kingsley needed money, and needed it fast. And if Luke Kingsley was scared, and needed money fast, he would pay good money to secure his inheritance, to know that Nathan Kingsley's fortune was definitely going to be his.

Campling had already taken steps to place advertisements in the Law Gazette and the local papers, to enquire as to the whereabouts of any known will made by Nathan Robert Kingsley. It was a moot exercise of course, because he knew there would be no responses to the enquiry, but one had to play the game.

He put down the pen and turned his attention back to the pile of manila folders, picking up each one in turn, the conveyancing documents for the rental properties in Scarborough, information received that afternoon from Marshall and Slaughter, notes taken during his meeting with Luke Kingsley. One folder remained untouched and he paused for a moment, and then opened it and pulled out a thin sheaf of papers fastened with a paperclip.

There was no question that three hundred thousand would be an admirable result for administering the Kingsley estate. But how much more, he wondered, would Luke Kingsley be prepared to pay to *ensure* that he inherited? He glanced down at the papers in his hand, the simple legal statement that spoke of Nathan Kingsley's love for Alice Blacklaws, and his lips curled into a crooked, disingenuous smile.

How much more would Luke Kingsley pay for Hector Campling to breach the regulated duties of his office, and destroy his brother's will?

8

Rose cast a glance around the ENB's staff canteen, a long noisy affair of white melamine tables and blue plastic chairs. It was barely eight thirty five, and a brisk succession of colleagues were crashing through the swing doors to her right in search of their first caffeine hit of the day. Most of them were young women, and most of them cast in the same high-heeled, highly-groomed mould. A petite blonde on her way out through the doors lifted a hand in recognition and the girl sitting opposite Rose smiled, and waved in reply. 'A friend of yours?' Rose asked.

'That's Lydia. She works in the branch with me.' Stacy Singleton shared the smile with Rose. 'We started work for the ENB on the same day, and we go out together at the weekend.' She lowered her voice. 'She's actually been out with Luke Kingsley. Can you imagine?'

'Really?'

'Mm. He took her out for dinner. To Umberto's. You know, the posh Italian in the Old Town. The one that all the footballers use.'

'Oh, goodness.' Rose didn't know, but she tried to make the right noises. 'Are you interested in football, Stacy?'

The girl turned her head away with a coy smile. 'Not really. My Dad is. He supports Kirkby, of course. I was a bit of a disappointment to him. You know, an only child and I turn out to be a girl.' She turned back to Rose. 'But he still talks to me about it. He's so chuffed that Kirkby got promoted at the end of last season. He reckons that was down to Nathan Kingsley. He's always said that Nathan was a better player than Luke.' She gave a gentle shake of the head. 'I wouldn't have a clue. But I do see Luke sometimes. You know, out in the pubs and clubs at the weekend.'

'So you know him?'

'No. Not personally. Lydia was out with another friend when she met him.' Stacy's face registered the disappointment of an opportunity missed. 'I suppose I'll get to meet him now, when he finally makes an appointment to discuss Nathan's affairs. But it's not the same, is it?' She wrapped a hand of long, slender fingers around the paper coffee cup in front of her and thought for a moment. 'I'm so glad that you're here, Rose. I know this isn't a particularly complicated case, but it is so high profile.' She gave a skittish shake of the head, tossing a glossy mane of brunette waves away from her shoulders. 'It's so important that I get it right. I don't want to let Clive down.'

'I'm sure you won't do that, Stacy. Clive speaks very highly of you.' Rose smiled at her with genuine amiability. 'And that's quite an achievement in itself. Clive is very picky about who he praises. I should know. I bend over backwards to keep him sweet, and he never has a good word to say about me.'

It was an honest compliment, but the young woman still looked uncomfortable. 'I just try to do my job, Rose. It's a responsibility, to deal with the bereaved. And the ENB still has such old fashioned values for some things. I just try to uphold them.' She breathed out a sigh. 'Of course, it's usually elderly customers that I deal with. It's very rewarding, to think that I'm helping them at such a difficult time. The bereaved have enough to cope with without worrying about mundane things like bank accounts. If I can take the weight of some of the simple things, it leaves them room to arrange the funeral and deal with their grief.' She turned a knowing eye towards Rose. 'And of course, it's so important that we handle everything correctly. We wouldn't want the ENB to be accused of mishandling something so sensitive.'

Rose felt an unbidden smile begin to tug at her lips, and she pursed them together and nodded sagely in the hope of suppressing it. No wonder that Clive, who had been known on occasion to let a fatuous interest in a colleague get the better of him, had been so lavish in his praise of Kirkby's young bereavement officer. He could probably scarce believe his luck. Dealing with the consequences of death was a curious occupation for an attractive young woman, and this particular young woman was certainly attractive. The collar of her white, standard-issue polyester blouse lay crisp against a perfect mid-tone spray tan that ran all the way from her dark, lustrous hair down through a curvaceous body and skimmed its way to a pair of highly-polished black stiletto shoes via the longest pair of legs Rose had ever seen. She had a coltish beauty, marred only by a studious frown that betrayed her concern for her role and her responsibilities to both the customer and the bank. It was the studious frown, Rose reflected, that Clive probably found most appealing.

'I'm sure nothing will get mishandled on this one, Stacy. And just to be clear, I'm not really here to participate in the interviews with Alice and Luke. Clive knows that you're more than capable of dealing with both of them. He's just a little worried because of the nature of Nathan's death. It is possible that the police might be interested in Nathan's financial affairs as part of their investigation, and ... well, to be honest with you, he thought it would protect both the ENB and you as an individual to have an independent witness at those meetings.' It was almost the truth.

Stacy bowed her head and parted glossy lips to reveal a near-perfect smile. 'Clive can be so kind. I must admit, I did hope that he would send someone to help me, given the peculiarities of the case.'

'Peculiarities?' Rose tried to make the question sound casual.

'Oh yes.' Stacy leaned forward a little over the top of her coffee, and lowered her voice. 'The current account will be straightforward to deal with, of course, because it's in joint names so it will simply pass to Alice. And the cars will be dealt with under the terms of the finance agreements.' She flashed her eyes to the right, and then to her left, to assure herself that no one was in earshot. 'As for the house, the property transfer itself isn't unusual, of course, given that Nathan and Alice were about to be married. And Clive has confirmed that the transfer will complete, even though Nathan has died since the request was submitted. But,' she licked at her lower lip, and knitted her brows over eyes that were staring directly into Rose's face, 'he paid so much off the outstanding account before the transfer was requested that there is virtually no mortgage left to pay. And yet there is so little liquid cash left in the accounts that he held with the ENB. He has an outstanding credit card balance with us of just over six hundred pounds and we would normally just settle this by transferring cash from one of his other accounts. But he doesn't even have that much on deposit with us.' She blinked her long lashes. 'I'm not sure what it means.'

Rose folded her arms onto the table and gave a reassuring smile. 'It might not mean anything, Stacy. Nathan had other accounts than those he held with the ENB. We just need to ask whoever is administering his estate to make sure that the credit card account is settled.' She scanned the girl's face for evidence that her answer was enough, but Stacy's brows were still beetled forward, some question still playing on her mind. Under different circumstances, Rose might have been amused by the girl's curiosity, encouraged it even. But not on this occasion. On this occasion, if pressed to the point, Rose might have admitted to being worried.

Stacy Singleton was an asset to the ENB. She was attractive, professional, even empathic. Such a woman could be dangerous in a man's world, if she knew how to put those talents to good use. She had even caught the eye of an incorruptible bore like Clive Barden. But Rose had seen a flaw in the perfect Stacy, a tiny chink of weakness in the few brief moments they had discussed Luke Kingsley, that unmistakable look of a single woman susceptible to the glow of minor celebrity. And she couldn't discount the possibility that an attractive, professional, empathic woman, when cursed with the disadvantage of an empty heart, could render herself vulnerable to predators.

Was this why Clive wanted Rose by Stacy's side? Had he already seen the warning signs, the subtle nuances in Stacy's personality that would render her not an asset to the ENB, but a vulnerable liability?

George Mulligan walked over to the window and looked out across the Kirkby skyline. He'd used this office for over twenty years now, and usually he hardly gave a second thought to the view. But this morning it seemed to take on a different significance for him. It was all there in front of him, the Kingsley case framed like a modern masterpiece by the aluminium strips that ran the length and breadth of the double-glazed, sound-proofed glass. Luke Kingsley's apartment building stood a quarter of a mile or so to the left of centre, and beyond it the spotlights of Kirkby FC's ground pierced the sky like so many antennae. Over to the right he could just make out the crenelated roofline of the Kirkby Manor Hotel. And behind it in the distance, thanks to the gentle climb of the landscape, the dark-slated rooftops of Haverland Street's Georgian houses.

He folded his arms across his chest and leaned against the window frame. He felt out of his depth, and the feeling was a novelty to him, one that he didn't much like. He'd never dealt with a contract killing before, there wasn't much call for them in a provincial backwater like Kirkby, and he was too old a dog to be learning new tricks. He had a wealth of local knowledge, but that wasn't going to be much use on this one. The killer wasn't local, of that he was certain. Rumours in the town complained of an incomer. Typical of the Kirkby criminal fraternity, he thought. A talented young footballer with his whole life ahead of him has been snuffed out by a killer, and all they can do is complain that it was an outside job.

He sniffed his disapproval. The killer would be miles away now, would have been miles away on Saturday. There was no sign of him on the CCTV footage received from the hotel, and apart from Patricia Hewitt's sketchy description he might never have existed. He was cool, clean, professional. The only way they were going to find him was by tracing the motive, and for someone to pay for a professional of that calibre it must have been a pretty powerful one. But where do you start looking for the motive when the victim was a model of perfection?

Thinking it through, he had three possible lines of enquiry. The first was obvious, to look at those closest to Nathan. He couldn't think of any conceivable reason that Alice would have wanted her fiancé murdered an hour before their wedding. She stood to lose so much. If there had been bad blood between them, trouble in paradise that no one had noticed in those days and weeks leading up to the wedding, surely she would have just broken off the engagement? And if she was cold enough to have wanted the financial comforts that Nathan had to offer, without the added encumbrance of Nathan himself, wouldn't she have arranged for the killing to happen *after* they'd taken their vows, so that she could ensure an inheritance? As things stood, unless a will turned up, Nathan's estate would pass to Luke, and Alice would be left with nothing. And as for Luke, Patricia Hewitt had given evidence to his shock and grief when Nathan was shot. He might be afraid, Mulligan mused, but his grief was genuine.

If those closest to Nathan were out of the frame, then Mulligan would have to consider the possibility of some unknown connection, someone that Nathan had crossed in love or business. The idea seemed fanciful to him. What was to be gained by such a senseless murder? Revenge for a love affair cast aside when the beautiful Alice came into his life? The security of knowing that he couldn't spill the beans about a dodgy business deal? He couldn't see it.

His eyes wandered towards Luke Kingsley's apartment building. The third possibility still intrigued him. He couldn't shake off the suspicion that the bullet was intended for Luke Kingsley, despite all of Kingsley's denials. There had been a definite flash of fear in those hawk-like eyes when Mulligan asked him if he had any enemies. And the lad was a liar. Anna Hill was adamant that Luke hadn't been anywhere near Haverland Street since Nathan's death, and yet Luke had told Mulligan to his face that he'd spoken to Alice and that she was coping.

But Luke Kingsley was, by his own admission, an average, provincial soccer player. Why would anyone pay good money to get rid of him? Who might have wanted him dead? He was a known womaniser, it could have been a jealous ex-girlfriend. And he gambled, but it was common gossip that Nathan Kingsley settled his brother's gambling debts. And anyway, Mulligan reasoned, if a gambler owed you money then snuffing him out wasn't going to get you your money back.

He turned away from the window and stared at his desk. Come on George, think about this logically. What do you already know, and what does it mean? Luke Kingsley is afraid. If Luke Kingsley is afraid, then he knows something, either who the killer is, or why his brother was murdered, and possibly both.

This isn't about Alice, and it isn't about some unknown jealous girlfriend or disgruntled business associate. This is about the Kingsley brothers. This is about something where their lives have overlapped. The answer to this one has to lie somewhere in their shared past.

What we have to do now is start digging.

Michael Spivey turned to look at Olivia through the car window and lifted his hand to wave to her. Safe in the arms of Vienna's sister Florence, Olivia waved back at him with a grin and blew her Uncle Mikey a kiss.

He swallowed down a lump in his throat and started the Vauxhall's engine, pushing it roughly into first gear, and pulling away from the kerb before his emotions got the better of him. *Poor little mare.* He tried not to think about her mother, about Alice, about what she was feeling. Love found, and love lost so ruthlessly. If he lost Vienna now, like Alice had lost Nathan, it would be the end of him.

At the end of the road he turned left, leaving the Barnfield estate and pointing the car back towards Kirkby. The traffic was light for a Wednesday morning, and he reckoned it would only take him twenty minutes to get back to the town centre. Vienna and Alice wouldn't need collecting from the bank until at least midday. He eased his foot up off the accelerator. There was no need to rush.

He put out a hand and switched on the radio, and fiddled with the tuner until he found a station that pleased him. He liked nostalgia, songs that reminded him of his mother and his Auntie Jen, and the times he'd spent with both of them in Scarborough, after the bad times had stopped. After the last time his father had battered his mother, and she'd taken him away to safety for good.

He turned up the volume and tried to drown out the memories, but he knew it would take more than the Beach Boys this morning to put the past to rest. He flicked the radio off again with an impatient finger, and travelled the next mile and a half in a petulant silence until a familiar junction came into view. He slowed the car and swerved left down the narrow side road, and bumped another quarter of a mile until he reached a familiar and much-loved place. He pulled the Vauxhall to a halt and opened the door, and closed his eyes as a waft of warm, sea breeze blew across his face, filling his nostrils with a familiar salty air.

Why had the bastard sent him another letter?

It had arrived that morning, Michael's name and address scrawled across the envelope in that familiar, spidery handwriting. What the hell did his father want? And how did he even get hold of the address? Was he watching Michael? Spying on him?

There had been no contact now for over twenty years. When he was a boy he'd wanted this father, even after his mother had taken him away. Or maybe he had just wanted any father, even a dysfunctional one. Better than no father at all. It had been tough as a teenager. His mother wasn't faultless, but she'd done her best. And yet there was still a big, gaping hole where his father was supposed to be.

He opened his eyes and stared out through the windscreen, across the scrub land in front of the car, over the edge of the cliffs and out to sea, across blue foaming waves and out into the distance. His mother had been dead for the best part of ten years, his Auntie Jen gone too. They died so young. It must have been the hard life they led.

He swallowed back a tear. His mother would be furious, to know that his father was trying to get in touch with him now. And even more furious to know that he was thinking of opening the letter. He couldn't decide if it would be disloyal, a betrayal of her memory, even just the fact that he wanted to know why his father was writing to him. Would it do any harm just to open it? He could always throw it away afterwards.

But could he? One letter was easy to throw away. You take a match to it, watch it burn, stamp on the ashes, the problem goes away. But this problem hadn't gone away, had it? He'd disposed of the first letter in just that way, much to Vienna's disgust, and plop, here's another one arriving on the doormat. If he disposed of this one, what then? Would another one come? And another, and another?

The only way he was going to answer the question, of course, was to open the damned letter. His father must have a reason for getting in touch with him, and it must be a good one to break the silence of twenty years. It wouldn't be to offer something, of course. He'd never offered anything to Michael, except perhaps his belt across the back of bare calves or his hand across the back of the head, reprimands, mistreatment, punishment. So if it wasn't to offer something, it could only be to ask for something.

Was that possible? That his father could want something from him, something so important that he'd write not once, but twice in the space of a couple of days, refusing to accept his silence, insistent that Michael listen to what he had to say? He thought for a moment, about the possibility of his father, the man who knocked his mother around, who was never there for him, now begging for some favour, some gift that only Michael could provide. Some need that only Michael could deny him.

Now that would be worth opening the envelope for. To turn the tables for once in his life, to know that his father wanted something from him, perhaps even needed something, and to know that he – Michael – was going to be in the position of power. The power to say *no*. To refuse his father some begged favour or gift which he, and he alone, could deny.

The thought was just too tempting. The letter was secreted in the Vauxhall's glove compartment, and he yanked it open and pulled the envelope out, and hastily slipped a nicotine-stained thumbnail under the flap to rip it open. He pulled out a single sheet of spidery scrawl and unfolded it with almost trembling fingers, and then ran his eyes quickly over the untidy writing. It wasn't what he expected.

He felt a sharp sting in his throat as the unexpected grief gripped him, and the hand holding the letter gnarled into a fist, curling the paper with it, and he blinked sharply to contain the tears beginning to sting at the back of his eyes.

He took in a deep breath to steady himself. He shouldn't have opened the letter, he knew that now, but it was too late. It was done. He couldn't put it back, couldn't seal it up and forget about it, pretend that he hadn't seen what was in there.

He understood now why his father had written to him again. And he knew that if he ignored this letter, as he had ignored the first, there would be another, and another, and another, until he finally caved in and responded.

Or until his father couldn't write any more letters.

9

The air in the ENB's small meeting room was stuffy with the scent of lavender. Rose had watched bemused as Stacy Singleton dropped a fragranced tissue into the waste paper basket just minutes before their meeting with Alice Blacklaws. It was supposed to create a relaxing atmosphere, Stacy had said, and put the customer at ease. Rose, whose nose was beginning to itch with the desire to sneeze, remained unconvinced.

Still, lavender or no lavender, she couldn't deny that somehow Stacy Singleton had managed to gain the trust of Alice Blacklaws with remarkable ease. The two were of an age and a gentle rapport, encouraged by Stacy's uncanny ability to mirror Alice's body language and patterns of speech, had soon developed. Alice had visibly relaxed as Stacy explained to her those parts of Nathan's financial affairs which they could and could not discuss, nodding her head in understanding and gentle agreement. Stacy was a born communicator, and Rose was just concluding that her own role in the meeting was unlikely to expand beyond that of quiet observer, when Alice tossed a curved ball into the conversation with such a gracious whisper that her words fell into an empty space in the proceedings for which Stacy had no planned response. 'It doesn't really matter to me what Nathan left behind. I don't want any of it.'

Stacy, seated to the left of Rose, had been smiling at

Alice with a kind concern, but at hearing these unexpected words the smile froze to her lips. The connection between herself and Alice broken, she turned startled eyes to Rose. 'I think, Rose, we need to discuss each financial item in turn?' It was an unmistakeable cry for help.

Rose leaned her forearms on the table and turned kind eyes towards Alice. 'From the bank's perspective, we can only follow the instructions that a customer has given us within the terms and conditions of an account. That means we must arrange for anything that legally belongs to you – like the contents of the current account that you held jointly with Nathan – to become yours. If, after that, you choose to give the money away for some reason, then that is your right. But it's not something that the bank can do for you, Alice. We have to follow a process.' She saw a flicker of understanding on Alice's face. 'Perhaps if Stacy takes you through each account in turn, we can explain what the bank must do with that account, and then you can decide afterwards what you wish to do with the money. There is only really the mortgage account and the current account. Everything else was in Nathan's sole name and must be dealt with during the administration of his estate. We are assuming that Luke will take care of that.' She turned back to Stacy with a nod.

Stacy, still discomforted by this deviation from her plan for the meeting, smiled wanly at Rose and picked up the first sheet from a small pile of papers in front of her. She passed it over to Alice, who took it and then placed it down on the table without looking at it. 'This is a statement of the mortgage account, Alice. The transfer to joint names has almost completed now, and ...'

'The house is nothing to do with me.' Alice gave a gentle shake of the head. 'The house belonged to Nathan. It was his decision to include me on the mortgage, because we were getting married. But now ...' She began to stumble over the words. 'Now that he's gone, the house is nothing to do with me. I'm not his wife. The house belongs to Luke.' She turned to Rose, looking for understanding. 'Even if I wanted to live there, I couldn't possibly afford to. Nathan paid me a salary to be his personal assistant. Even my job died with him. I only have a small amount of savings to live on until I can find work. And even when I do find work, my pay will be so small that I couldn't possible raise the mortgage, let alone meet the repayments on my own.' She paused, and then added 'there must be some way to reverse the transfer, so that the property stays in Nathan's name, and passes directly to Luke.'

Rose lifted her arms from the table and leaned back in her seat. She folded her hands into her lap, but kept her eyes on Alice's face. 'Did Nathan tell you, Alice, that he had paid a lump sum into the mortgage account before he requested the transfer to joint names?'

Alice blinked. 'No, he didn't.' It appeared to be genuine surprise. 'Why would he do that?'

'Well, I would think so that the house wasn't encumbered by a mortgage.' Rose pointed a finger at the mortgage statement. 'If you take a look at the document which Stacy has passed to you, you'll see that Nathan settled virtually the whole mortgage by a number of transfers from accounts held with both the ENB and with other banks. The ENB has checked out all the transfers, to ensure that the funds were legitimate, and they were. Each transfer came from a savings account in Nathan's name. The current outstanding balance on the mortgage is fifty pounds. That is the minimum sum required for the ENB to retain possession of the title deeds to the property. It's a service we provide so that the customer doesn't have to pay a solicitor for secure storage.'

Alice was blinking rapidly now, and a faint panic was beginning to show on her face. 'I don't understand why he would do this? Why would he do this?'

Rose and Stacy exchanged glances, and then Rose said quietly 'probably so that you would have a home without a mortgage. Perhaps he wanted you to start your married life with that amount of security. Of course,' she added after a moment, 'as he decided to make you a joint tenant of the property, it means that when the transfer is complete, the whole property will belong to you. Free of a mortgage. The ENB doesn't apply interest to the fifty pounds left in the account for deed storage. It just gives us the right to hold the deeds on your behalf.' Rose paused, and then said gently 'the house belongs to you, Alice.'

The gentle fragrance of lavender in the room appeared to be losing its effect. Alice Blacklaws was struggling to hold back a convulsive sob, her lips folded in to hold back the sound, her eyes closing to stem the tears beginning to flow. 'Why would he do that? Why would he do that to me?' The words escaped her lips as an agonised wail.

Rose stretched out her right hand and grasped the fingers of Alice's left hand tightly. 'I don't think he did it *to* you, Alice. I think he did it *for* you. I think he did it because he loved you.'

The Kirkby Central Library was a large Victorian sandstone building a quarter of a mile south of the police headquarters. Originally a workhouse, its lofty ceilings and clinical corridors were not unknown to DS Scott, who was usually pleased to volunteer when an investigation called for a trawl through the archives of the local newspapers. But today he was embracing the task with less than his usual amiable enthusiasm. Because George Mulligan was having lunch with Rose Bennett, and he hadn't been invited.

Ian Scott liked Rose. He'd always had an eye for a slim redhead, and Rose came with the added attractions of a quick brain and a sense of humour. He'd enjoyed a relaxing supper with her when their paths had crossed last November, but the opportunity to repeat the experience had eluded him until now. He knew there was a boyfriend in the background, but Rose herself had admitted doubts that the relationship was going anywhere, and Mulligan's announcement yesterday that she was back in Kirkby and working on the Kingsley case had been music to his ears. Shame, then, that George had decided to keep her all to himself.

He stretched out his arms above his head and forced a yawn to expel stale air from his lungs. He had been in the archive room for over an hour now, trawling through back copies of the Kirkby Evening Press on microfilm, and his eyes were beginning to ache with over-use. It hardy compared with lunch at Umberto's. It might not have been so bad if the Kingsley brothers had played rugby. At least an interest in the sport might have left him feeling less hard done by. But football? It didn't stir a heartbeat.

He lowered his arms and rolled his head around first to the left, and then right, easing out the tension forming in his neck muscles. He had to admit that his efforts weren't a complete waste of time. Press coverage of the Kingsleys in this one provincial newspaper alone, beginning with the death of their parents in 2012, had revealed an interesting trend in the brothers' relationship.

The newspaper had given extensive coverage to the funeral held at St Benedict on the Hill. Pictures showed Nathan and Luke Kingsley at their parents' graveside, their arms around each other for support. From there, throughout the following football season, the brothers had been inseparable. The sport pages carried glowing reports of their performance on the pitch, and the gossip pages revelled in their social life around the bars and clubs of Kirkby. Both brothers were reported in equal measure, but it was clear which Kingsley was the party animal, and which the serious sportsman.

Towards the end of 2013 the newspaper carried a different kind of story, reporting that Nathan Kingsley had accepted a role on the committee of a local charity supporting under-privileged kids. And here there appeared to be a parting of the ways. As coverage grew of Nathan's interest in the charity, of the time he spent coaching young players at evening training sessions, and the support he gave to fund-raising initiatives, his brother was conspicuous by his absence. At least, by his absence from Nathan's side. As Nathan threw himself into his charity work, Luke Kingsley's partying appeared to go from strength to strength.

Throughout the following year the trend continued, the brothers appearing to grow further and further apart. Kirkby FC were playing well, holding their position near the top of their league, but with promotion always just out of their reach. Reports in the sports pages seemed to confirm that on the pitch at least Nathan and Luke were playing with their usual sense of team spirit, but occasional photographs in the gossip column showed them looking strained, Luke frequently drunk, Nathan just as frequently disapproving. A full page article in the autumn of 2014 reported that Luke Kingsley had started a fight in a local nightclub, a tasteless brawl in which a young woman in the wrong place at the wrong time had ended up with a broken wrist.

Ian Scott took in a deep breath and fixed his eyes back on the screen in front of him, and turned the machine's handle to feed the next set of images through the reader. He bent his head forward and focused his eyes on the small print whizzing past as the handle turned, scanning the images for more news of the Kingsleys. It came at the end of 2014.

Just as the Christmas party season began a new set of stories began to emerge, of a smiling Nathan Kingsley out on the town with a beautiful and delicate looking blonde. DS Scott turned the machine's handle slowly, running his tiring eyes down the small print, searching for anything that might be of use. Headlines talked about the local beauty who'd captured the heart of a local hero, and photographs showed the couple together at charity events and business dinners, and on one occasion even a visit to the children's ward at a local hospital. And as the pictures of Kirkby's new golden couple increased in frequency, so did reports of Luke Kingsley going off the rails. Stories of his boorish behaviour off the pitch began to increase. As Nathan's happiness grew, if the sports pages were to be believed, so did his performance on the pitch. And as Luke's behaviour deteriorated, his own performance on the pitch began to suffer. Cause and effect. Action and reaction. As Nathan's love and energy found a new direction in Alice Blacklaws, so his brother's star began to fade.

Scott slumped back in his seat and turned his head away from the screen. It almost pained him to think it, but this particular line of enquiry was beginning to look interesting. The growing rift between the two brothers was clearly visible with each passing newspaper report. He'd reached the end of 2014, and there was one more reel of microfilm to go. He straightened his back, rolled out his shoulders, and swapped out 2014 for 2015.

Nathan Kingsley and Alice Blacklaws announced their engagement on Valentine's Day. Pictures in the newspaper now were showing not just the couple, but little Olivia Blacklaws too. By contrast, Luke Kingsley was becoming more and more isolated. Pictures of him taken in local nightspots showed a sullen, angry young man, abandoned by his brother and partying hard to forget it. But on the plus side, his sporting performance somehow seemed to improve. Kirkby FC were doing well, and for the first time in nearly twenty years they looked like a contender for promotion. As the season progressed praise upon praise was heaped on Nathan Kingsley. There was even a suggestion that Alice and Olivia were to thank for Kirkby's upturn of fortunes, that having settled down and found a family, Nathan Kingsley was finally at peace and had found his stride in the game. Everyone was winning as a result. A back page banner at the end of April 2015 carried an optimistic headline, crying "Kirkby finally for promotion?" and Scott, close to the end of the season and therefore close to the end of his task, rattled the handle of the film-reader round, only for the end of the film to fly off the spool.

He lifted his hands in a gesture of frustration, and muttered under his breath. 'Where the hell is the rest of the paper?' He looked about him and caught the eye of a passing archivist. 'Excuse me? The Kirkby Evening Press,' he pointed at the film reader, 'the spool has run out at the end of April?'

The archivist, a prim looking young woman with an armful of dog-eared periodicals, peered at him over the top of her spectacles. 'We only transfer to film once a month, and in arrears. The May copies won't be done until the end of June.' She turned to carry on her way, but he called her back.

'I'm investigating a police matter. Can I see the actual papers, if they haven't been transferred to film yet?'

The archivist rolled her eyes and tilted her head towards a desk at the back of the room. 'You'll have to fill in a request slip.'

He pulled his warrant card from out of his trouser pocket and flicked it open so that she could see it. 'I need them now.'

Her eyes widened for a moment, and then narrowed again. 'We bring original documents every thirty minutes. Make sure that you leave your request slip in the tray on the right hand side.' And she was gone before he could say "that would be wasting police time."

Stacy Singleton rested the phone in the crook of her neck, and swivelled round on her chair to reassure herself that Rose was out of earshot. She lowered her eyes to the mouthpiece and spoke quietly into it. 'Thank you so much for calling us, Mr Kingsley. We were hoping to hear from you today.' She pivoted the chair from side to side, a girlish, almost flirtatious movement that was completely wasted on a caller who couldn't see it.

At the other end of the line, Luke Kingsley's voice was smooth and amiable. 'I was hoping to come into the branch this afternoon and sort out my brother's affairs. Would that be convenient?'

Stacy felt her cheeks flush with a sudden excitement. 'This afternoon? That would be ideal.' She lifted her eyes up across the office to where Rose was taking a phone call of her own. 'I wonder, would it be possible for you to come in after three o'clock? I have a colleague in the office today who was hoping to sit in on our meeting, and she has a late lunch appointment. Apart from that, our diary is completely free. If we pencilled you in from three until five that would give us plenty of time to discuss your brother's accounts.'

There was a pause while Luke considered the possibility. He gave a quiet, self-conscious laugh. 'I'm sorry Stacy, I have to meet again with my solicitor after three. Would it be possible to meet at two? If your colleague isn't available, I'm sure the two of us will manage.'

The two of us? For a moment Stacy lost the ability to breath. Alone in an office with Luke Kingsley? She blew out a breath and glanced again at Rose. What was she supposed to do now? She couldn't force him to come in at a time to suit Rose, he was the customer. And Rose herself had been insistent that they speak to him as soon as possible. She could book the appointment for two o'clock and ask Rose to change her lunch appointment. That was the obvious thing to do. But then, perhaps, Rose wouldn't be able to change her appointment. Oh hell. *Oh hell.*

'Stacy, are you still there?' Luke's voice was soothing. She hadn't expected him to be so gentle. There were rumours about him, that he had a temper, that he could play the fool. But here, on the end of the line, he sounded nothing but charming.

'Yes, sorry.' She tried not to sound flustered. 'Yes, two o'clock. I'm sure that would be fine.'

'Is there anything you'd like me to bring in to the bank? Any documents, paperwork, whatever?'

'There were some items outlined in the letter we sent to you, Mr Kingsley. We'll need the death certificate, or an interim certificate to confirm the death. And a copy of your brother's will, if there is one.' She was back on script now, talking quickly, almost gabbling at him. *Play it cool, Stacy. You don't want him to think you're an idiot.* 'We'll need details of the executors for his estate, and his legal representatives. Oh, and please could you bring some form of identification for yourself? As you're a customer of the ENB, we just need one form of ID, your debit or credit card will suffice.'

'OK, I can do all of that. Stacy, can I ask you …' He broke off and laughed. 'You don't mind me calling you Stacy, do you?'

'No, no, of course not.' She was babbling now, the excitement of finally meeting him face to face beginning to overtake her. 'What is it that you'd like to ask, Mr Kingsley?'

'Please, call me Luke.' His voice was beginning to sound hypnotic. 'Just exactly what will we be covering at the meeting?'

'Well, as it outlines in our letter we'll review all of your brother's accounts, and give you an up to date position on their balances. We can discuss any payments due on any of his accounts, like his credit card account, and how you might want to settle those. And we can talk about any immediate expenses, such as funeral expenses.'

He was silent for a moment, thinking, and then he asked 'has Alice been in to the branch to speak to you?'

Stacy's heart skipped a beat. 'Alice?'

'Yes, Alice. Alice Blacklaws. Nathan's … fiancée.'

For a moment she was tongue-tied. There was no reason for him to ask about Alice, and every reason for her to maintain Alice's confidence. But this was Luke Kingsley, and reason didn't come into it. There was no desire to deny him an answer, and every wish to try and impress him. She cleared her throat. 'We have spoken to Miss Blacklaws, yes. But only in her capacity as a personal customer. I mean, we didn't discuss … Well, we only talked to her about those accounts which were held in joint names.'

This time his silence before speaking was longer. 'Accounts in joint names?' The tone of his voice had changed too, still friendly, but now there was a hint of disdain.

She felt the colour in her cheeks deepen, a self-regulating rebuke for having spoken out of turn. 'Perhaps we could discuss that further when you come in this afternoon?'

'At two o'clock.' His tone had softened again. 'Yes, I'll look forward to it. It will be good to put a face to the name, Stacy.' And he hung up without waiting for her to reply.

Stacy closed her eyes and let out a sigh of self-reproach. What the hell was she doing? She had a clear instruction from Clive to make sure that Rose was at any meeting that took place with either Alice Blacklaws or Luke Kingsley. And Rose was a sweetheart. Having her there at the meeting wasn't going to be any sort of hardship. Except, of course, that if Rose was there it would only ever be a meeting. A professional meeting. There would be no opportunity for small talk, to take the conversation onto a personal level. No opportunity for flirtation. And if Rose wasn't there, then …

She put her hands up to her face, cupping her own cheeks in a moment of sheer dismay. *For God's sake, Stacy, he's not just Luke Kingsley, he's a bereaved customer.* She would have to tell Rose. Of course she would have to tell Rose. Rose would have to rearrange her plans, and be at the meeting at two o'clock. But what if she couldn't? Stacy lifted her eyes and cast another glance across the office, to where Rose was just beginning to pack her bag and depart for her own lunchtime meeting. She swivelled round in her chair and grabbed her handbag from under the desk, then without a backward glance she stood up and headed quickly for the door leading to the staff restaurant. She needed a coffee, and needed it fast. So fast, in fact, that talking to Rose would have to wait. And preferably until after she had met with Luke Kingsley.

10

'Essex? What the hell do you want to go back there for?'
Benny Bradman lounged back in his office chair and
folded his arms across his chest. He fixed his eyes on
Michael Spivey's face. It was two years now since they'd
headed north together to Market Melbourne, Benny to
start a new life after the loss of his wife, and Michael
because Benny was all he had in the world. Neither of
them had been back to Essex since.

Theirs was a curious relationship. The late Mrs
Bradman had defended Michael Spivey on a charge of
petty larceny and taken him under her wing after his
acquittal. Benny, who never questioned an instruction
from the woman who lit up his world, had employed the
hapless criminal in one of his betting shops. They had little
in common except Catriona Bradman and a shared passion
for sport, and for some time, both before and after her
death, it had been a tenuous relationship. But in recent
times, and largely due to Vienna Fielding's growing
influence on Michael, they had developed a sort of
grudging, mutual respect. Benny, baffled that a feisty and
intelligent girl like Vienna would look twice at a weasel like
Michael, found himself looking at his sidekick in a
different light. Michael, influenced by Vienna's view that
Benny had an old-fashioned kind of integrity that deserved
a degree of respect and admiration, found himself
appreciating his boss for things he had never before

thought important.

But appreciation was one thing, and candour was another. Michael sniffed at Benny's question, and shrugged his shoulders. 'It's private. Family business, like.'

'Family business?' Benny's tone was incredulous. 'You ain't got any family.'

Michael looked peeved. 'Yes I do. I've got a cousin in Dagenham.'

'And that's who you're goin' to see, is it? This cousin in Dagenham?'

'You owe me a day. I covered the first day of Royal Ascot on my day off, and you said I could take it back this week.'

Benny nodded. He could see that he wasn't going to get anywhere with this line of questioning. 'And you're plannin' to go tomorrow.'

Michael's face relaxed and he managed a half-smile. 'You won't even miss me, Boss. I'll drive down first fing in the morning, and I'll be back the same day. There ain't much business on tomorrow, the girls in the shop can cover it without me.'

'Vienna's goin' with you tomorrow, then, is she?'

'Vienna? Nah, she wouldn't be interested.' Michael glanced down at his fingers, and looked suddenly shifty.

'Not interested in your family? That don't sound like the Vienna I know. She loves family. And for some utterly inexplicable reason, Michael, she loves you as well.' He watched a blush creep into Michael's cheeks and laughed to himself. 'I find it very hard to believe that she wouldn't want to meet this mythical cousin of yours.'

'You ain't catching me out like that, Benny. It ain't a myffical cousin. And Vienna, well, she would have come but she's busy with Alice.'

'So how come I've never heard about this cousin before?'

'We lost touch, like. You know how it is.'

If Benny knew how it was, he didn't concur. 'And so he

just got back in touch, did he? Out of the blue?' He was watching Michael's face closely. 'It is a bloke, is it? I hope you're not thinkin' of playin' away.'

Indignation flooded into Michael's face. 'You know I wouldn't do that to Vienna.' The words hissed out like a jet of steam.

'And so I should damn well hope.' Benny rested his elbows on the desk and fixed Michael with a firm stare. 'Alright, you go off to Essex and hook up with this cousin. And when you get back you can come and tell me all about it.' He watched as Michael got to his feet, and waited until he was almost out of the door. 'Michael.'

Michael turned and looked at him. 'Yes, Boss?'

'There are things we left behind in Essex that might be better off forgotten. If I thought ...'

Michael blinked, and then he shook his head, eager to appear reassuring. 'It's just a cousin, Benny. Like I said. A bit of family business.' He dropped his eyes to the floor and turned out through the doorway, closing the door behind him.

Left alone, Benny raised his eyes to the ceiling and tried to recall what he knew of Michael's family. There was a mother, dead and gone, and an Auntie Jen up in Scarborough who had married a fisherman. There was no cousin in Dagenham that he knew of. But there was another relative, one that no one with any sense would want to remember.

It wasn't his place to tell Michael not to go to Essex. If Michael wanted to visit his father, it was up to him to make a decision like that for himself. But Benny couldn't help but feel that no good was going to come of it. Perhaps the best he could hope for was to be around to pick up the pieces when it all went horribly wrong.

'I've never known so many people want to get rid of a fortune.' Rose drained the remaining drops from a glass of iced pineapple juice and gently placed the glass down on the table. She ran a finger absently around the rim of the tumbler, studying it, and then looked up at George Mulligan. 'In the last few weeks of his life Nathan Kingsley settled a small fortune on Alice Blacklaws without telling her. He paid off his mortgage and then took steps to make her a joint tenant of the property so that it would belong to both of them equally. The transfer wasn't quite complete when he died, but it will go through, and when it does Alice will own the property outright. In addition, in the days before his death, he transferred large sums of money into savings accounts held at the ENB. One in Alice's name, and one in her daughter Olivia's.'

'When you say large sums, what are we talking? Thousands? Tens of thousands?'

'Between the two, the total runs to almost two hundred thousand pounds.'

The policeman expelled a soft whistle through his teeth. 'And she claims she didn't know?'

'I'd swear she didn't know, Mr Mulligan. She knew that Nathan had requested the change of ownership for the house, but she was genuinely shocked when I told her that he'd paid off the mortgage.'

'And the savings?'

'She had the passbooks with her. There was an amount of interest due on both accounts and she'd planned to have the books updated while she was in the branch. The original balances totalled around fifteen hundred pounds. We had the books updated and handed them back to her. I thought she was going to pass out when she saw the balances.'

'So she came into the bank with almost nothing, and left knowing that she was a millionaire.' Mulligan gave a soft laugh. 'King Cophetua and the beggar maid.'

Rose smiled at him. 'You think that Nathan lifted her out of the Barnfield estate to turn her into a princess?'

'Don't you?'

'No, I don't. I'm too cynical for that.' She leaned her head closer to his. 'Clive thought it was a simple case of money laundering, that Nathan was siphoning funds into Alice's name. But we've had all the sources of that money checked, and it's squeaky clean. Most of it came from savings accounts with other banks, and the balance had built up over a number of years. It was a combination of legitimate earnings and a legacy from his parents. No,' she shook her head, 'he wanted her to have the money.'

'They were about to be married. She would have had the money anyway.'

'But what if he believed his life was at risk?'

'He could leave a will.'

'Then people would ask questions. He was going to be married in a few weeks' time. The marriage would have invalidated any will made previously. Why would someone make a will just before they married, knowing that it would be overturned so soon? And in any case, a will can be challenged. Actually giving the money away of your own free will … that's not something that can be challenged, unless other potential beneficiaries suspect that either you're not in your right mind, or you've acted under some sort of duress.'

'Are you suggesting that Nathan Kingsley knew that someone wanted his money, and that he gave it to Alice to put it out of harm's way?'

Rose leaned back, away from him, and turned her head to glance around the restaurant. They were in Umberto's, the elegant Italian eatery favoured by Kirkby's wealthy elite, waiting for lunch to be served. Idle waiters were scattered at key points around the room, polishing glasses and fiddling with cutlery. Apart from the staff, they had the place to themselves. She turned her smile back to him. 'This is a curious place to bring an informant for lunch, Inspector Mulligan. Do you bring all your narks here?'

'Are you avoiding my question?'

'Not at all. I'm just flattered. And a little awed by the

coincidence.' She thought for a moment, and then said 'this place came up in conversation at the bank this morning. Apparently it's a favourite haunt of Luke Kingsley's. He brings his one-night stands here.'

'I hope you're not suggesting that I make a habit of doing the same.' Mulligan chuckled to himself, amused by the thought. 'I've seen the prices on the menu, this lunch will take my expense budget for the whole month.'

'But you know I'm worth it. Just look at all the help I'm giving you.'

'With respect, Rose, all I've had for my money so far is the suggestion that Nathan Kingsley wasn't money laundering.'

'No, you've had the suggestion that he was deliberately divesting his fortune.' She leaned forward again and lowered her voice. 'Luke Kingsley is Nathan's natural beneficiary if he died intestate, which looks likely, since no one seems to know of any will. Now I can't see the full picture of Nathan's estate, because I can only see details of the accounts that he and Alice held with the ENB. But he's already settled money on Alice in a way that Luke can't challenge. And here's the most curious thing about it. *Alice doesn't want it.*'

'She *what?*' Mulligan's voice bellowed across the restaurant, and every waiter in the room turned to look at him. He lowered his head and spoke more quietly. 'What do you mean, she doesn't want it?'

'Simply that. She wants to give it away. Initially, she wants to give it to Luke, and if he won't take it – which I think is unlikely, by the way, given the amount of cash it must take to fund his lifestyle – she wants to give it to charity.'

'Does she think it's tainted in some way?'

'I don't know. But it's causing her a lot of distress. She had Vienna Fielding with her at the bank this morning. Vienna didn't join us for the meeting, but we explained the situation to her afterwards, and she's taken Alice home to try to talk some sense into her. It could be the grief of course, still coming to terms with the fact that Nathan has gone.'

'Or it could be something more.' Mulligan pulled absently at his ear. 'Are you aware that Luke and Alice don't get on?'

'I am. I also know that Luke Kingsley paid a visit to Alice yesterday evening. To discuss Nathan's affairs.'

'Did he, now?' The policeman frowned. 'Why is it that I'm the last to hear the things that matter most?' He shook his head. 'Do we know what that was all about?'

'According to Alice, he came to discuss the funeral. She wouldn't say much more than that.'

'But you think there *was* more?'

'There must have been. She said he'd come to discuss the funeral, and to ask whether she knew if Nathan had made a will. She said not. She said she gave him the documents she believed he needed to begin settling Nathan's estate. And then she clammed up.'

'Luke Kingsley still hasn't shown his face at the bank, then?'

'No. I was hoping he would come in today, but it's not looking hopeful.' She glanced at her watch. It was almost twenty past two, and they were still waiting for their main course. 'I promised Stacy Singleton I'd be back by three o'clock. There's a slim chance that Luke might have set up an appointment for later this afternoon. If he has I'll be sure to let you know.'

The air in the small meeting room at the back of the ENB's Kirkby branch was warm and humid. The temperature outside on the street was rising well into the high seventies, and Luke Kingsley ran a finger around the inside of his shirt collar, pulling the fabric away from the clammy flesh of his neck. The room must have had air conditioning, why on earth wasn't it switched on? An unfamiliar scent that lingered in the cloying air was filling his nostrils and catching at the back of his throat, something that smelled sickly and sweet, like the old-fashioned bath cubes his mother used to buy for his grandmother. He glanced down at his watch, a furtive, secretive movement that he hoped she wouldn't notice. It was just coming up to twenty five minutes past two.

He fidgeted in his seat, trying to find a more comfortable position. The plastic of the chair was beginning to draw against his flesh, luring moisture from his pores, and his trousers were becoming damp with the unwelcomed perspiration. He didn't like being uncomfortable, and he could feel his own impatience beginning to grow.

Across the small table, Stacy Singleton was diligently checking through the thin sheaf of documentation that Luke had brought with him to their meeting. She had some sort of checklist, and as she worked through the papers she ticked the list to acknowledge every document seen, the interim death certificate from the coroner's office, the letter of introduction for Hector Campling, his own evidence of identity. He couldn't help noticing that the pen she used, clutched tightly in her left hand, was shaking. She was nervous, he thought. Hell, why were some women so unsure of themselves?

She pushed the pile of papers to her right and smiled nervously into his face. 'I'm sorry that I had to ask you to provide some evidence of identity, Mr Kingsley. It's just routine. I mean, of course we all know who you are, but the process ...'

He put up a hand. 'There's no need to explain, Stacy. And please, call me Luke.' He saw her cheeks colour under the film of carefully applied fake tan, and her eyelashes flutter with an excited anticipation. He folded his brows over his eyes quizzically, and pointed a finger at her. 'I know you, don't I, Stacy? You're a friend of Lydia's.'

Stacy's eyes widened at the recognition, and she

nodded in agreement. 'Yes, yes I am.'

'I thought so. I've seen you out on a Friday night.' He tried to sound more interested than he was. 'It's good to know it's not a complete stranger that's going to be helping me with this.'

The hand holding the pen began to quiver, and she rested it on the desk to steady it. 'I've prepared a list of all the accounts held at the branch by your brother.' She stretched out her other hand and pushed a piece of paper towards him. 'As you can see, there is a current account, a credit card account and several savings accounts which were in his sole name.'

He gave a casual shake of the head. 'I don't plan to look at the numbers myself.' He pointed to a sealed manila envelope beside him on the table. 'I got a pile of stuff from Alice last night, I haven't even opened it.' He tried to sound indifferent, as if the money didn't matter. 'I guess I'm just not a detail kind of guy. Just let me have the paperwork and I'll add it to this. I'm going to see my solicitor later this afternoon, I just plan to drop it all off with him. He'll do the legwork.' His brow puckered with another thought. 'Is the paperwork there for the house?'

For a moment Stacy looked uncertain. She looked away towards the wall, as if perhaps just averting her eyes would absolve her of the need to answer the question. She cleared her throat and looked back at him. 'By the house, I take it that you mean the property in Haverland Street?' She spoke so quietly that he could hardly hear her. 'You are aware that the property was jointly owned by your brother and Miss Blacklaws?'

Jointly owned? It took a few moments for the words to register. 'Sorry, Stacy. I don't follow. The house belonged to my brother. He bought it long before he met Alice. It was nothing to do with her.'

'Miss Blacklaws is a co-owner of the property.'

'But I'm his next of kin. There's no will.'

'Perhaps if you spoke to your solicitor …'

'I will. But right now, Stacy, if you understand what's going on here I'd be grateful if you would share it with me. Are you trying to tell me that she owns half the property?'

Stacy looked distinctly uneasy now. 'She owns the whole property. Your brother took steps to make her a joint tenant, which means only she can inherit your brother's share.' She paused, and then added 'unless your brother was to be declared insolvent after death, of course. In which case a court could ask for your brother's share to be returned to his estate to meet his debts.'

Luke spluttered a spontaneous laugh. 'There won't be any debts, Stacy. My brother didn't believe in debt. He was too busy squirreling his money away.' Something in her expression caught his eye. 'What?'

'Your brother had an outstanding credit card balance of just over six hundred pounds. I'm sure there will be sufficient funds lodged with another bank to pay the bill, but …'

'Another bank?' Luke's confusion was growing. 'Nathan had deposits with this bank. It's just a few hundred quid. Can't you take it out of one of his savings accounts?' He was watching her face closely. She was agitated now, and avoiding his gaze. 'He must have thousands on deposit, I can't see what the problem is?'

'I really think it would be a good idea to speak to your solicitor.'

'I don't need to speak to my solicitor. I'm speaking to you. Are you trying to tell me that my brother owes this bank more than he has on deposit?'

He watched as Stacy pursed her lips and stared down at her hands, and realised that he'd gone too far. He really needed this girl on side, especially if things weren't going to be as straightforward as he needed them to be. He put a hand up to his face and rubbed at his temple. 'Stacy, I'm so sorry.' He puffed out a breath. 'It's all just a bit too much. I didn't mean to snarl at you like that.'

She responded to his apology in an instant. 'Oh please,

there's no need to apologise.'

'But there is. Look,' he glanced at his watch, 'I'm going to have to get out of here now, I need to get these papers over to the solicitor's office. But I want to make it up to you. Why don't I take you out for dinner this evening? We could go to Umberto's, do in a bottle of wine. What do you say?' It was an insincere and gaudy piece of bait, but she looked to him like the sort of girl who would bite on it without a thought. And he wasn't mistaken.

The anxiety on her face melted into a smile of almost pathetic delight. 'Dinner?'

'Sure. It would be my pleasure.' He began to gather up the papers scattered over the desk, shuffling them into an untidy pile on top of the manila envelope. 'Just one more thing, though, before we finish up here.' He dug deep and turned on his most charming and insincere smile. 'I could have sworn that Nathan told me that he still had a mortgage on that property. I can't help wondering how on earth Alice is going to take that on by herself?'

11

'Is that Lu Aylesbury's dog?' Mulligan peered down under the table at the small, untidy terrier curled up next to Benny's feet.

'He used to be. She's goin' to have trouble gettin' him back from me.' Benny looked down at the terrier. 'Ain't she fella?' On cue the dog lifted his head from his paws and looked up at him adoringly with his one good eye.

'Well I don't envy you that conversation.' Mulligan lifted an illicit half pint of bitter to his lips and took a long gulp. They were sitting in the small courtyard at the back of The Feathers pub in Market Melbourne, a fifteen-mile journey out of town that Mulligan had been pleased to make. Technically he was on duty, but he'd spent his usual lunch break discussing the case with Rose, so he'd decided that technically he was clawing the hour back so he could do as he pleased. It was a presumption he would never have dared during working hours in his ambitious days, but the closer he got to retirement the more comfortable he felt sailing close to the wind. He put his glass down on the table and nodded at Benny Bradman, who was staring at him with undisguised amusement. 'Everything alright?'

Benny shrugged his shoulders with a laugh. 'You tell me, George. From where I'm sittin', it looks as though you needed that drink. Was that because you were thinkin' of Lu? I heard that you once fancied your chances in that direction.'

'Did you?' Mulligan arched an eyebrow. 'That was over thirty years ago. She was my "one that got away." Nope,' he sipped again on the bitter, 'if I need a drink, it's more to do with the Kingsley case. It's tying me in knots.'

'Is that why you're out here in the sticks enjoyin' a bit of downtime with me and the dog?'

'This isn't downtime, its investigation. I need information, and I think you can provide it for me.'

'Is this official, or off the record?'

'As you can see, I'm enjoying my lunch hour.' Mulligan nodded towards his glass. 'So we'll call it off the record. The thing is, Benny,' he folded his arms onto the table, 'I don't know much about football. But I know that you do. Between you and me, Ian Scott has been doing some digging into the Kingsleys' background this morning, and he's found something that we'd like to know more about. I've tried to get hold of Kirkby's manager, but he's on a family holiday in Menorca, and I don't want to set hares running with anyone else in the club.'

'So you thought of me.'

'So I thought of you. You're an honest bloke, for a bookie. I know you'll tell me straight if there's anything I need to know.'

'I'm not quite sure how to take that, George, but I'll try to take it as a compliment. What do you need to know?'

'You know the Kingsleys, don't you?'

'I knew Nathan pretty well. I've met Luke a few times.'

'What's your opinion of them?'

'Nathan was a shrewd lad. He had his fingers in a lot of pies, but as far as I could see everythin' was on the level. He didn't really need to get into anythin' dodgy, he was makin' enough money by legitimate means.'

'People get greedy.'

Benny nodded. 'They do. But Nathan was an old head on young shoulders. He wasn't the sort.'

'What about his brother?'

'Luke is a different kettle of fish. He's like the junior

prince, second in line and always battlin' to be noticed. Nathan was born with the sensible gene. Luke just likes to indulge himself. Gamblin', women, livin' like a second-rate footballer.'

The policeman laughed. 'And is he? Second rate?'

'Nathan was the better player. You really don't know much about football, do you George?'

'No, I'm a cricket man.' He thought for a moment, and then said 'I've heard that Luke and Nathan Kingsley had a barney on the pitch during the first half of the last match of the season. They were lucky not to be booked, and afterwards the club played it down. Have you any idea what that was about?'

Benny thought for a moment. 'It never did come out.'

'Were you there?'

'Me? Yes, I was there. So were several thousand other people.'

'Don't be coy, I thought we were mates.'

Benny shrugged. 'It was a critical game for Kirkby. They needed to win or draw for a promotion. They played a bit slow in the first twenty minutes. A couple of times I saw Luke approach Nathan and say somethin' to him. It could have been anythin'. He might have just been complainin' that Nathan was keepin' the ball to himself. But then ...' Benny closed his eyes and shook his head. 'There was a pause in play while Kirkby took a corner. I saw Luke go up to Nathan and say somethin', and Nathan turned on him. He looked angry. Well, as much as I could see from where I was sittin'. Luke shoved him, and Nathan shoved back. The referee moved in on them and looked like he was goin' for a card. I thought he was goin' to send one of them off. But Nathan put his hands up and backed off, and the ref had second thoughts.' He paused again, deep in thought.

'Something else?'

'Nathan turned round and signalled to the bench. I couldn't see exactly what was goin' on. But they took Luke

Kingsley off the pitch ten minutes later. He went kickin' and screamin'. He was red in the face like a toddler, yellin' at Nathan.' He laughed to himself and shook his head. 'He's a proper little drama queen when he gets goin'.'

'Kirkby won that match, didn't they?'

'Blimey George, I know you ain't interested in football but even you must know the answer to that one. They were celebratin' in Kirkby town centre all weekend, it must have dented your police budget keepin' up with the drunks.' He laughed again. 'They deserved the win. Nathan Kingsley played his socks off.'

'And what about afterwards? Was Luke happy with the result?'

'Happy with …?' Benny's words trailed off. It was obviously something he hadn't considered. 'They got promotion. Why wouldn't he be?'

'Maybe the victory was just a little bit tarnished, given that he was taken off?'

'I wouldn't know about that.'

'I keep hearing rumours that there was bad blood between the brothers in the run up to the wedding. Some trouble about Alice?'

Benny shook his head. 'Siblin' rivalry, George. Nathan was the sensible one and Luke was the liability. Luke relied on his big brother to dig him out of scrapes in the same way a little lad would expect his big brother to fight off the bullies at school. And Alice was queerin' the pitch.' He turned a questioning eye on Mulligan, serious now. 'Tell me you ain't seriously considerin' that Luke had anything to do with Nathan's murder. Bloody hell, George, he was there when Nathan was shot. Nathan died in his arms.'

'He didn't have to do the job himself.' He puffed out a sigh. 'Brothers fight. Nathan and Luke Kingsley fought. They fought off the pitch, and they fought on it. Everyone watching that match saw it.'

'That was different. They were under pressure. They were players disagreein' about tactics, not brothers bayin' for each other's blood.'

Mulligan drained off the contents of his glass and placed it gently back on the table. The bitter had gone down too quickly. 'Are you sure about that? It's a funny thing, rivalry.' He grinned to himself, distracted momentarily by a different train of thought. 'By the way, did I hear that Rose Bennett was meant to be your guest at Nathan Kingsley's wedding?'

The conversation's change of direction threw Benny, and he frowned. 'I did invite her, yes. But she couldn't make it.' His face broke into a grin. 'Why George, are you jealous?'

'Me? No. Not me.' Mulligan wrapped a hand around his empty glass, tilted it towards him, and stared mischievously into the empty interior. 'But I know a man who might be.'

The air in Hector Campling's office was sour, a musty mix of parched leather and aging paper, with a hint of stale tobacco. Luke put a hand up to his face and rubbed at his temple. His head still ached from his meeting with Stacy Singleton, and the fusty vapours of the solicitor's room were vying with the cloying smell of lavender still lingering in his nostrils. He hoped he wouldn't have to wait too long for the solicitor to make an appearance.

The manila envelope he'd received from Alice lay on the desk in front of him, and he looked down at it now, at the jagged, ripped edge where he'd torn into it angrily after his meeting with Stacy Singleton. There was plenty in there relating to Nathan's estate, he couldn't argue with that. But now he'd seen the contents he couldn't shake off the feeling that he'd sorely underestimated Alice Blacklaws. He'd been taken in by those pale blue, limpid eyes as she'd passed the sealed envelope over to him, and he'd taken it from her without a word, never thinking to open it, never thinking to challenge her there and then about some of the contents. Bank cards for accounts that had nothing in them. Pass books for savings accounts that had been wiped out. He felt his pulse begin to quicken, his anger building, and he took in a deep breath to calm his nerves. He couldn't show his rage in front of Hector Campling. Earlier that afternoon his temper had almost cost him Stacy Singleton's confidence, he couldn't afford to alienate the solicitor as well.

He swallowed hard and tried to rationalise his thoughts. He was here to give the solicitor a clear set of instructions. There were still assets in Nathan's estate that now belonged to him as next of kin, and he needed the money freeing up from those assets as soon as possible. The two rental properties in Scarborough would have to be sold, and the insurance policies secured against their mortgages cashed in. The envelope had brought him a bonus in the shape of a pension policy he didn't know existed, so that would have to be surrendered too.

Wresting the house in Haverland Street from Alice and Olivia was going to be more difficult, but Campling would have to come up with a solution, that's what Luke was paying him for. Campling had a reputation for being creative in his methods. After all, that's why Luke had chosen him for the job. It was nothing to do with the fact that the solicitor had carried out work for his brother. It was because he was dishonest. Because the word on the street had left Luke in no doubt that Hector Campling could be relied upon to do pretty much anything for money, no questions asked, providing the price was right.

And when it was all over, when Campling had confirmed that his instructions had been understood, and the wheels had started to roll, he could send a text to Larry.

A familiar lump of fear began to form in the back of his throat and his eyes wandered subconsciously down to the pocket of his light, linen jacket where his mobile phone was tucked away. Texts from Larry were beginning to come through more frequently now, demands for money, and threats of what would happen to Luke if he didn't produce it, and produce it quickly. There was no chance now of an escape to Spain, of ducking out and lying low until everything was forgotten. Each passing text was a reminder that Larry didn't forget anything.

His only chance now was to raise as much money as he could and hope it was enough to make the danger go away. Perhaps, he thought, if he could tell Larry how much it would be, that would keep things quiet for a while. He closed his eyes and tried to calculate how much cash would be released when all of Nathan's assets had been liquidated. The two flats would yield him about two hundred thousand when the insurance policies paid out to cover the mortgages. There was a statement with the pension policy that he didn't really understand, but he'd seen a figure of two hundred and seventy thousand, and that would do for now. That made four hundred and seventy thousand. Nowhere near enough to keep Larry off his back.

It was going to take time to raise the money, too. He needed cash now, something on account to keep Larry sweet. He needed the savings that Nathan had given to Alice and Olivia as a gift.

He shook his head and swore quietly under his breath. Thank God that Stacy Singleton was such a stupid bitch. All it took for her to break Alice's confidence was a bit of false flattery, and the offer of a free dinner at Umberto's had been enough to buy him the knowledge that Nathan had paid off the balance of his mortgage and shovelled all his spare cash into accounts in Alice and Olivia's names.

He needed that money. He needed it back from Alice, and he needed it fast. Hector Campling must know a way of bringing that about. If he could get his hands on the house and the savings, if he could find some way of showing that the money should have been his, and not Alice's, then he might be home and dry. Four hundred and seventy thousand, plus maybe nine hundred thousand for the house, plus another two hundred thousand in cash, plus whatever was in the business account, that would be … hell, almost two million, give or take the odd hundred thousand. That had to be enough to get them off his back.

The plan outlined in his head, he was about to turn his attention to a lesser problem, what to do about Stacy Singleton, when the door behind him opened and Hector Campling breezed into the room. Luke rose to his feet and extended his hand. 'Mr Campling. Thank you for seeing me again. I've been to the ENB, and I've managed to get hold of Nathan's financial paperwork from Alice.' He sat down again, and slid the manila envelope across the desk. 'This is everything I've managed to find so far.'

The solicitor dropped into his chair without looking at Luke, and adjusted his spectacles, pushing them down to the end of his nose and peering through them at the manila envelope without touching it. He looked up at Luke with a smile, a self-satisfied smirk that smacked of superiority. 'Well, that will be most useful, Mr Kingsley. Because I have news of my own to impart. We should be able to begin work on your brother's estate today, and have things wrapped up much more quickly than I expected.'

'We should?' Luke frowned at the unexpected parry. 'But I haven't given you any instructions yet.'

'Instructions?' The solicitor regarded him over the top of his spectacles, and licked his lips. 'I already have my instructions, Mr Kingsley. I have them from your brother.'

'From Nathan? I don't understand.'

'Indeed.' Hector Campling leaned over the desk towards Luke with a self-assured smile. 'I'm delighted to tell you that we have found a copy of your brother's last will and testament, and its terms are most clear, most clear indeed. Your brother has made provision for only one beneficiary.'

'A will? You mean Nathan actually left a will?' Luke's

pulse began to race. He knew that Nathan wouldn't have let him down. 'And that means I'll get access to the money sooner than we thought?'

'Certainly the estate could be administered more quickly than expected. As to accessing the money, I think perhaps there is a conversation we need to have before work on the administration begins. It is possible that you may not wish me to proceed, given the terms of the will.'

'I don't understand.' Luke rubbed again at his forehead. He felt that Campling was playing some sort of game with him, but so far he couldn't tell what it was. 'If there is a will, don't you have to abide by it? Why would you think I wouldn't want you to begin?'

'Ah yes, how can I put this?' Campling leaned his elbows on the desk and steepled his fingers, and regarded Luke through narrowed eyes. He cleared his throat with a cough and when he spoke again his voice was lower, his tone almost sinister. 'When I share with you the terms of your brother's will, it is possible that you might … well, not to mince words, Mr Kingsley, it's possible that you might prefer me to forget that the will ever existed.'

12

'I'm not really sure why you think I should apologise.' Rose had been on the receiving end of Clive's temper before, and these days it flowed like water from a duck's back. 'I undertook to support Stacy during her interviews with Alice Blacklaws and Luke Kingsley, to report anything notable back to you, and to keep George Mulligan off your back at the same time. I'm a consultant, Clive, not a bloody miracle worker.' She turned away from the telephone and looked across to Stacy Singleton's desk, where a chastised and subdued Stacy was avoiding her gaze by diligently clicking away at a computer keyboard.

'I trusted you to keep things under control.' Clive's tone was distinctly chilly. 'I cannot believe that you left Stacy to meet with Luke Kingsley alone.'

'And I can't believe that you still expect me to nurse-maid your staff. You know what, Clive? Nothing ever changes in the Kirkby office. They're process-perfect, and emotionally unreliable. They can recite whole tracts of the Consumer Credit Act like reciting their eight times table, but show them a decent six pack or give them a whiff of designer aftershave and they lose all sense of reason. Maybe you should think about commissioning me to introduce a new element into all the business processes. We could create a new decision-point where any colleague has to decide whether or not they find the customer attractive, and if the answer is yes, then that customer has to be passed over to another colleague who doesn't.' She sucked in her cheeks. 'That wouldn't take into account the colleague lying of course. They could always say they weren't attracted to the customer when really they were, just to get the customer on their own in a meeting room. We really wouldn't have any way of validating the answer.'

'Rose, you are being unforgivably flippant. You know that I cannot deal with you when you are in this frame of mind.'

'Then don't put me in this frame of mind. I specifically, clearly and without any degree of ambiguity whatsoever instructed Stacy Singleton that she was to ensure that any meeting with Luke Kingsley included me.'

'Did you forbid her to meet him without your attendance?'

'I beg your pardon?'

'Did you forbid her to meet him without your attendance? Did you make it abundantly clear that she was not to meet him under any circumstances unless you were there?'

'No, Clive, I didn't. And before you ask me, I'll tell you why I didn't. It's because I'm not her mother. I'm not her mother, or her nurse-maid, or her probation officer. Stacy is a professional young woman with six years' experience of working at this bank. It's her responsibility to know better, not my responsibility to keep her in check.' Rose expelled an audible sigh, an hour's worth of pent up frustration and disappointment. 'Look, it's done now. She's had the meeting, and she can't have discussed that much with him. He was barely here for half an hour, by all accounts.'

Clive was silent at the other end of the phone, his own frustration simmering just below boiling point. Eventually he said 'has she tried to explain herself?'

'She knew that I was going to be out until three o'clock, and she said that he couldn't meet after three because he had an appointment booked with his solicitor. And she claims that although I made it clear I needed to be there, she thought it was more important to get him into the branch today so that we could get things moving with Nathan Kingsley's accounts.' Rose snorted a gentle laugh. 'She actually had the brass neck to say that she thought we – that's you and I, Clive – would have been pleased that she'd used her initiative.'

Some of the indignation was diffusing from Clive's tone. 'I've invested a lot of time and effort in personally coaching that young woman, Rose. I suppose I only have myself to blame. I suppose woman, as much as man, is susceptible to folly when dressed in a little brief authority.'

'The Merchant of Venice?'

'Measure for Measure.'

Rose smiled to herself. Her knowledge of Shakespeare was as good as Clive's, but as a ploy to play to his temperament it always paid dividends to let him think that he knew more than she did. And it also didn't hurt, she mused, to let him think that he was in control of the situation. 'So what would you like me to do now?'

'Await further instructions from Luke Kingsley. Consider the risks. Providing Stacy has only given him the information that he's entitled to, there shouldn't really be anything for us to worry about. I appreciate your assurance that there is no evidence of money laundering in the case. You've provided some background information to Inspector Mulligan regarding Alice Blacklaws and the property transfer. Luke Kingsley has slipped through our fingers today but now that we know that the transactions made by Nathan Kingsley are legitimate there doesn't appear to be any real risk to the bank. He's made contact, we can begin closing the accounts, and we have the details of the solicitor dealing with probate. I think perhaps, unless you yourself can see any pressing reason to stay in Kirkby, we have done everything we need to do at this stage. It might serve us better to back away now and disassociate ourselves with the case. I will, of course, leave it to your discretion.'

'In that case, Clive, I'll stay here one more night and be on my way tomorrow. I'll touch base with George Mulligan about Luke Kingsley before I go.'

'Very well. I'll ask Moira to contact you about your travel arrangements.' He paused, somehow reluctant to end the conversation. 'I wonder, Rose, if I might trouble you for an opinion on something else?'

'Of course. If I can help.'

'Stacy. Stacy Singleton. What is your initial impression of her? Do you feel she is management material?' His rage blown out, he was being fatuous again.

Rose turned her head to look at Stacy. The girl was presentable, personable, professional, empathic. But was she reliable? Rose sighed. 'If you'd asked me that question this morning, Clive, after I witnessed the way she handled Alice Blacklaws, I would have been in no doubt how to answer it. But now?' She pouted, and shook her head. 'If I were you, I would wait to see how this Kingsley thing pans out. We know what Stacy has told us, and at this point we have no reason to disbelieve her. But unpalatable truths have a way of wriggling to the surface. I don't want to accuse the girl of anything, but there's a gleam in her eye when she talks about Luke Kingsley that makes me feel uncomfortable.'

'You think she's untrustworthy?'

Unseen by Clive, Rose bowed her head and shook it gently. 'No Clive, I think she's vulnerable.'

The afternoon sun had been beating down through the windows of Luke Kingsley's car for almost an hour, and the temperature gauge on the dashboard registered thirty one degrees. He turned the key and started the engine, twisting his neck towards an air vent and closing his eyes so that the icy blast of the car's air conditioning system could cool his face. God knows he needed to cool down.

His face was burning, more from the sting of Hector Campling's words than from the heat of the sun, and his head was pounding. He'd received another text from Larry, short and to the point. *If I don't get good news today, it's bad news for you.*

Good news? His head sank forward onto the rim of the steering wheel and he shrank back instinctively as his skin made contact with the red-hot leather trim. Even the car was against him. He leaned back, resting his shoulders against a leather seat that burned through his shirt. It felt like the lesser of two evils.

Barely an hour ago it had seemed like everything was in the bag. It should have been a breeze to persuade Hector Campling to come up with a plan to overturn Nathan's gifts to Alice and Olivia, and to liquidate the estate as soon as possible. Luke had been so certain of his position he could almost smell Nathan's money making its way into his bank account. But it had taken merely minutes for the mendacious solicitor to show his true colours. The only plan Campling had in mind was to produce Nathan's will like a rabbit out of hat, and screw an extra hundred thousand out of Luke in return for "losing" the document so that Luke would by default inherit everything that Nathan had to leave.

Except, of course, that when it came down to it, Nathan didn't have that much to leave him. Campling's eyes had widened at the news that Alice already had possession of the house in Haverland Street, and narrowed to hear that she also had a substantial portion of Nathan's liquid cash. Barely a glance at the pension documents secreted in the brown manila envelope had brought forth a throaty laugh of derision, and the news that the small print made it abundantly clear that Alice Blacklaws was already the sole beneficiary of the policy.

If Campling was to be believed, even if the will was destroyed there would barely be enough left in Nathan's estate to cover his inheritance tax liability, settle his remaining debts and obligations, and meet the inflated fees that the solicitor intended to charge for dispersing the estate. Why would he even bother?

Luke was beginning to feel sick now, with the heat of the sun and the rising panic in the pit of his stomach. How could things change so much in the space of twenty four short hours? Yesterday he was convinced that everything Nathan had to leave was going to be his. He'd found the courage to face Alice, to play his hand with an outward confidence, to give no hint of his inner fears. And he thought it had paid dividends. Alice had bent to his words so readily, and handed over that manila envelope full of documents with barely a murmur. And now?

Now he had nothing. Alice had the house, the cash, the pension, and by the end of today she would know that there was a will, and she would have everything else. He had nothing to show for his play acting with her last night, for his charm offensive with Stacy Singleton, or for his misplaced confidence in Hector Campling. He didn't even have a plan any more. Larry was waiting for news, news that the money was his, that everything was going to be squared. But Nathan's money wasn't his, and there was no other way he could get his hands on the sort of money it would take to make Larry and his threats go away.

He felt his mobile phone vibrate in his trouser pocket, another incoming text, and he pulled it out, heart thumping, and glanced at the screen. The message consisted of one simple word. *Well?*

How the hell was he going to answer this? How could he use a simple text message to convey the failure of his plans, the misery of his situation, the burgeoning fear that another Kingsley was at risk of losing his life? How could he tell Larry that whichever way this played out, Alice had won? That there was a will after all, but that it didn't really matter whether Alice knew about it because she was already in possession of the only parts of the estate worth having? That Alice had the house, the cash, the pension …

that everything else was only going to go west in taxes, and expenses, and in paying the exorbitant fees of a shyster solicitor?

He rested his elbows in the lower rim of the steering wheel and rested his head in his hands. There had to be a way to dig himself out of this hole. There had to be. Nathan wouldn't have wanted this to happen to him. Nathan would have done anything, absolutely anything to protect him, to keep him safe from Larry. Wouldn't he?

He snuffled a laugh of self-deprecation. He was fooling himself. Nathan didn't give a shit. Nathan had known what was coming, he could see that now. And he'd cleverly, calculatingly moved his money out of harm's way. Out of Luke's way, and ultimately out of Larry's way. He'd moved it to Alice. He'd known his own life was at risk, and he'd made sure that Alice was safe regardless of whether they married or not. He'd placed Alice's safety above his brother's, another brutal, heartless demonstration that Alice, and not Luke, was the most important thing in his life.

There wasn't much point in fighting now, was there? Being angry at Nathan wasn't going to bring him the money he needed to buy Larry off. And being afraid of Larry, afraid of the reprisals, well … that wasn't going to save his life, was it? He could see that now. There was only one avenue left to him, to surrender to his failure and go out on a high. He sighed out what was left of his anguish, and turned his attention back to his mobile phone. His message back to Larry was a simple one. *Everything has gone to Alice.*

He tossed the phone onto the passenger seat and for a few moments he sat still in the car, unable to think, unsure of what to do next. The surrender had brought him an odd peace, an acceptance that the struggle was over. There was nothing more he could do but wait for Larry to do his worst. There was no telling when the end would come. Today, tomorrow, it wouldn't be long. There were things, he was sure, that a man in his position would have to do. Speak to Alice, tell her the truth. Perhaps even speak to Inspector Mulligan, for all good it would do him. He doubted that even the protection of the police could save him now. Larry wasn't known for letting the law stand in his way. But first he was going home to shower and change. Perhaps he would go out and get drunk. Perhaps he would take Stacy Singleton out to dinner after all, and give her a night to remember.

He braced himself at the steering wheel and then pushed the car into first gear and flicked on the indicator, glancing in the wing mirror to check for a gap in the passing traffic. He was about to swing away from the kerb when his mobile phone vibrated again, and he swore under his breath, and flicked off the indicator. He grabbed at the phone and glanced at the incoming text.

It wasn't what he expected. The words brought a lump to his throat and made tears sting at his eyes. He couldn't. Not that. He beat his fist against the steering wheel. Defrauding Alice out of her inheritance, that was one thing. But this? He couldn't. *He couldn't.*

Why the hell couldn't Larry just send a contract killer for him too, and get it over with?

It was cool in the office above Benny Bradman's betting shop. Benny closed the door gently behind him, and went straight to the tantalus on his desk. He was still troubled by George Mulligan's suggestion that Luke Kingsley might not have been so pleased that Kirkby FC had won their long-awaited promotion.

The tantalus wasn't locked, and he poured himself a modest Scotch before settling down in the comfort of his leather chair and picking up the remote control for the TV opposite his desk. He had recorded Kirkby's last match of the season in the way that he would record any other significant sporting event on which he'd taken a substantial number of bets, but he hadn't so far had any need to watch the recording. He clicked on the remote's buttons as he sipped on his drink, finding the match easily and fast-forwarding to the point at which he believed the skirmish between Luke and Nathan Kingsley took place.

Benny himself had been privileged enough to have a seat in the Director's box that day, thanks to a large donation to the charity which both he and Nathan had supported. During the match his only real interest had been the game itself, and its outcome, not the behaviours of the individual players. His seat had given him a privileged view of the game, but his own recollection of the argument was of a momentary spat, tempers flaring, the pushing and shoving of two players under pressure. The scene unfolding before him on the screen now told a different story to anyone who cared to look more closely.

The commentator was focused on a corner being taken, over to the left of the screen, and seemed impervious to the drama unfolding to the right. Benny leaned in to the screen and watched closely. Luke Kingsley walked up to his brother and put a hand on his arm, and appeared to be asking for something. Nathan shook his head and brushed Luke's arm away, and began to walk backwards away from his brother. Luke followed him, and pointed towards the other end of the pitch. Nathan's head shook again and he picked up his pace, jogging backwards now with Luke still trotting towards him. Suddenly Luke lashed out, shoving Nathan off balance. Nathan stopped, stiffened, and turned to look at his brother before pushing him back. Their altercation was becoming heated. The commentary turned to the squabble. "Something's going off at the side of the pitch. It looks as though the Kingsley brothers are fighting".

It was over in seconds. The referee's attention had turned to the Kingsleys and he was heading towards them with a hand in his pocket, but before he could pull out a card of any colour Nathan Kingsley bowed his head and held up his hands in supplication. For reasons best known to himself the referee drew his hand out of his pocket and wagged an admonishing finger in Nathan's direction before backing away and turning his attention back to the game.

Benny watched for five, maybe ten minutes more as the game progressed and then stalled as a Kirkby player was brought down by a bad tackle fifteen yards short of the goal. But it wasn't the tackle that caught everyone's attention so much as activity on the edge of the pitch. An official at the edge of the pitch was signalling a substitution to the Kirkby team, and the camera swung round to point at the player being substituted. Luke Kingsley was standing gazing into the distance.

Benny picked up the remote control and zoomed the image up to focus as best he could on Luke Kingsley's face. Luke was distraught, his eyes wide, his head shaking violently towards his manager. He glanced around, searching for Nathan, but Nathan was avoiding his gaze. And then his head turned and he looked up into the crowd, high up into the stand, and shook his head again. Benny paused the recording and wound it back a few second before pressing play. He watched again as Luke Kingsley turned away from his brother and looked up into the crowd, his eyes clearly searching for someone lost in the multitude of supporters lining the terraces, fear drawn on his face.

Up into the crowd? Who was he looking at? Who was watching him? Benny wound the recording back a second time and watched again. Luke was terrified, and he was trying to communicate with someone in the crowd. What the hell was all that about, then?

What on earth would make a grown man behave like that? Fear? Fear of what? They had everything to play for, the team was on form, the promotion was in the bag. Hell, even the referee was on their side. What could Luke have wanted Nathan to do, wanted so much that to not achieve it would reduce him to tears of anguish?

He pressed the pause button and stared again at the grainy image of Luke Kingsley's face, the wheels of his brain beginning to turn, reaching conclusions that he really didn't want to think about. He raised his eyes to the ceiling in momentary contemplation, and then turned his attention to the phone on his desk, lifting the receiver and jabbing at the keypad with a stubby finger. 'Sal, is Michael down there?' At the other end of the line the head cashier concurred. 'Send him up, will you?'

As he waited, Benny contemplated what he knew of Luke Kingsley. He was stupid enough, and greedy enough, and cowardly enough. There was no doubt in Benny's mind of that. But was he really dishonest enough? He put his hands up to his face and rubbed at his eyes. He knew the answer to that question without thinking too hard about it. He would be dishonest enough if the stakes were high.

A quiet tap at the door caught his attention and he looked up to see Michael Spivey peering around the door. 'Yes, Boss?'

Benny nodded towards the empty chair at the other side of his desk. 'Take a seat, Michael, I've got a job for you.' He waited until Spivey was seated and then leaned across the desk and fixed him with an earnest stare. 'I want you to go out and put yourself about. Take two hundred from the petty cash, and start with the pubs in Kirkby. I want to know everythin' there is to know on the street about Luke Kingsley and that last game of the season. I want to know if he found a way to place a bet himself, and if he did what he placed. I want to know if he gave anybody tips before the match, or if he warned anybody off.'

Michael Spivey was dense about most things in life but when it came to sport or gambling he always caught on quickly. 'You fink it was fixed.' It wasn't a question, just a sober statement of fact.

'Let's just say I'm keen to know that it wasn't.'

'I'll start with The Kings Arms. The supporters club drink in there.' Michael got to his feet and turned towards the door, and then he paused. He looked back at Benny over his shoulder. 'Is this about Nathan?'

'I don't know, Michael. It's just a hunch. Do your best?'

'Of course, Boss. Anyfing to help Alice.'

Alone again, Benny sank back into his chair. If he was right, and Luke had been trying to persuade Nathan to fix the match, it didn't bear thinking about. But then again, neither did Nathan's death.

Nor Alice's grief.

Stacy shifted her weight from one leg to the other, and tried to loosen the knot of tension in her lower back. The blue sandals with a four inch wedge would have been a much more comfortable option for standing, but the white ones with a five inch stiletto heel had an attractive ribbon fastener that wound around her slim ankles and tied in a bow, enhancing the glossy, tanned skin of her long, lithe legs.

She turned her head and glanced nonchalantly in through the window of Umberto's restaurant. It was an intimate venue, just a dozen small tables, and only the one table remained empty. She turned back to the street and glanced first to the left towards the railway station, and then to right towards Kirkby's modern town centre. There was still no sign of Luke.

She had been waiting for the best part of twenty minutes now. Barely recognisable out of her sensible polyester bank uniform, she was beginning to feel uncomfortable, like a slab of meat in a butcher's shop window. An additional application of fake tan, bare legs and a mini-skirt so short it could pass for a belt had seemed like a good idea when she was getting ready for her evening out. But now, in full view of the town's midweek drinkers, and after being honked at by more than one lecherous passing motorist, she was beginning to realise her mistake.

She turned again to look through the restaurant's window and wondered whether it would be acceptable to go in and announce herself, and wait for Luke at their reserved table. She could order a glass of wine to steady her nerves, and sitting down would be bliss compared with standing in the muggy heat in shoes that were now feeling so uncomfortable she could barely stand still in them. Through the glass a tall and swarthy waiter caught her eye, and encouraged by his smile she stepped towards the door and stretched out a hand to the handle, but as she did so a smartly dressed man in his forties also stretched out a hand, and their fingers collided.

Stacy blushed and drew back her hand. The man merely smiled and proceeded to turn the handle, before ushering his companion, an elegant blonde in a modest navy silk two-piece, in through the door. The young woman turned to cast a smile at Stacy, with an unmistakeable smugness that hinted at superiority. Stacy turned her head away, embarrassed by the encounter, but reassured by the notion that the young woman would be equally embarrassed when she and her partner discovered that the only vacant table left was already reserved.

Minutes passed, and the couple did not reappear. She didn't have to look back through the glass to know that they had been seated at the one remaining table. A tear of humiliation prickled behind her eye, and she blinked it back and pulled her mobile phone out of her handbag. She hadn't dared to ask Luke Kingsley for his phone number, but she'd dared to help herself to it from his banking records, and had optimistically stored it ready for regular use in her list of contacts. The number dialled, it rang and rang without response, not even from a voicemail service. She brushed an unpleasant thought to the back of her mind.

There could be any number of reasons why Luke Kingsley was late. He could have been held up at his solicitor's, or just unable to get a taxi. Except it was hours since he'd been due to meet with Hector Campling, and he lived in the town centre, just a ten minute walk away from the restaurant. There must be another explanation. Perhaps she'd just got the time wrong. Perhaps he'd said eight thirty, and not eight o'clock. That would explain it. And it would explain why all the tables in the restaurant were taken at the moment. He had booked a table that would come free at eight thirty. Relieved by her own explanation, and confident in her conclusion, she decided to go into the restaurant and order a drink at the small bar in the corner. After all, it would only be fair to give the elegant blonde a ringside seat when Luke Kingsley finally arrived and greeted her with a kiss.

Inside the restaurant the air was cool and scented with oregano, and the tall waiter who'd caught her eye through the window a moment or so earlier left his post at the bar and stepped forward to the doorway to greet her with expectant eyes. 'May I help?'

She returned his smile with a nervous fluttering of eyelashes. 'I'm waiting for ... for a friend. I think he's booked our table for eight thirty. May I wait at the bar until he arrives?'

'Of course. With pleasure.' He gave a gracious nod of the head, and turned to a large appointments book which lay open behind the restaurant's till. 'The name, please?'

'Kingsley.' She spoke a little louder than intended, and several diners turned to look at her.

'Kingsley?' The waiter ran a finger down the list of the evening's bookings, and then looked up at her with an uncertain stare. 'Kingsley? Signor Kingsley is a regular customer here, yes, but there is no booking for him this evening. You are sure this is the right restaurant? He sometimes dines at La Lanterna, our other restaurant.'

For a moment Stacy couldn't speak. Tears were

pricking fiercely at her eyes now, and her throat felt tight. She swallowed hard and forced a smile at the waiter. 'I'm so sorry. I've come to the wrong restaurant.' She threw up a hand. 'What am I like? I'd better get over there, Luke will be wondering where I am.' She knew he was staring at her, and that his sympathy was practiced, as if apologising for Luke Kingsley was part of his regular duties. But holding his gaze was preferable to turning her head towards the restaurant's diners. She could feel eyes burning into her, silently laughing at her, another silly tart taken in by Luke Kingsley's lies. Unsteady on her heels, legs shaking, she turned towards the door and stepped out on to the pavement without another word, letting the door slam shut behind her.

For a moment she just stood outside the door, swaying dangerously atop her vertiginous heels. Lydia said he was a bastard. Lydia said he would use her. And she put it down to Lydia being jealous, because Lydia couldn't hold on to him herself. She'd let herself be used, she'd given him information she shouldn't have given him, endured the wrath of Rose Bennett, and risked her glowing reputation with Clive Barden, and the bastard hadn't even booked a table. The date being cancelled, being let down by an excuse, that was a humiliation that she could have borne. Dates were made and broken all the time. But to be invited out to dinner and then publically humiliated by the knowledge that he hadn't even booked a table?

She couldn't go home yet. She couldn't face her family. She couldn't face anyone that she knew. She needed to calm down, to think, to work out a way to save face. She glanced around her, absently, looking for a place of safety, and her eyes latched on to a burger bar directly across the road. It appeared to be empty, save for a family of four in the window, tired-looking parents watching two small boys rip the pieces out of a burger and chips. Slowly, carefully, she picked her way across the pavement to a pelican crossing a few yards to her left, and navigated her way across the road.

The burger bar was next to a newsagent's shop, and as she passed it something on the pavement caught her eye, a small news board a few feet away from the shop's open door. The Kirkby Evening Press had claimed another scoop, and as she took in the words on the board time for Stacy stood still. An elderly man emerged from the doorway and, seeing her distress, took hold of her arm and steadied her on her feet. She looked at him with blank eyes, and then turned her attention back to the board.

He followed her gaze and gave a sad nod of the head. 'Aye, it would shock anyone, that bit of news. Who would have thought it so soon after Nathan?'

Luke Kingsley Dead.

The words barely registered before the mist descended. Stacy gave a strangled sob and tried to hold on to the stranger, but her knees were already buckling dangerously, and without another sound she slumped, unconscious, onto the pavement.

13

'Someone's idea of a joke?' Ian Scott put his first coffee of the day down on the edge of George Mulligan's desk and lifted up the poster, holding it up in front of him at arm's length to get a better look. 'It looks authentic. Does it constitute a crime?'

Mulligan folded his arms across his chest and eyed Scott over the top of his glasses. 'Not that anyone can think of. Under normal circumstances I'd chalk it up to a prank, but in the light of Nathan Kingsley's death we'll have to follow it up. Anna Hill was on duty last night, and she volunteered to deal with it. That one,' he pointed to the paper in Scott's hands, 'was taken from a news board outside a newsagent's in the city centre, just around the corner from the bus station. But there were more. The desk took around a dozen calls from shop owners over the course of the evening.'

'It looks like the official Kirkby Evening Press banner printed across the top. Who supplies these things?'

'The Evening Press have them printed, and supply a pack to any business selling their newspaper. They're supplied as blanks, so that the vendor can write on it whatever headline they think will sell the newspaper in their area. Anna called the Press yesterday evening and was told that they keep a record of how many blank posters are supplied to each vendor, but I doubt that will help us much. They supply them to thousands of local businesses.

That one could have been taken from anywhere.'

'And what about Luke Kingsley?' Scott dropped the poster back onto Mulligan's desk.

'Very much alive and kicking. Anna called him after the first call came in. He was at home, and he told her that he planned to spend the evening there, so she asked if she could stop by and speak to him. She showed him one of the posters and he turned white as a sheet, but he refused to be drawn on it. She reckons he played it down, and tried to make out it would be one of his team mates trying to wind him up.'

'That's a bit weak, isn't it?'

'Even for Luke Kingsley.' Mulligan's smile was disparaging. 'If someone murdered your brother, Scottie, and then a few days later posters appeared around the town announcing that you were dead, what would you do?'

'Panic? Ask for police protection, and make myself scarce if I didn't get it?'

'Me too. Unless I had an idea who was responsible, and I didn't want to draw too much attention to it.'

'There is another reason he might not be panicking. He might have put those posters up himself.'

'To make it look as though he was being threatened? Why would he do that? To draw us off the trail?' Mulligan thought about it. 'I suppose it's possible. But then he wouldn't have blamed it on a prank, would he? Surely then he would have demanded that we do something about it, to make it look as though his own life was at risk? No,' Mulligan shook his head with a scowl, 'he knows something alright. I think he knows who murdered his brother, and I think he knows why.'

'So why doesn't he tell us?'

'Because he's scared shitless, Scottie.' Mulligan took off his spectacles and laid them down on his desk. 'Think about it. Every time we've spoken to him he's been twitchy. We both agreed there was something else going on behind the grief. But we've respected that grief, and we've given him the benefit of the doubt through all his explanations, weak or otherwise. I think we've been pussyfooting around his sensitivities for long enough. These posters are some sort of threat. Maybe he's already had threats, and now the killer is going public, putting the pressure on.'

'So what does the killer want, George?'

'I don't know. But I've got a pretty good idea. Nathan Kingsley gifted a serious amount of cash to Alice Blacklaws in the last few weeks of his life, and she claims she knew nothing about it. If that's true, then he was trying to move that money to a place where only she could benefit from it.'

'I thought that Rose confirmed that money was all legitimate?'

'She did. Just because it's legitimate doesn't mean someone else can't lust after it. Maybe he owed it to the killer. Or maybe,' Mulligan nodded to himself, jigsaw pieces finally beginning to fall into place in his mind, 'maybe the killer wanted him to settle someone else's debt. According to Benny Bradman, Nathan had a reputation for settling his brother's gambling debts. Maybe there was one debt too many, and maybe the Bank of Nathan Kingsley just stopped paying out.'

Ian Scott blew out a sigh. 'Are you sure this isn't just another one of your wild speculations, George? We've got no evidence of extortion. We don't even have any evidence of Luke Kingsley's gambling debts.'

'Not yet, we don't. But that's not going to stop us paying Mr Kingsley a visit.' Mulligan put his hands onto the desk and pushed himself to his feet. 'Get that coffee down you, Scottie, and then get your jacket. I think it's time we started playing hard ball.'

Stacy picked up the long-handled spoon and lowered it slowly into the cappuccino. She gave it a half-hearted stir and then pulled the spoon out, scraping it along the edge of the glass to remove the coffee's frothy deposits. Normally she would take pleasure in licking the spoon clean but somehow today it was an indulgence she felt that she didn't deserve. She glanced at her watch, and saw that she was ten minutes early for her meeting with Rose. Another ten minutes, then, to contemplate last night's disappointments and muse on her own failings.

She had chosen a table in the corner of the staff restaurant, as far away from the doors and the service counters as she could. She didn't want to see anyone she knew this morning, and didn't want anyone she knew to see her. Rose she couldn't avoid. But other colleagues? Well, word would have travelled, wouldn't it? She'd told Lydia yesterday about Luke's invitation to dinner, and Lydia wasn't the sort to keep that kind of news to herself.

She slumped back into her seat, turning her head a little to the left so that she could look out of the window. The restaurant was on the third floor of the building, and the windows gave out onto Kirkby's main shopping street. It wasn't quite nine o'clock and the pavements were busy with that spike in pedestrian traffic when late-running office workers collided with the first wave of early-morning shoppers. She lifted her eyes up to the skyline, where the upper levels of Luke Kingsley's apartment building rose up from behind a row of ageing department stores, and blinked to hold back an unbidden tear. It wasn't the first time she had been used, but it was damn well going to be the last.

That poster had been nothing more than a hoax, of course. Passers-by had picked her up off the pavement last night, and dusted her down, and one of them had gone into the shop to buy a copy of the Evening Press to show her. There was nothing in the newspaper about Luke Kingsley. The newsagent, ignorant of how the poster had found its way to his notice board, had called the paper's news desk, the news desk had denied all knowledge of the story, the police had been called, and Luke had been found alive and well and spending the evening alone in his apartment. The waiter at Umberto's had been telling the truth. He hadn't even booked a table.

She drew in a deep breath to steady her nerves. She would have to come clean with Rose. She would have to tell her everything, that Luke had invited her out to dinner, that she'd been taken in by him and betrayed Alice's confidence, that she'd given him confidential information about the mortgage account and about Alice and Olivia's personal savings accounts. It would probably mean the end of her career. It would certainly mean the end of her privileged working relationship with Clive Barden.

And all for what? The distant possibility of a fling with a second-rate footballer, a liar, a cheat, a man so devoid of integrity he hadn't even had the decency to book a table at the restaurant and at least make a decent pretence of it before standing her up. She felt an angry flush rush into her cheeks, and her breathing quickened. How dare he? How dare he humiliate her like that? Who the hell did he think he was?

And what did it matter? Whoever Luke Kingsley thought he was, he wasn't the man Stacy Singleton had expected him to be. And what did it matter to him what Nathan had done with his money? She was glad Nathan had given his money to Alice Blacklaws, glad that he'd loved Alice more than his shallow, grasping brother. Luke had been angry when she told him about Alice inheriting the house, and angrier still when she told him about the money Nathan had gifted to Alice and Olivia. He'd frightened her for a moment, and he knew it. Oh, he'd recovered well, but he knew his temper had been flaring.

Maybe this had all worked out for the best. Maybe the stories she'd heard about Luke Kingsley, the stories that she hadn't wanted to believe, were true. And perhaps this hadn't been a disaster so much as a lucky escape. She turned her head and glanced across the restaurant. Rose

Bennett was at the end of the service queue, paying for a coffee, and perhaps sensing Stacy's eyes upon her she turned and smiled and fluttered her fingers in a friendly wave before pocketing her change. Stacy forced a smile and waved back. Perhaps, she thought, a serious display of humility to Rose might be enough to persuade the consultant to plead her case with Clive Barden.

A serious display of humility to begin with, and then perhaps a searingly honest account of her conversation yesterday with the duplicitous Luke Kingsley.

Benny perched awkwardly on the edge of the armchair and waited for Alice to regain her composure. She was sitting on the Chesterfield sofa, Olivia sleepily cradled in her arms, gently rocking back and forth. He couldn't decide if she was rocking to reassure the child, or to soothe herself. He wanted to hug her, as a father might hug a grieving daughter, but he didn't know her well enough. A more confident man might have hugged her anyway, but Benny's confidence was restricted to worldly matters, running his business and pursuing his hobbies. Displays of warmth and affection made him uncomfortable, especially with women.

'Would you like me to make a coffee, Alice? You look all in.'

She gave a gentle shake of the head. 'I've been up drinking coffee all night. I haven't slept.' She bent her head over Olivia and kissed the top of the child's head, a natural, comforting gesture. Her eyes were directed towards Benny's knees, rather than his face, but her focus was somewhere in the distance, far away from the present moment. 'I'm sorry to be like this. And I'm sorry I had to call you this morning, but I didn't know what else to do. There's no one else to ask, and Vienna …' She broke off and snuffled a humourless laugh. 'I already know what Vienna will say. I need to talk to someone who knew

147

Nathan, and who won't stand in judgment of Luke without considering all the facts.'

Benny closed his eyes and thought for a moment. He wasn't necessarily the best person to ask, if Alice was looking for someone who wouldn't stand in judgment of Luke Kingsley. He'd spent most of yesterday evening trying to put a few facts together for himself. The footage of Kirkby's last game of the season, the argument on the pitch between Nathan and Luke, the fear on Luke's face, his glances up into the crowd to an unseen spectator. And more than that, after Michael had called him late in the evening from a city centre pub. Give Michael his due, he didn't have many talents but he knew how to gain the confidence of a fellow drinker or punter, and how to turn that to his advantage to obtain information without it looking like more than a bit of harmless gossip.

The word on the street was that Luke Kingsley hadn't placed any bets on Kirkby's last game himself, and he hadn't given anyone a tip. But a couple of weeks before the game he'd appeared unexpectedly flush with cash. He'd settled overdue accounts with bookmakers in the town, and then enjoyed running them up again. He'd boasted about a shopping trip to London to buy designer clothing, and spent heavily in the town's smarter bars buying drinks for friends and hangers on and even strangers, if they took his fancy. This run of affluence seemed to last until the end of the season, and those hangers on who enjoyed spending his money were looking forward to the extravagant blow-out that was bound to come after Kirkby's win in that final game.

But those hangers on had been disappointed. Sent off during the game, tail between his legs, Luke Kingsley had slunk away after the match to drown his sorrows away from public gaze. Gossip in his favourite haunts that night had speculated on his behaviour, his tantrums, his public humiliation in being substituted, a player of much less ability being sent on in his place. He'd been seen, someone said, drowning his sorrows twenty miles away in a spit and sawdust place on the outskirts of Scarborough. For Benny, it painted a picture he didn't want to think about.

And now this.

He looked closely at Alice. Her flawless skin was drawn and pallid today, and dark circles ran around her eyes. The blonde hair that usually flicked and curled around her lovely face hung in lank rats-tails around her sallow cheeks, and her eyes, those eyes that so studiously avoided staring directly into his own, were lifeless.

He got up from the armchair and looked down at her, wanting to make things better but afraid to overstep the mark. But there were tears on her cheeks now, and she was beginning to sob. He sank down beside her on the Chesterfield and without any more hesitation wrapped her safely in the best bear hug he could manage. 'I can't promise to be any better than Vienna, Alice. Luke Kingsley is a lyin', devious little toe rag.' He hugged her closer. 'But whatever it is he's done, you can tell me about it. And if you want me to just listen, I'll just listen.'

Under his embrace she seemed to relax a little. She lifted her head, and tried to sniff away the flow of tears. 'He came to see me last night, Benny. Late. Really late. Almost midnight.' She sniffed again. 'He said he was sorry to call so late, but he needed to speak to me. He needed to tell me that he was in trouble, and that I was the only person who could help him. He was in a really bad way, crying and trembling. I didn't know what to do, so I let him in and I made him a coffee.'

'Had he been drinking?'

'Yes, I think so. But he wasn't just drunk. He was scared. I've never seen him like that.'

'Did he admit that?'

'Oh yes. That was why he'd come, you see. To tell me why he was scared, and to ask me to save him.'

'Save him?' Benny uttered a humourless laugh. 'The only thing Luke Kingsley needs savin' from is himself.'

149

She shook her head violently and lifted her face up and around to look at him with hollow, anguished eyes. 'He's in such trouble, Benny. And he says I can sort it all for him. But I don't know where to start. I need someone to help me. He says it's all Nathan's fault.'

'Nathan's fault?'

She nodded. 'He said that it's Nathan's own fault that he was murdered. That Nathan took a bribe to throw Kirkby's last game of the season, and now the man who bribed him wants his money back because Kirkby won.' Tears were flowing steadily now despite her efforts to stop them, and her words were coming in spurts between sobs and snuffles. 'He said that Nathan wanted Luke to help him, to deliberately play badly so that Kirkby would lose the game, and Luke wouldn't do it. That's what the argument on the pitch was about. And he said that after they argued, Nathan daren't do anything else to try to throw the match, because Luke had threatened to tell everyone what he'd done.'

Benny closed his eyes and swallowed hard to suppress the bile that was beginning to rise in his stomach. 'And Luke says this was all down to Nathan? That Nathan took the bribe, and then decided at the last minute not to sabotage the game because he was afraid that Luke would blow the whistle on him?' He ground his teeth together to keep the anger in. 'And after that, I suppose that whoever bribed Nathan would want his money back? And then, when he didn't get it ….'

She was weeping heavily now, and he could barely make out her words between sobs. 'He said it was worse than just paying the bribe back. That punters overseas had been gambling on the game, that they'd lost thousands and thousands of pounds, and they wanted their money back. They wanted it back from Nathan, and he wouldn't pay, so they murdered him.' Her voice became a hoarse whisper. 'And he said that Nathan had to die before we married, so that Luke would inherit everything. They've been threatening Luke ever since the day of the wedding. Demanding that he hand Nathan's money over to them.'

'Is that right?' Benny's cynicism was evident in his voice. 'So where's his problem? There's no will, so now he inherits, doesn't he? And I've heard that he's got that little scumbag Hector Camplin' running his errands, why does he need you to be involved?'

'Because Hector Campling has found a will. Luke says that Nathan has left everything to me. And unless I sign it all over to Luke ...' She shrank down into his arms and sobbed convulsively. 'He even knows that Nathan already gave some of his money to me before he died. I don't know how he knows. But he wants me to go the bank, to transfer it to his bank account. He wants me to go first thing this morning. But I don't think that's the right thing to do. I don't want the money, but I don't think it right for him to give it to these criminals, and he won't let me talk to the police.'

Benny rested his chin on the top of her head, and when he spoke again his voice was unexpectedly calm and soothing. 'Now you listen to me, girl. I don't know what the hell Luke Kingsley is playin' at, but I can promise you one thing. Nathan did not take a bribe to throw that match. I know that, and if you look deep into your heart you know that too.' He gave her a gentle squeeze. 'And here's somethin' else I'll promise you. I don't know about this will, or who inherits, or what the hell is goin' on with Nathan's money. But we're goin' to talk to Rose Bennett about that. And then we're goin' to talk to George Mulligan about these lies that Luke's peddlin'. And when we've done that, we're goin' to sort you out with a solicitor. A proper one. Not a devious, theivin' lowlife like Hector Camplin'.'

'But Luke said I mustn't tell anyone.'

'I'm sure he did. But you've told me, and I'm glad that you did. Luke's not here now, but I am. And I'm tellin' you straight, we're playin' this by the book. Nathan was as honest as the day is long. And Nathan loved you. And I'm not goin' to stand by and watch Luke Kingsley ruin your life, or little Olivia's life, in the way he's ruined his own.'

14

It was late morning when Michael Spivey turned the ageing Vauxhall off the A10. He'd been driving for almost four hours without a break, and his shoulders were beginning to burn with the tension of holding the steering wheel at speed. But it hadn't been a bad journey, all things considered.

He'd made an early start that morning, extracting himself from Vienna's solicitous gaze well before breakfast. She'd hugged him tightly and told him to be safe, but to keep his heart and mind open and listen to what his father had to say. He couldn't imagine that, listening to what his father had to say. All he could remember of his father's voice was a drunken slur, an angry word, a coarse laugh as the leather belt made contact with the back of his own spindly eleven-year-old legs.

He was almost at the Essex border now, and it felt strange to be crossing into a county that he hadn't visited since Benny Bradman had taken him north to Market Melbourne more than two years before. Truth be told, he wouldn't be going back there now if it weren't for some inexplicable urge driving him on. He didn't need Benny to remind him that there were some things they'd left behind that were better left forgotten. But some demons had to be faced in order to be rid of them.

At least he had a bit of spare cash in his pocket this morning, the means to show his father that his life was on the up, that he could earn his keep and pay his way. Benny had his faults, but failing to show his appreciation of a job well done wasn't one of them. An envelope containing five crisp twenty pound notes had been slipped through his letterbox at some point early that morning, probably when Benny had been making his way to the shop. It was a pity that Benny had spoiled the gesture by writing "remember what I said" on the outside of the envelope. A simple thank you would have done nicely. Vienna said that Benny was just looking out for him, and maybe he was, but it still felt as though Benny didn't trust him, as though he was always expected to screw up. How was he supposed to prove his ability if people were always ready to put him down, if every word of encouragement came with a balancing word of derision?

The thought annoyed him, and he switched on the radio and began to sing along under his breath. It was a sunny day, and he'd chosen a scenic route for his journey, branching off the A1 at Huntingdon and heading down across country by Royston and Ware. The road was long and straight, and for some reason he remembered that it was the old Roman road of Ermine Street, a long forgotten fact from schooldays that overall hadn't made much of an impression on him. It made for a pleasant drive, the unswerving line of the road cutting sharply through the undisciplined landscape of rolling hills, past thatched cottages and country pubs, and on into the outer reaches of the Home Counties, where a rural way of life had long since been replaced by the London commuter's daily toil, and the price of a house was now measured by its proximity to a railway station rather than by its size and stature.

Heading east now, towards Harlow's modern New Town, a growing tightness in his chest was beginning to join the ache in his shoulders, but this new tension had nothing to do with the length of the drive. He was drawing close to his destination now, and thoughts of his father were beginning to creep back into his mind. He hadn't bothered to write back to the old man, to let him know that a visit was on the cards. There hadn't really been time to write back. Or maybe that was just an excuse. Maybe he thought there would be power in surprise, that if he could catch his father off guard with an unexpected visit, it might somehow give him the upper hand. And if he had the upper hand, he reasoned, it might make the past just that bit easier to deal with.

The car was coming to a major junction, and he turned right at the roundabout, and headed towards the address he'd been given. It was a name he recognised from long ago, an unappealing block of council maisonettes that had housed a number of his school-friends. It was barely a quarter of a mile from the place they'd been living when his mother had taken him away to the safety of a halfway house in Chelmsford. He felt a prickle of fear across his body, and he banished it away with a thought of silent bravado. *I'd like to see the old man try to beat me down now.*

He drove about a mile and a half, and then turned the Vauxhall left at a familiar junction. The block of maisonettes was just a few hundred yards along the road on the left, and he swung the car into a small car park at the side. His heart was beginning to beat within his chest, slow, steady thumps that rippled through his body, and his mouth was turning dry at the thought of coming face to face with his father, that half-God, half-demon, whose presence, and then whose absence, had coloured just about everything that had happened to Michael Spivey in the last twenty years.

For a fleeting moment he contemplated backing out of the parking space, of turning the car around and driving straight back to Market Melbourne, to the familiar comfort of Vienna's smile and Benny's banter, the betting shop, and his own shabby but homely flat, four safe walls where this half-God, half-Demon couldn't touch him. But he'd come this far. And it was a test. He knew it was a test, and he knew that he would never forgive himself if he backed down now. He swallowed hard, and took a glance at his own face in the car's rear view mirror. Beads of sweat had formed on his forehead, and he took a clean linen handkerchief from his pocket and dabbed at it before getting out of the car.

He found the house, number eight, in the middle of the block, identified by an oval, cast iron name plate decorated with painted daffodils. The door was spotlessly clean, and a new doormat proclaiming "Welcome to our Home" was flanked by a pair of large plant pots containing geraniums and petunias. She was house-proud like his mother, then, this unknown woman who had stood by his father for so many years.

He paused for a moment, and tried to remember why he was here. He was here because his father was dying, because his father wanted to talk to him, but above all because he wanted to put the past to rest. He hadn't seen his father for the best part of twenty years, but the man still had a hold on him. A couple of letters was all it had taken for Michael to ignore the past and drive two hundred miles to see him. He knew that if he'd ignored the letters, he would never be free. He knew what his father was, and knew what his father was capable of, and he could carry that burden through the rest of his life, or he could face his past now, stand up to the man for the first time in his life, and set himself free. There was no contest, really.

The door had a heavy brass knocker placed at eye level, between two panes of frosted glass, and without another thought he put up a hand and gripped it, and rapped loudly once, twice, three times on Jack Canning's front door.

'I'm sorry, Mr Kingsley, but your accounts have been frozen.' The bank teller regarded Luke with suspicious eyes. 'We have a clear notification on our systems that accounts in the name of Luke Kingsley are no longer active.'

Luke leaned across the counter and stared directly into the young man's face. 'How the hell am I supposed to access my cash if the bank has frozen my accounts?' He hissed the words through clenched teeth. 'I'm expecting a large transfer into my current account this morning, I need to check the balance to confirm that it's gone through, and I need to access the cash as soon as possible. How the hell am I supposed to do that, if this pathetic, tin-pot little shit-hole you call a bank has buggered up my accounts?'

The teller observed him coolly for a moment, and then glanced right to exchange knowing glances with a colleague. He turned back to Luke. 'Perhaps it would be better if we discussed this in private.' He stepped out from behind the counter and held up an arm to shepherd Luke into a small meeting room tucked into the corner at the front of the branch. 'Please, take a seat.'

Taking a seat did nothing to improve Luke's temper. He could feel the tension growing in his shoulders and his neck, and his breathing becoming deeper. He knew he needed to stay calm, that losing his temper wasn't going to get him anywhere, but his anger was instinctive, born of panic rather than of reason. He waited while the young man clicked at the keyboard of a small computer on the desk between them. The man was frowning, his eyes flicking as they ran down the screen taking in information that was hidden from Luke's view. 'Are you able to tell me what the hell is going on?'

The young man nodded to himself, and turned calm eyes towards him. 'I'm afraid all of your accounts have been frozen as a result of a notification received yesterday by one of our other branches.'

'A notification?'

'I'm not quite sure how to put this to you, Mr Kingsley, but according to our system, well ... I'm afraid you're dead.'

'Dead?' Luke frowned, and thought for a moment. 'Is this some sort of sick joke? Do I look dead to you?'

The young man risked a quiet laugh. 'Of course not. But our system …'

'Your system is evidently wrong. I'm here, alive and kicking, and I need access to my bank accounts, and …' Luke paused, troubled by an invading thought. 'Can you see the balance on my current account on that thing?' He pointed at the computer. 'Has a transfer been made in this morning, a large transfer from another account with the ENB?'

'I can see the closing balance, yes, but I'm afraid no transfer has been made today. You see, we were notified of your death during business hours yesterday, and your accounts were disabled overnight. Any transfers in progress before the accounts were disabled would have gone through, but anything actioned this morning would be rejected.'

'In plain English?'

'If someone tried to transfer money into your account this morning, the transfer would have been rejected because the account is no longer active.'

Luke put his hands up to his face and rubbed at his temples. 'Let me see if I've got this right. Someone told the bank yesterday that I'm dead, and so the bank has disabled my accounts. Even though I'm clearly not dead, because I'm sitting here in front of you?' He didn't wait for a response. 'So, I'm guessing …' He paused, and looked quizzically at the young man. 'What's your name?'

'Daniel.'

'Daniel.' He nodded. 'So, I'm guessing, Daniel, that what we need to do now is reactivate the accounts so that I can access my money, and the transfer I'm expecting can go through?'

'In order to reactivate the accounts, I'm afraid you'll have to go into your home branch. It's not something we can do for you here.'

'My home branch?'

Daniel glanced back at the screen. 'Your home branch is the Kirkby Head Office branch. If you visit the branch with two forms of identification …'

Visit the Kirkby Branch, and run the risk of bumping into Stacy Singleton? That wasn't going to happen. Luke held up a hand. 'Identification? You want me to take time to travel to another branch, and take identification to prove … what? That I'm not dead? Isn't it enough that we're sitting here having this conversation?'

'I can understand your concern, but …'

'Can you? Can you really? Thanks to the ENB I've just discovered that I'm dead. I have no access to my bank accounts, I have to go out of my way to visit another branch just to prove that I'm not dead, and the only way I'm going to be able to pay for things until you sort this mess out is to run up a bigger balance on my credit card.'

Daniel cast his eyes down at the desk. 'I'm afraid that's been frozen too.'

'So I have no credit either?' Luke placed his elbows on the desk and rested his head in his hands. 'I'm obviously missing something here. Just exactly what is it that makes the ENB think that I'm dead? Don't you need evidence of a death before you start messing around with people's bank accounts?'

'We have evidence, Mr Kingsley. Perhaps if I show you?' Daniel clicked at the keyboard, and then took hold of the side of the computer's monitor and twisted it round so that Luke could see the grainy image on the screen. 'This was scanned into our system yesterday, when it was received by the bank. It's a verified copy of a death certificate, which we accepted in good faith as a legitimate document, and it says …' Daniel moved his head closer to the screen and peered at the image. He blinked once, twice, and then glanced uncomfortably at Luke. 'It says quite clearly that you died two days ago from a brain haemorrhage as a direct result of a gunshot wound.'

'We were just on our way to see Luke Kingsley when you called.' Mulligan directed his words at Benny Bradman, who was sitting beside Alice on the sofa. She looked exhausted today, wrung out by the events of the last few days, and he felt a lump in his throat where a grizzled, case-hardened police inspector had no right to feel one. The murder of her fiancé on their wedding day was more than one woman should have to bear in a week. But with Nathan's murder she had lost her job, almost lost her home, believed herself to be penniless only to discover that she was a millionaire, and now this – the suggestion by her fiancé's brother that he was a criminal, a fixer, someone who would take a bribe to throw a football match. If he'd read Alice Blacklaws right, that would be the cruellest blow of all – to have trusted Nathan Kingsley, and find herself wondering now if she'd ever really known him at all. To be wondering whether he'd really cared for her, or whether she was just another pawn in a game that she hadn't even realised he was playing.

Benny pointed to an armchair. 'Take a seat, George. I'll make a brew in a minute.' He turned to Alice with a smile. 'It'll be alright now, girl. I've told George all about it on the phone. He's only got a few questions for you.'

She returned his gaze with quiet resolve. 'Could I speak to Inspector Mulligan alone?' Her voice was calm. 'There's something I'd like to say to him.'

Benny looked hurt, and he studied her face for a moment. It showed a calm determination. 'Of course. Why don't I make that brew now, and take Sergeant Scott with me?' He put his hands on his knees and pushed himself to his feet, and motioned for DS Scott to follow him.

Alice waited until they were gone, and then turned swollen, bloodshot eyes to Mulligan. 'I'm not sure exactly what Benny has told you, Inspector Mulligan. But Luke is in trouble. He needs help.'

Had she been taken in, then? Mulligan pouted his disappointment. 'I've heard that Luke has accused Nathan of taking a bribe to throw Kirkby's last match. And I've heard that Nathan supposedly lost his bottle and didn't go through with it because Luke called it out. And frankly, Alice, I don't believe it.'

She gave a wan smile. 'I'm not sure what to believe any more. I thought I knew Nathan, but he had secrets from me. Even if I've benefitted by his gifts of money and the house, they were still secrets, he still wasn't open with me.'

'Perhaps he was trying to protect you.'

'Perhaps. But I thought he knew how important the truth was to me. Perhaps,' she suggested, 'he didn't know *me* as well as I thought he did.' She glanced across the room, avoiding his gaze, and spoke into the distance. 'I believe that someone did want the game to be fixed, and it didn't happen. And I believe that particular someone is responsible for Nathan's death. They want Nathan's money, and I'm in the way. Luke has asked me to give the money to him, all of it, so that he can settle the unpaid debt.'

She was going too fast for Mulligan. 'Alice, you don't have to give anything away. You don't know if Luke's story is true, for one thing. Didn't you wonder why it's taken him days to lay this story at your door? Why didn't he tell you straight away that he knew who'd murdered Nathan? Why didn't he tell us? Wouldn't it make sense for him to tell the police, so that we could offer protection and seek out the murderer?' He shook his head. 'He could have invented this story just to extort the money from you because he found out that Nathan had made a will, and that it disinherited him.'

'He could. But I don't believe that he did. After all, someone did kill Nathan. There must be a killer, and there must be a reason.'

'Well, we plan to talk to Luke today, to press him to tell

us what he knows. We were already planning to speak to him before Benny called. What you've told us just makes us all the more certain that he knows who killed Nathan, and he knows why. He's kept it to himself for five days now, that means he's either somehow responsible for Nathan's death …'

'… or he's afraid for his own safety.'

'Is he afraid for your safety, Alice?'

'*My* safety?'

'Aren't you at risk? You and little Olivia? Nathan gave you all the money. And for what it's worth, I believe he did that because he knew his life was at risk. He was trying to pass his wealth to you so that you would be secure if anything happened to him.'

'I can't think about that now. One way or another, Luke needs help.' She turned her gaze back towards him. 'On Saturday, Inspector Mulligan, you asked Vienna to pass a message on to me. You said "tell her I'll get the bastard who did this". I know that you'll keep that promise, but I have something else to ask you. I have to ask you to help Luke, to keep him safe.'

'Help him? After everything he's done … everything he's trying to do, to you and Olivia?'

'Whatever else he is, he's Nathan's brother. Nathan isn't here to look after him now, but I am. Nathan would want me to. And he's all I've got left of Nathan. I can't be Nathan's wife, but I can be a sister to Luke. I know that you'll do the right thing, if I ask you to. I know that you have to trace Nathan's killer, but please don't hang Luke out to dry, Inspector Mulligan. If you can do anything for me right now, then please keep Luke safe.'

15

'So much for you not needing me today.' Rose rested her mobile phone in the crook of her neck and stretched out a hand to take hold of her small suitcase, pulling it from the side of her chair and pushing it gracelessly under her desk.

At the other end of the line Clive Barden sounded tired. 'You will allow, Rose, that this turn of events is not something we could have foreseen. I gather Luke Kingsley became rather angry when staff refused to re-open his accounts.'

'And this was at the Scarborough branch?'

'Yes. Daniel Collier dealt with him. Most professionally, I understand, given the customer's rudeness.' He clicked his teeth in disapproval. 'Daniel advised that Mr Kingsley should visit the Kirkby Branch, which is his home branch, and arrange to have the accounts re-opened there. I suggested that in addition they might provide him with a taxi to travel between branches at our expense, but I understand that he would prefer to come into the branch later this afternoon. He's asked for an appointment at three o'clock. Can you be available to see him? I don't want to entrust this to anyone else, especially after Stacy's escapade yesterday afternoon.'

'I can, yes. But I've checked out of the Kirkby Manor now. Could you ask Moira to book me in for another night? And my travel arrangements will have to be changed. She booked me on to the 14.23 to Kings Cross. '

'Of course.' He coughed to clear his throat. 'How is Stacy this morning?' He tried to make the question sound impersonal, like the casual interest of a senior manager, but wasn't wholly successful.

'She'll live. We had a chat first thing this morning, and she's quite contrite about the whole thing. But ... well, not to put too fine a point on it, there's something else I need to tell you. Stacy didn't stop at meeting Luke Kingsley on her own during office hours. She accepted a dinner invitation from him, to meet up at a restaurant in Kirkby yesterday evening. She thought it was a date.'

'A date?' He sounded horrified. 'You mean a personal assignation? With a customer?'

Rose suppressed a laugh. 'Well, I suppose that's another way of putting it. The thing is, it all turned a bit unpleasant for her. They'd agreed to meet at eight o'clock and he didn't show up. She called into the restaurant to claim their table, in case he'd been held up, and he hadn't even made a booking.'

'You mean he'd arranged to meet her, with no intention of turning up?'

'So it would seem.' She gave a sigh. 'Anyway ... Stacy set off across the road to get herself a coffee in a nearby café while she decided what to do next, and found herself caught up in a hoax aimed at Luke Kingsley. She practically fell over a fake news board outside the newsagents next door. It had a poster on it claiming that Luke Kingsley was dead.' She waited for Clive to think about the implications. 'You can see how awkward this is now, Clive? A hoax yesterday evening suggesting that he's dead, and now we have a copy of a death certificate stating the time and cause of his supposed death?'

'You think it's more than a hoax.'

'I don't think we can overlook the possibility that these are threats.'

'And whoever is making them has had the audacity to embroil the East & Northern Bank in their plans.' She heard him draw an exasperated sigh at the other end of the line. 'The sooner we can establish how the death came to be recorded with us the better. Have you spoken to Inspector Mulligan yet?'

'No, I wanted to speak with you first. We have a rigorous procedure around bereavement notifications. There will be an audit trail, the system wouldn't close the accounts unless all the supporting documentary evidence was in place. Although ... I'm not sure how we would validate whether the death certificate presented was authentic. If someone could come up with fake news boards for the Kirkby Evening Press, I suppose it's possible they could also come up with a fake death certificate. '

'I'm not sure, Rose, whether the presenting of a false death certificate is a crime as such. I will consult with our legal department. From our perspective our staff are well-trained, and I'm confident that we acted in good faith accepting the certificate as evidence. Can I ask you to set up a call with the branch responsible, and find out exactly what happened? The process would ask for the informant to provide identification so that we could be certain of their right to notify of the death. Find out who that informant was and bring me up to date before you pass the information on to Inspector Mulligan. He will need the informant's details, and a copy of the false certificate.'

'And what about Luke Kingsley's accounts? He claimed that he was expecting a large transfer into one of his accounts this morning, and that our mistake has resulted in the money not hitting his account.'

'Re-open them. We have no grounds to keep them inactive, and given the nature of the police investigation, I don't want the ENB to be accused of muddying the water. We don't know what transfer he was expecting, although I suppose you could take a chance and ask him. The information may be of use to the police.' He was silent for a moment, and then said 'it would appear that Stacy has had a rather disagreeable twenty four hours. I hope she hasn't taken it all too badly.'

Rose looked across the office to where Stacy was clicking away at her keyboard. Some of the colour had returned to her cheeks, and she had coiled her long, brunette hair up into an up-do that made her look less like a footballer's prey and more like a professional bereavement officer. 'I think she's fine now, Clive. She's apologised for her mistakes, and she's apologised for arranging to meet Luke Kingsley without letting me know. I might even let her sit in when I meet with Luke, it would do her good.'

'Do you think that's wise?'

'Yes, I do. In fact, I think it's the perfect opportunity for her to demonstrate just what the whole sorry episode has taught her.'

Benny dropped the remnants of his steak sandwich onto the plate and pushed it away from him. Out of the corner of his eye he saw a shaggy white head lift optimistically from the dog basket under the window, and turn in the direction of his desk. He pulled a piece of cold meat from between his discarded crusts and tossed it towards the dog. Mac's head tilted skilfully, and his lips parted to catch the morsel with the barest of exertions.

Benny watched as the dog chewed contentedly on the gristle of his leftovers. It was going to be hard to give him up when Lu returned from her holiday to reclaim him. It was going to be hard to give a lot of things up when this week was over.

He turned his gaze to the photograph of Catriona on his desk and leaned back in his chair. *She's only a mate, Trina. Just a mate.* He sighed. *But I don't half wish she didn't look so bloody much like you, girl.*

The words stayed firmly in his mind, soundless, as if just thinking them rather than speaking would leave him feeling less guilty. *The stupid thing is, you'd like her. She don't have your finesse, but she's got your spark.* His mobile phone was sitting idly on his desk and he picked it up, and opened the messages folder to look again at the text from Rose. The message had been unexpected but welcome. She'd have to cancel lunch because something had come up at work, but could he do dinner instead? She had to stay another night in Kirkby.

'She's just a mate.' He nodded to himself, the words spoken out loud now, and Mac turned his head again and eyed him cynically with his one good eye. He scowled at the dog. 'You keep your bark shut, if you know what's good for you. Anyway, I need her help with Alice.'

That at least was true. It was beginning to tax his abilities, soothing a grieving young woman, and he was out of his depth. Vienna was a diamond, the best of friends for Alice, but she didn't have Rose's nous when it came to dealing with the business side of things. And anyway, Vienna was biased against Luke. She had a bit too much to say for herself in that direction, it was clouding her judgment.

Then again, his own feelings about Luke weren't anything to be proud of at the moment. The lad had taken a bribe to throw the game, he was certain of that. But throwing the game on his own was too difficult, and he must have tried to take Nathan along for the ride. As if Nathan would have involved himself in anything criminal. Luke had been taken off the pitch, the game had been won, and any crooked bets placed had been lost. The punters would want their stake money back from the fixer, and he would want that – and the initial bribe – back from Luke. But Luke had already burnt through the money, and Nathan had shown himself no longer inclined to settle his brother's debts.

Benny rubbed at his forehead to ease a growing tension. He knew the sort of people who arranged for matches to be fixed. And he knew the sort of pond life that arranged for crooked bets to be taken. He'd nearly been caught up in it himself, years ago, and been glad to distance himself from it. They weren't the sort of people you crossed. People who wouldn't take no for an answer, who would do anything they could to recoup their losses and make sure that at best you didn't let them down again, and at worst you never forgot your mistake. There was no wonder that Luke was running scared, and there was no way that he was going to risk naming names.

He leaned further back in his seat and closed his eyes. He couldn't remember taking any bets himself on Kirkby to lose, and not secure promotion. But then it was unlikely that any crooked betting would take place so close to where the match was being played. Somewhere else in the country, then. Or possibly even overseas. There were ways of finding out. Maybe if he could get a lead on the betting, it would bring them closer to whoever murdered Nathan. He opened his eyes and picked up his phone again, flicking stubby fingers at the key pad, searching through the list of numbers stored for later use. The one he wanted was just a short way down the list. David Campbell was a specialist, a data genius who could examine a raft of gambling numbers, smile enigmatically, and pinpoint the nub of a fix with such apparent ease he'd quite easily built a thriving business around it. Benny had no doubt that if anyone could spot the origin of the bribe that had tempted Luke Kingsley, David Campbell could.

He was about to dial Campbell's number when his eye caught the next name down in his contacts list. *Hector Campling.* He paused, and then dropped the phone onto the desk, and turned his eyes towards the office window, looking through the glass but not really seeing the Georgian conversion across the road which served as Campling's office premises. He needed to call on Hector Campling today, to get hold of the will which Luke claimed had been made by Nathan in the weeks before his death. Alice needed that will, it was hers to administer, and so far Campling had made no attempt to hand it over.

His eyes narrowed at a troubling thought. Nathan's regular solicitor was Richard Fleming. Why had Nathan used a lowlife like Hector Campling to draw up a will? And why draw up a will at all leaving everything to Alice, when the very act of marrying the girl a few weeks later would render any such will null and void? There was something about making a will before marriage that was playing on his mind, something he remembered Catriona talking about in respect of a case she was representing. Something about making a will *in anticipation* of being married. Damn it, he couldn't remember, and he didn't know enough about it to even know if it mattered.

His eyes came suddenly into focus and Hector Campling's name, etched on the glass of the window in his office, came sharply into view. The call to David Campbell could wait. He needed to see the will. If Nathan had felt it necessary to make a will just weeks before his wedding to Alice, then that implied that Nathan wanted to make sure she would inherit if anything happened to him *before* the wedding.

And if that were true, then Nathan had spent the last few weeks of his life looking over his shoulder, wondering if he would still be alive on his wedding day.

Michael Spivey watched with some misgiving as Lucy closed the front door of the maisonette behind her, leaving him alone with Jack Canning. Without her generous warmth and smiling eyes the room felt suddenly dark and cold, and he rubbed his hands together nervously, alone at last with the devil.

'She seems a nice sort.' He nodded towards the direction of her exit. 'It's a shame she had to dash off like that.' He cast a sideways glance at Jack, and then looked away again. He hadn't known what to expect after all these years. He hadn't even been certain he would recognise his own father. But he hadn't expected this. In his memory, and in his imagination, his father was a big man, a bruiser, a bully. But his memory had played a trick on him. Jack Canning was small and wiry, and clearly very, very sick. Michael could see it in the pallor of his skin and the hollows of his eyes.

Jack smiled at the thought of Lucy and nodded, more to himself than to Michael. 'She's the best. She's stood by me for years now. She asks no questions, and she tells me no stories. You can't ask for more than that in a woman.' His voice was soft and rasping, the deepening illness beginning to take its toll. 'And she knows when to make herself scarce. She's gone shopping so that we can have some time on our own.'

There was a time when being alone with his father might have frightened Michael, but there was nothing to be afraid of here, at least nothing physical. They were just two strangers talking about nothing in particular. 'I've got a girl now. Vienna, her name is.' He couldn't hide the pride in his voice. 'We've been going out for over six months now.' He fished in his pocket for his mobile phone and slid his fingers deftly over the screen until it filled with an image of himself on the seafront at Scarborough, his arm around a slim, pale girl with raven black curls and shrewd, intelligent eyes. He passed the phone over to Jack.

'She's a looker.' Jack looked at the picture and for a moment his eyes widened with surprise, and he nodded. 'You've done well there, son.'

Son. *Son?* What right had this man to call him "son" after playing no part in his life? Michael felt his cheeks begin to burn and he swallowed hard. He hadn't been sure whether this wraith of a man who claimed to be his father was still capable of hurting him emotionally. The sight of his father dying hadn't done it, all he felt about that was pity. Pity, and a little disappointment.

But now he had the answer. All it had taken was that one word that carried with it all the hurt and pain of his childhood, and he was eleven years old again, back in his grubby bedroom, his calves stinging from the whip of Jack's belt, his face dirty with tears of shame and sorrow. He cleared his throat and licked his lips. He'd promised himself that he wouldn't let Jack get to him. And he'd promised Vienna that he wouldn't lose his temper. When he could trust his voice not to tremble he said 'that picture was taken a couple of weeks ago. We went to the seaside with her sister and the kiddies. She has free. Her sister, I mean. Her sister has free kiddies.'

If Jack was aware of the nerves in Michael's voice he didn't give any sign of it. 'Well, she looks like a keeper.' He leaned over towards Michael and handed him the phone. 'My Lucy is a keeper.' His face straightened, and he looked suddenly vulnerable. 'That's one of the reasons I wanted to see you. Only one of the reasons, mind. I … I wanted to apologise to you, first.'

'There ain't no need.'

'There is.' Jack held up a hand. 'I know you're going to think this is just the illness talking. And you're probably right. But there's nothing like the kiss of death to remind a man of his failings. It makes you take stock of your life. I've never done right by you, Michael. And I want to make that up to you.'

'Like I said, there ain't no need.' Michael shook his head at the prospect of a conversation that he didn't want to have. 'I've got everyfing that I need. I've got Vienna, and a decent job. I don't need nuffing from you now.'

Jack closed his eyes and nodded quietly to himself. 'You're angry. And I don't blame you for that, you've got every right to be angry. But I want you to know that when I've gone, and that won't be long now, when I've gone there's some money for you.'

'I don't want your money.' Michael was hissing now, angry and hurt in equal measures. 'I've managed alright without you all these years. Give the money to Lucy.'

'I am giving something to Lucy. I've left a will dividing

everything I have equally between the two of you. It's witnessed and everything, kosher. It's locked in the middle drawer of that desk.' He jerked his head towards the small, old-fashioned desk in the corner. 'What money I have is in a building society account. The passbook is in the drawer, and the key to that drawer is taped to the back of my bedside cabinet. Lucy doesn't know about it, and I don't want you telling her. When I've gone, I want you to come back here, take the will and the passbook from the drawer, and help her to sort things out. She's got no family beyond me, no one who can help her.' His face darkened. 'There's a canvas sack in that drawer as well, Michael. When I've gone, I want you to take everything else in that drawer and put it in the sack, and dump it. Somewhere where no one will find it. Take a drive out to the coast and dump it in the sea.' He looked at Michael with hopeful eyes. 'You know what I'm saying? She mustn't ever know about it.'

'What's in it? What are you asking me to get rid of?'

Jack turned his face away. 'I ain't going to tell you about that now, son.' He looked down at his hands. 'No questions asked. If you won't do it for me, do it for Lucy?'

'Why should I do it for her? She's not my mother.'

His father was tiring now, his face grey from the strain of asking favours he had no right to ask. 'She's got nobody, Michael. I'm asking you to look out for her.'

'Why the hell should I do that for you?'

Jack turned his gaze back to Michael and stared directly into his eyes. 'You have every right to ask that. And every right to refuse to do it for me. I deserve that.' He braced himself. 'So if you can't do it for me, then do it to spite me. This is the best chance you're ever going to get to prove that you're a better man than I am.'

16

'And you can assure me that the bank is going to do something about this mess? Because so far, I've just been passed from pillar to post.' Luke Kingsley lounged back in his seat and fixed Rose Bennett's back with a hawk-like stare.

Rose, who was busy lowering the blinds which hung along the glass partition wall of the meeting room, looked over her shoulder and beamed at him with a vacuous smile. 'I'm sure there's nothing we can't sort out, Mr Kingsley. I'll just secure us a bit of privacy first. We don't want everyone staring in at us, do we?'

He scowled in reply. 'My dealings this week with the ENB have been appalling. They've frozen my bank accounts for no reason, and caused me a great deal of inconvenience by failing to process an important money transfer into my account. The staff in your Scarborough branch refused to help me this morning. And on top of all that your bereavement officer has been next to useless. She was no help at all with my brother's affairs.'

'I will try to address each of those concerns in turn, if you will bear with me.' Their privacy secured, Rose took a seat opposite him at the small meeting table. 'There is a limit to my authority, of course, but I will try to answer your questions. Now, if we can begin with your accounts?' She glanced down at a set of documents on the table, and began to sift through them. 'Ah yes, here we are.' She pulled a photocopied document from the pile. 'You are aware, of course, that your accounts were frozen because another branch of the ENB was notified of your death. This is a copy of the death certificate we received from the informant.' She slid the document across the table until it was in front of him. 'The bank freezes accounts after bereavement to protect the estate, pending further instruction from the estate's administrators. Having frozen your accounts in good faith, we now need to decide whether or not to reactivate them for you.'

Luke's eyebrows beetled forward and his eyes clouded. 'That certificate is a fake. The whole thing is a hoax. That much is evident from the fact that I am sitting in front of you. Why in God's name would you not reactivate my accounts?'

Rose gave another inscrutable smile. 'I'm afraid it's not that simple. You see, the ENB is under no obligation to offer banking services to an individual. It's a matter of discretion. If you are certain that this was a hoax, then it's possible that you know who is responsible. And if that is the case, the bank could take a very dim view of their business being used for the purposes of fraudulent activity.'

'Are you telling me that the bank might refuse to reactivate my accounts?'

'I'm telling you that they are under no obligation to do so until they are satisfied of the circumstances surrounding this fake death certificate. Of course, if you are so dissatisfied with the ENB that you don't want to do business with us any more, then you are welcome to take your custom elsewhere. I'm sure another bank would be more than happy to open an account for you.' She frowned. 'Of course, it would still be necessary to settle your overdraft with us before your accounts could be closed.'

His mouth twitched as he considered the possibility of settling an overdraft which ran well into five figures. The beetled eyebrows almost knitted together, and then suddenly his face relaxed and he broke into a smile. 'Look, Rose – may I call you Rose? I'm as much in the dark about this fake certificate as you are. And I will admit it's not very pleasant to be on the receiving end of that sort of malice. But in my game – you know I play for Kirkby FC? – there's a lot of jealousy and spite. I've had threats before, they never amount to anything serious. It's usually just some celebrity-hating nobody trying to get their kicks by bringing me down.' He smiled, and for a moment looked less like a hawk, and more like a crocodile.

Rose thought for a moment, under no illusion that he was trying to turn on the Kingsley charm, and decided that just because she was impervious to it was no reason not to turn it to her advantage. She blinked vacantly, and presented her best girlish smile. 'Of course we'd be delighted if you decided to retain your accounts with us, after all the necessary checks. Perhaps now we could discuss the money transfer that you claim has gone missing? If you could give me the details, I can tell you exactly what's happened to the money, and we can take steps to expedite the funds into your account as soon as it's been re-activated.'

His smile became a grin. 'I would appreciate that, Rose. The amount I'm expecting is substantial, certainly tens of thousands.'

'You're not able to tell me exactly?'

He frowned again. 'It's coming in from a family member, as a gift. I can't say what the exact amount will be.'

'And the source of funds?'

'Excuse me?'

She looked up at him and smiled. 'The name of the account holder transferring the funds to you?'

He looked uncomfortable now. 'Why do you need to know that?'

'It helps us to locate the transaction. If we can't see the

transfer waiting to go into your account, we can trace it further back up the line and see if it has left the source account. If it has, it may have gone into the bank's suspense account, in which case it needs to be released to you.'

It wasn't a completely accurate explanation, of course, but it was enough to satisfy Luke. 'Alice Blacklaws.' He said the name so quietly it was almost a whisper.

'I will check that out for you as soon as we finish speaking.' She put down the pen and regarded him with a serious look. 'With respect to our Scarborough branch, I can only apologise if you don't think they did enough to help you. They are bound, of course, by our internal procedures.'

'Did I really have to come all the way back to Kirkby to sort this out?'

'I'm afraid so, yes. We would have been pleased to arrange a taxi for you.'

He laughed. 'It wasn't just the transport. I was worried that you were going to leave me with that bereavement officer again. What was her name? Stacy, was it? She was useless the other day. But I can see I didn't have anything to worry about. You've been more than helpful, Rose.'

'It's very kind of you to say so, Mr Kingsley.'

'Please, call me Luke.'

Rose gave a gracious tilt of the head without making eye contact. 'You have given me something of a dilemma here, of course. I did mention, I think, that there was a limit to my authority. We do still have to follow the bank's process when it comes to reactivating your account. There is a strict procedure, and I'm afraid I'm not authorised to execute that procedure. In this situation there is only one colleague, useless or not, who can decide whether or not your accounts can be reactivated.'

Almost on cue, the door of the meeting room began to open, and Luke turned to see Stacy framed in the doorway. She was breathing heavily, nervous of the task ahead, but there was a defiance in her eyes that reflected her determination to show both Rose and Clive that she would only need one chance to regain her professional reputation. She avoided Luke's gaze and smiled at Rose. 'Are you ready for me now?'

'Oh I think so, Stacy.' Rose swept up her notebook and pen from the table and pushed back her chair, holding out a hand as she got to her feet. Luke stared at the hand with a look of sudden bemusement. 'It's been a pleasure to meet you, Mr Kingsley. As I promised, I'll look into that missing transaction for you.' Her smile was beginning to tug at the corners of her mouth now, and threatening to turn to laughter. 'Just in case you were wondering, as you have been listed as officially deceased on the bank's systems, the only colleague with sufficient authority to reactivate your bank accounts is our bereavement officer. And that, as you already know, is Stacy.'

Hector Campling forced an insincere smile and steepled his fingers. 'Well, this is an unexpected pleasure, Bradman. What brings you to my office?'

'I'm here representin' Alice. Alice Blacklaws.' Benny folded his arms across his chest. 'We understand from Luke Kingsley that you have a copy of Nathan's will.'

The solicitor raised an eyebrow. 'Mr Kingsley told you that in person?'

'Mr Kingsley,' Benny repeated, with contempt in his voice, 'told Alice that in person, and Alice told me. What we'd like to understand is why you've taken so long in comin' forward with this bit of information. And why you haven't been in touch with Alice about it.'

Campling gave a gentle nod of the head. 'I find your concern for Miss Blacklaws quite touching, Bradman. But you will have to forgive me. You are not her legal representative, nor are you a member of the family. I am under no obligation to answer your questions, nor indeed to share any information with you.'

Benny leaned forward and rested his elbows on Campling's desk. 'Look Hector, I know you don't have time for me. There ain't no love lost between us, and I don't think either of us lose any sleep over it. But this is about Alice. That young woman lost her fiancé on her weddin' day, and spent days wonderin' whether or not she was goin' to be turfed out on to the street. She's got a little girl to think about. You could have saved her a lot of heartache if you'd come clean about this damned will right at the start.' He stopped short of any accusation that Campling might be milking the situation for his own ends. Riling the solicitor further wasn't going to gain him the information he wanted.

Across the desk Campling had stopped smiling, and was chewing thoughtfully on his lower lip. 'I was waiting for the correct protocol.'

'Meanin'?'

'I was waiting for Miss Blacklaws to appoint a solicitor to represent her interests. The first action of the solicitor would be to advertise in the press for any information regarding a will. At that point I would, of course, have contacted the solicitor to discuss the matter.'

'Instead of which you just decided to share it with Luke Kingsley.' Benny had to work hard to keep his rising anger under control. 'Even though he weren't a beneficiary of the will.'

'Luke is Nathan Kingsley's next of kin. He is entitled to the information. Painful though it may be to Miss Blacklaws, she is not Nathan Kingsley's next of kin.' He frowned, and then added 'although as beneficiary of the will, had she asked for a copy I would of course have provided one.'

Benny lifted his arms from the desk and leaned back in his seat. 'Are you goin' to provide me with a copy of the will now, so that I can take it to Alice?'

'No.'

'But you'll provide her with a copy if she asks you for it directly?'

'I will provide a copy to Miss Blacklaws, or to an authorised legal representative. Of course,' the insincere smile returned, 'if Miss Blacklaws has yet to appoint a legal representative, my firm would be most happy to assist in any way we could.'

Benny resisted the temptation to laugh. There was a time when Campling's petty jibes and innuendos would have wound him up, but not any more. 'Well that's very decent of you. I'll be sure to pass that message on.' He grinned at the solicitor. 'Tell me, Hector, didn't you think it a bit odd that Nathan Kingsley asked you to draw up that will. I mean, you're not his usual solicitor, are you?'

'Mr Kingsley had purchased some investment property from me, and I had provided the conveyancing service. I viewed making the will as simply a piece of additional business.'

'And you didn't think it odd that he was making a will so near to the date of his marriage?'

'Why should I? The prospect of marriage often leads an individual to consider their financial affairs. If anything I thought it rather circumspect of Nathan Kingsley to make a will.'

'Yes, but his marriage to Alice would have invalidated the will, wouldn't it? Why would you make a will to someone who was goin' to become your natural beneficiary in a matter of weeks?'

Campling took in a deep, slow breath and then let it out again. 'I know what you want me to say, Bradman. You want me to say that Nathan Kingsley made that will because he was expecting something to happen to him. But there is no evidence to suggest his life was at risk.'

'Apart from the bullet that entered his brain barely an hour before his weddin'.'

The solicitor sucked in his cheeks. 'I think it's time for you to leave.'

'Was Nathan troubled when he asked you to make that will? Did he seem scared, or nervous about somethin'?'

'I have nothing to say on the matter.'

'Did you have a flutter on the game, Hector?'

'A flutter?'

'Yes. Did you fancy Kirkby to win? Or did you think there was a possibility they might lose?'

'I don't know what you're driving at, Bradman. But I would be grateful now if you would leave my office. Please pass my regards to Miss Blacklaws and let her know that I am here to assist in any way I can.'

Benny leaned a little further forward over Campling's desk and stared straight into his eyes. 'You want to be careful, Hector. You might be out of your depth with this one. You made a will for Nathan Kingsley that seems to have upset a few people. And if I'm right about that, it might be useful to know that they're the sort of people it doesn't do to upset.'

'Are you threatening me?'

'No Hector, I'm warnin' you. I'll pass your message on to Alice. But you take my word for it, you might want to get that will out of your office and make it someone else's problem.' He got to his feet. 'You know I ain't a bettin' man. I take bets for other people, I don't waste my own money on them. But I'll give you any odds you like that Nathan's will had a "contemplation of marriage" clause in it.'

The solicitor became suddenly cagey. 'I don't see why you would think that. It would have been rather pointless. The purpose of such a clause is to ensure that beneficiaries other than the new spouse would not be disinherited as a result of the marriage. I thought you already knew that Nathan left everything to his fiancée.'

'Oh yes, I knew that, Hector. But I think on this occasion that clause had another purpose. It was to make sure that if anythin' happened to Nathan before his wedding took place, there would be no basis to challenge the will. Nathan Kingsley was makin' it as clear as he could that he intended Alice Blacklaws to inherit everythin' he had, whether he married her or not.'

Luke glanced at his watch and sighed out his irritation. It was almost ten past four, and he was still waiting for Stacy Singleton to return to the small meeting room and confirm that his bank accounts were reactivated. The air in the room was stifling, and he reached into his trouser pocket for a handkerchief, and dabbed with it at the back of his neck to mop the perspiration gathering around his collar of his shirt. It barely helped. He shoved it back into his pocket, and began to tap impatiently with his fingers on the table in front of him.

His mobile phone was on the table, dormant and expectant, and he tapped on the screen to spark it to attention. The newly-received text message from Larry was still present at the top of the screen. It was short and to the point.

Not long now.

Not long until what? He couldn't bear to think about the possibilities. He'd already had a number of hints, the fake news boards, the phoney death certificate. These were just the sort of sick tricks that Larry liked to play. He cast his mind back to the text he'd received yesterday. *If it isn't good news for me today, it's bad news for you.* That's what the fake news boards were all about. Bad news for Luke. Just another example of Larry's twisted sense of humour.

And the fake death certificate? He couldn't help wondering how the hell Larry had pulled that off, how he had persuaded the ENB that the certificate was genuine and his death was confirmed. Rose Bennett had given him a copy of the document, and he glanced at it now, lying on the table beside his phone. Was this Larry's way of telling him that he was facing the same end as Nathan? A bullet in the brain? Rose hadn't given anything away about who presented the certificate to the bank, just that they were still looking into it. He couldn't help thinking that there were more questions he should have asked of her, but he didn't know what was important. Nathan would have known. Nathan always knew what to do.

Still, his bank accounts were being reactivated. It had been a sticky moment when Stacy Singleton had come back into the picture. He really thought that she was going to be spiteful and refuse to help him. But she hadn't. In fact, she had been surprisingly nonchalant about the whole thing. There had been no mention of the previous evening, nothing said about the way he'd humiliated her. Perhaps he'd underestimated her.

It would hardly be a surprise. He was beginning to realise that underestimating the women in his life was a mistake he seemed destined to repeat. He thought about Alice, and his eyes narrowed. Rose Bennett had confirmed to him that there was no sign anywhere in the bank's system of a payment making its way from Alice's bank account to his own. It had never occurred to him that Alice wouldn't follow his instructions. He'd told her that his life was at risk, for God's sake, and she still wouldn't give him the money.

Perhaps, he thought, she hadn't swallowed his story about Nathan and the bribe after all. Which was ironic, because it wasn't a million miles from the truth. Nathan *had* been murdered because he wouldn't pay back Larry's losses. Alice didn't need to know that it was Luke who'd taken the bribe. Knowing that wouldn't bring Nathan back. It hadn't been easy for him, blaming his blameless brother for his own sins. But it had been better than Larry's latest suggestion, that he take little Olivia when no-one was looking and then blackmail Alice for the money. Even he couldn't stoop quite that low.

He was going to have to talk to Alice again, try harder to get her on side. If he was lucky, he had this one day left to try to put things right with Larry. "Not long now" could mean anything, and Larry had a short fuse, but Luke thought it likely that he would at least wait the day out to see if Alice came through with the cash. Larry had no way of knowing that she hadn't transferred the money yet, and there was still time if only Luke could find a way to persuade her.

He glanced again at his watch. There was time, but it was running out fast. He picked up his phone to send Alice a text, a message to let her know that he was planning to pay her a visit. He had barely begun to type when the phone began to ring with an incoming call. It was from a mobile number that he recognised, and that he didn't want to acknowledge. George Mulligan had called him five times already today using that number, leaving messages, asking for his calls to be returned. Mulligan was keen to speak to him as "a matter of some urgency". If it was urgent for the police, he reasoned, then it was urgent for him to avoid the conversation. At least until he'd got Larry off his back.

He waited until the phone stopped ringing and then completed his text to Alice. He planned to be with her in half an hour, he only needed Stacy to come back and confirm everything was OK with his bank accounts. It couldn't be long now. She couldn't leave him sitting here for much longer. Perhaps he ought to remind her that he was here, make the point that he didn't have all day to wait around. Perhaps, he thought, she wasn't as cool about yesterday evening as he'd believed. Perhaps she was doing this on purpose to wind him up, making him wait to punish him for what he did to her. In which case, he needed to do something about it.

He started to get to his feet, intent on leaving the room in search of Stacy, but as he did so the door of the small meeting room began to open. He sank back onto the seat with barely disguised irritation. 'I thought you'd forgotten about me.'

'Did you, Luke? I find that hard to believe, given how

many messages I've left for you today.'

It wasn't the voice that Luke expected to hear. Momentarily thrown, he jerked his head up to look at the speaker. Framed in the doorway, where he'd hoped to see Stacy Singleton brandishing evidence of reactivated bank accounts, was the unwelcome sight of a grinning Detective Inspector George Mulligan.

'It's a shame we haven't a spare room to put them up in. It would have been nice to have them visit. Just the once.' Lucy kept her eyes fixed on the phone's screen as she spoke, and Jack knew she was avoiding eye contact. He also knew that "just the once" meant "before the end". It didn't make it any easier.

'Michael's done alright for himself.' He pointed a bony finger at the phone in her hand. 'That picture was taken in Scarborough. That's him and his girl. Her name's Vienna.' He'd persuaded Michael to send him the photograph that afternoon, afraid that if the moment passed Michael would return to Yorkshire and forget all about it.

'Vienna? That sounds very exotic.' Lucy nodded to herself. 'And look at all those wild curls. I bet she's a handful.' She wrenched her eyes away from the photograph and handed the phone back to him. 'I'm pleased he came, Jack. I didn't think he would.'

He took the phone from her with a grim smile. 'I didn't think he would, either.' But he had. Michael had answered his appeal and paid him one last visit. He knew he didn't deserve it, knew it even more so now that he'd met his son again.

'Are you pleased?'

It was the sort of question she didn't normally risk, and he feigned a scowl. 'Pleased?'

'That he came. That you've seen him?' She was looking at him with loving, solicitous eyes.

'Don't make a thing out of it, Lucy. I asked, and he came.' It was difficult enough for him to feel the emotions of the day without being drawn into talking about them. But he saw her eyes blink at the shortness of his words, and more kindly he said 'yes, I'm pleased. Alright?'

'I'm glad.' She nodded. 'Is it serious, then? Him and this Vienna?'

'I think so. It's good that he's got somebody.' Her gaze was making him uncomfortable now, and he turned his eyes down and back to the photograph. 'He's got a ready-made family with this one. She's got a sister on her own, and a niece and two nephews. They all look out for each other.' He couldn't tell her how much he hoped that Michael would invite her to be a part of this ready-made family that looked out for each other, and how much he didn't want her to be alone when he'd gone.

'Well, let's hope you hear from him again.' She settled back into the comfortable curves of the sofa and closed her eyes. 'I'll make a start on supper in a minute. Steak and chips tonight?'

'Fine. But don't be too long about it. I've a match on at the snooker hall at eight.'

'And I've got a bingo game at seven thirty. It's not all about you.' She clicked her teeth in disapproval, but when she spoke again her voice was gentle. 'You ought to stay in tonight. You need a rest after today. It's tiring, dragging up all these feelings.'

He closed his own eyes and smiled to himself, a weary but wry curl of the lips. He couldn't argue that he needed to rest. Michael's visit had warmed and drained him in equal measures. The meeting had left Jack tired, and yet with a strange sense of pride. There were no good looks in his gene pool to be inherited, no hidden talents in the family. But he'd passed on the Canning nose, strong and aquiline. And perhaps also the one talent that Jack Canning himself valued above all others: the ability to survive against the odds. He'd condemned the boy to a hard life, the back of his hand, the deprivations of single parenthood, the brain-washing of an angry, bitter mother.

And yet even if Michael hadn't thrived, at least he had survived, in spite of his childhood injuries.

He opened his right eye a fraction and stole a glance at Lucy, round and warm and content on the sofa, and wondered again. Might things have been different if she'd been the boy's mother? They might, but he would never know. And he wasn't going to live long enough to know if a bond would grow between them. He could only hope that the boy had understood, that even if Michael couldn't forgive his father, he was to be there for Lucy. It was the only hope he had.

He closed his eye again and considered the evening to come, turning his head away from her to distance himself while he thought. There would be hell to pay when she got back from bingo tonight and discovered that he wasn't just playing snooker. But there was one last job that he needed to do. He'd like to tell her about it now, at least to let her know that there was a job, even if he couldn't tell her the details. But he didn't want to worry her, and he didn't need the earache. He would leave her the customary note with a plausible story: a trip to Bristol at short notice to deliver a car, a vehicle needed first thing in the morning, a customer too important to refuse. He could tell her it was an overnight stop, and that the firm had arranged for him to stay in a hotel overnight. It wasn't a million miles from the truth. She'd huff and she'd puff, but she wouldn't ask too many questions when he got back. She'd learned early on to save her breath and not ask questions that he was never going to answer.

Of course, he wasn't going to be travelling anywhere near Bristol. But she didn't need to know that either. Nor that he was doing this job to earn a last decent wedge of cash to leave for her and Michael. Any hint of a job and she would try to talk him out of it, all the more so if she didn't agree with his motives. It troubled him that in his present state of mind, emotionally moved by Michael's visit and uncharacteristically sentimental about the two people in his life that mattered, it might be easy for her to talk him out of it. That was the last thing he wanted. Because he wanted the money from this one last job. He wanted it for her and for Michael, and nothing was going to dissuade him.

And in any case, when it came down to it neither he nor Lucy would have the casting vote on this one. Because when Larry told you that there was a job to do, you just didn't risk saying no.

17

George Mulligan rubbed wearily at his forehead with the fingers of his right hand and expelled a sigh that contained all the day's frustrations. Suddenly aware that both Rose and Ian Scott were staring at him expectantly he gave a smile. 'Luke Kingsley is as slippery as a barrel full of eels.' They were in the small meeting room, Mulligan and Scott still in the seats they'd occupied while questioning Luke, and Rose standing across the table from them, her hands resting on the back of a chair. Mulligan winked at her. 'But we appreciate the tip off, Rose. And the use of your meeting room. We've been trying to get hold of him all day. At least now we've managed to pin him down.'

Rose shrugged. 'It was lucky timing, really. You arrived here to see the fake death certificate, and he just happened to be in here with Stacy. I wouldn't have thought anything about it if you hadn't mentioned that he wasn't returning your calls.'

'Well, we're grateful all the same. Of course he claims he has no idea who would pull a stunt like that. Someone is threatening him, but he's scared witless and he won't talk. He's sticking to his story that Nathan took a bribe and left him to sort out the mess. We can't force the truth out of him. But it's pretty clear to me that whoever advised the ENB that Luke Kingsley was dead is the same person behind his brother's death.'

'For what it's worth, he told me the same story. About

the death certificate, I mean.' There was a document folder on the table in front of Rose, and she pulled a copy of the certificate from it and bent her head to study it. 'It looks authentic to me, although I will admit that we don't have a check in the process to verify that a death certificate is genuine. I can't imagine that many circumstances where a customer would want to present a false certificate. Heaven knows where you would get something like this.'

'You'd be amazed at the kind of thing that can be produced if you have enough money. The people frightening Luke Kingsley are professional criminals, Rose. They'll have the contacts to come up with a false certificate.' Mulligan put a hand up to his mouth and chewed thoughtfully on a nail, and then asked 'is there anything in the bank's process that would help us find the person who reported Luke's death to the bank? You must keep details of the informant?'

'Of course.' Rose pulled another sheet of paper from her folder, this time of hand-written notes. 'I've started to look into that. At first sight it looks as though the process has been followed. We only accept notification from an authorised person – a family member, or an official such as a doctor. And we take two forms of identification from them, to confirm that they are the person they claim to be. Luke's accounts wouldn't have been frozen unless that part of the process had been completed. At this stage, the only thing I can tell you is that the notification was made at the ENB's Saffron Walden branch.'

'Essex?' Ian Scott broke his silence.

Rose gave a wry smile. 'Unless there's another Saffron Walden I don't know about.' She glanced down again, and ran her eyes over the paper. 'Stacy – that's our bereavement officer here in Kirkby – has spoken to her equivalent colleague who covers the Essex area. He says the death wasn't notified to him, but he will speak to the Saffron Walden branch first thing in the morning to get all the details. As soon as I have them, I'll pass them on to you.'

'I hate to sound impatient, Rose, but can't you just look it up on the system now?'

Rose laughed. 'This is the East and Northern Bank, Sergeant Scott. You can't assume that everything is computerised, we're years behind everyone else.' She pushed the papers back into her folder.

'Wait a minute.' George Mulligan put up a hand. 'If Luke's accounts were frozen, there must have been a flag set on the account to indicate the fact. How could that have been set if the notification of death isn't stored on the system?'

'Ah, I was hoping you wouldn't ask me that.' Rose winced, and looked suddenly reticent. 'I haven't notified any of this to Clive yet, and ...'

'Rose, this is a murder case. I'm not interested in the bank's bloody processes. Just tell me what I'm missing here.'

'As I said, we check the identification of the person notifying us of the death. We take photocopies of the documents they've shown us as evidence of their identity. And eventually those photocopies are scanned onto a document imaging system, which is indexed. But it isn't linked to our core banking system.'

'Which means?'

'Our core banking system has a number of data fields against a customer record which are used when a customer is deceased. The colleague updating the system can set a flag manually to confirm the customer is deceased, input the date of death, the date of notification, and the name of the informant. But the system doesn't hold images of the documents used to confirm the informant's identity. It just holds a flag to confirm whether the documents have been checked. If we ever need to refer to them we have to go to a separate system to look at the images.'

'So you *do* have some information on the system you can share with us?'

Rose was uncomfortable now. 'I really ought to have Clive's authority to proceed, because customer data is confidential. But … for Luke Kingsley's customer record, the deceased flag was set to "yes", the date of death was given as Monday of this week, the date of notification was given as Wednesday, and the document flag was set to "yes".'

'And an ENB employee keyed that information directly into the system?'

'Yes.'

'And the name of the informant?'

'I really ought to get verification on all this data before I share anything else with you. It may not be accurate.'

Mulligan arched an eyebrow. 'Accurate?' Inside he was growing unexpectedly angry. 'Who are you trying to protect, Rose? The bank? Or the informant?'

'I'm not trying to protect anyone. But just because a name has been keyed into a system … can't you see that the informant named might not be …'

'And they damned well *might* be.' Mulligan's words came out so fiercely he surprised even himself. 'Nathan Kingsley is dead, and if we don't do something soon Luke Kingsley will be going the same way. Just give me the name, Rose. Just spit it out.'

Rose turned for a moment and looked at Ian Scott, her expression unfathomable, almost vacant, betraying no evidence of her thought processes. And then she looked back at George Mulligan and nodded to herself with a quiet smile. 'I would be grateful, Inspector Mulligan, if you would respect my advice on this matter. The name I'm about to give you was keyed into the system by an ENB colleague. We have yet to speak to that colleague to confirm that documentary evidence was taken to confirm the informant's identity. If you choose to act on what I'm about to tell you, please note that neither I – nor the East and Northern Bank – can be held responsible for any outcomes until we have verified absolutely that the name of the informant is accurate.'

Mulligan's eyes narrowed. 'The name, Rose.'

She nodded again, her face inscrutable. 'The name, Inspector, is Alice Blacklaws.'

Alice placed the bottle of Chablis down on the table and then lowered herself into the chair opposite Vienna. It was warm in the garden, the blissful heat of a perfect June evening. She turned her head to look across the lawn, to where Olivia was playing at tea parties, a well-rehearsed script enacted almost daily with a small plastic dinner service and the obedient attention of Poo, Tigger and Piglet. It was past the child's bedtime, but there had been few moments of calm like this in the last few days, the peace was too precious to shatter just yet. She turned back with a smile and watched as Vienna poured the chilled wine into generous glasses. 'Have you heard any more from Michael?'

'Another text. He's stopped off at a service station to get something to eat. He'll be home in a couple of hours.' She took a slow sip of wine, savouring the flavour before swallowing. 'He's making good time, anyway.'

'Has he said anything about his Dad?'

'No, not yet. I know he thinks his Dad is a bad lot, but I don't know what he means by that.' Vienna sighed. 'I hope I did the right thing persuading him to go and build bridges.'

'I'm sure you did. He's still Michael's father, whatever he's done in the past.'

'I wanted to go with him, you know. But he wouldn't let me.' Vienna frowned into her glass. 'His mother's gone, and his Auntie Jen that he was close to. I feel like meeting his father would be my only hope of understanding more about him, about why he's like he is.'

Alice gave a gentle shake of the head. 'You're good for him, Vee, and that's enough. Maybe it's better that he's all future and no past. Anyway,' she sipped on her own drink, 'he hasn't lost everyone from the past. He's got Benny. Michael worked for him in Essex, they must go back a few years?'

'Yes, but he won't tell me anything. About Michael's past, I mean.'

'Have you actually asked him?'

'I've hinted. He just grins and shakes his head, and says I'm better off not knowing.'

'Maybe he's right.' Alice looked thoughtful. 'Benny's been an angel for me. He's been to see Hector Campling today, about the will. And he's arranged for Rose Bennett to come and see me to talk through Nathan's bank accounts. She couldn't do that before we knew about the will. Now I'm the beneficiary she can tell me about the accounts that were just in Nathan's name.' She looked back at Vienna and her eyes creased with an inquisitive smile. 'Benny's having dinner with Rose tonight. Have they got history?'

'Not the kind you're talking about.' Vienna's smile was coy. 'But it wouldn't surprise me if Benny wished they did. Michael says she reminds him of his wife. It's a shame he's still grieving after all this time. Rose could be good for him. It would take his mind off it.'

'If I wasn't grieving for Nathan, I would try to take his mind off it.' Alice's face flushed pink, and she broke into a spontaneous giggle, the wine beginning to go to her head. 'Oh I don't mean to be irreverent to Nathan's memory. But it feels good to laugh about something.'

Across the table Vienna fought to keep in a smile of her own. 'And I don't mean to be unfaithful to Michael, but if I was still a single girl you'd have to get behind me in the queue.' She put down her glass. 'You're right, it *is* good to laugh. But there are still serious things to think about. All this is yours now, Alice. I know it doesn't make up for Nathan, but at least you don't have to worry about being homeless. And the money ...'

'You're right. The money doesn't make up for losing Nathan. And this house is too much for me and Olivia. We need somewhere smaller, somewhere cosy. And anyway,' she looked away to where the child was still playing, 'I've been thinking about what to do next, and I've made my decision. I'm not going to give everything to Luke. But I am going to sell the house. And when it's sold, and Nathan's estate is finally settled, I'm going to give Luke half of everything.'

'You're crazy. Luke will hand the money over to whoever is threatening him. Is that what you want? For Nathan's money to go to the scumbag who killed him?'

'No, of course not. But I've been thinking about how Nathan arranged everything. I don't believe that he would ever have completely disinherited Luke. The deposit he put down on this house was a legacy from his parents. It was family money. It's only right that Luke should have that back. Maybe Nathan arranged for everything to come to me so that whoever was threatening them couldn't get their hands on it. Perhaps moving the money to me was meant to keep Luke's share safe from the criminals too. Perhaps he knew that I would help Luke afterwards. He knew that I wouldn't see Luke left with nothing.' She shook her head. 'No, half of everything would be more than enough for me and Olivia.'

'Do you believe Luke's story, Alice? Do you believe that it was Nathan who took the bribe?'

'No, of course not. I wasn't sure at first, it was all too much to take in, coming so soon after Nathan's death. But Benny was right. If I look into my heart I know it wasn't Nathan. I thought I'd lost him, Vee. He was so distant and moody in those last few weeks. But it wasn't because of me, was it? It was because of Luke.'

'He could have told you. He could have told you what Luke had done, and what it meant for him.'

'He wouldn't want to frighten me.' Alice was solemn now. 'He must have been so afraid.'

'He could have told the police. Have you ever asked yourself why he didn't?'

'Perhaps in his own way, he was still protecting Luke. And it was all so close to the wedding. I think he knew he was taking an enormous risk. That's why he made the will so close to the wedding. Maybe he was just holding on to some sort of blind faith that the wedding would go ahead, and then he could speak to the police afterwards.' Alice was still troubled. 'But if he had told me ... well, I would have postponed the wedding, encouraged him to speak to the police. Maybe I just didn't know him as well as I thought he did. And maybe, after all ... maybe he didn't know me.'

The taxi swung sharply onto the bypass and headed in the direction of Kirkby. Mac, forbidden the luxury of the vehicle's leather seats and sulking at Benny's feet, rolled to the left and lost his balance. Benny looked down at him with sympathetic eyes and whispered an encouragement. 'Not long now, mate.' He dropped a hand down to Mac's shoulder and rubbed his fingers in the fur, encouraging the terrier to lie down. Not long now until they would reach Haverland Street. 'Alice is goin' to look after you for a couple of hours while me and Rose have a little chat.'

The dog settled, Benny leaned back into the seat and turned his head to watch the rolling countryside fly past at speed. They would be in Kirkby in a little over ten minutes, and it would take him barely another ten to walk from Haverland Street to the Kirkby Manor Hotel. Twenty minutes to make sense of his day and organise his findings into a logical sequence to present to Rose for analysis.

He laughed under his breath. It was a long time since he'd taken a woman out to dinner. Supper at The Boar with Rose the other evening, well that had felt like a couple of mates catching up on the gossip. But the formality of the Kirkby Manor's a la carte menu and an impressive wine list? That felt like something different. It felt like a

195

dinner date. And for all his bad memory when it came to dinner dates, he couldn't recall anything about parcelling up a day's worth of angst and presenting it to your date for analysis.

Still, this Kingsley business was unsettling him now, and they were both caught up in it. Rose would have met Luke for the first time today, and Benny was keen to know what she made of him. For his part, he was beginning to wish he hadn't been so quick to offer his help to Alice. It wasn't that he didn't want to help the girl, rather that it had never occurred to him that offering to help might rake up things from his own past that he would rather have left forgotten.

He looked down at the seat beside him, and a roll of papers gently swaying with the motion of the taxi. It hadn't taken David Campbell long to come up with some betting data on Kirkby FC's last game of the season. With his usual flair Campbell had provided him with page after page of numbers and algorithms, evidence, he said, of an identifiable pattern of betting. Evidence that suggested a fix was on for Kirkby to lose the game.

Benny hadn't paid too much attention to the numbers. He didn't really need to know how many punters were involved, or how much money had been staked on that particular Saturday afternoon. Rather it was the pattern of bets taken that interested him, that curious, barely-noticeable web of secrets shared, conversations overheard, risks taken on a clever hunch, a knowing look, a crafty wink. He'd seen it more than once before, and been caught up in it more than once before, more than he would care to remember.

The fix was never broadcast, never shared beyond those few interested parties who were part of the scam. But even the fixer could never be sure there wasn't a joker in the pack. There was always some tyke who couldn't keep it to himself, a rogue chancer who would pass, or even sell, the information to a friend or relative. And once the knowledge was out there it would pass in whispers and hints from friend to brother to workmate to uncle, seeping across the local betting shops a tenner here, a pony there, a flutter in Harlow, a couple of bets in Romford, a stake against the odds in Saffron Walden.

Benny knew all about taking bets in the ancient county of Essex. And he knew who called the shots there when it came to crooked outcomes. He folded his arms across his chest and pursed his lips, displeased at the direction of his thoughts. Michael had been down to Essex today. He had no suspicions about Michael, or his honesty when it came to gambling. But it didn't take a genius to work out just who it was that Michael had been to visit. Michael only had one living relative as far as Benny knew, and that living relative had connections to people that no-one with any sense would get involved with.

An uncomfortable realisation was beginning to dawn on Benny now, a glimmer of coincidence too awful to contemplate, even for a hardened cynic like himself. He put his hands up to his face and rubbed at his temples to ease a growing tension. Memories were beginning to come up thick and fast, unbidden and unwanted. It wasn't just Catriona's death that had driven Benny north, at least not in the way that everyone believed. It was his desire to stay on the right side of the law. He'd never been a natural criminal, but he'd never balked at sailing close to the wind. When the proximity got a little too close he'd always backed away, never getting himself in so deep that he couldn't back out. Marrying Catriona had lifted him away from that sort of temptation. Losing her had left him vulnerable to the scum who wanted to drag him back down again.

It had never occurred to him before today that the same scum who'd drawn Luke Kingsley into their grubby little games might be the scum who tried to pull him into their illegal betting scams in the weeks after Catriona died. He'd been told in no uncertain terms that if he didn't want to play, it was time to move on. The wrecking of one of his betting shops had given him something to think about. Arson at another had convinced him that they meant business. When it came to his own skin, he wasn't afraid. If anything, in those days, he would have welcomed death, anything to wipe out the grief. But there wasn't just his own safety to consider. There was Craig, their son. There was the hapless Michael, Catriona's pet rehabilitation project. And his staff, all girls, all young and pretty, all with everything to live for. There were too many lives at risk, too many bright futures at stake.

He'd thought it was all behind him. But it wasn't. It was here again, snapping at his heels, reminding him of his past, kicking him back down just as he was on the way up. He felt suddenly and painfully alone and he leaned forward and wrapped his hands around Mac's middle, and lifted him up onto his lap. 'Alright, fella?' Out of the corner of his eye he saw the taxi driver's reflection in the rear view mirror, a sour scowl at the sight of the dog. He ruffled Mac's ears with his fingers, and glowered back at the driver. 'You said not on the seats. There's no reason he can't sit on my lap.'

They were turning into Haverland Street now. Ten minutes' walk and he would be at the hotel. Ten minutes left to decide whether to tell Rose, to share his suspicions, to reveal his past, to spoil the dinner. He pulled the dog closer to him. 'What do you think, then, fella? Do I spill?' Mac craned his neck around and looked up at him witheringly with his good eye, and Benny could only chuckle to himself. 'You're right, pal. This is Rose we're talkin' about. I can't believe I even thought about bein' economical with the truth.' He shook his head. 'It ain't goin' to be worth the earache.'

'Alice? It's Luke.' He jammed the mobile phone into the crook of his neck and tilted his head to hold it fast, and then jabbed at the lift's control panel with his free hand. The doors slid silently shut.

At the other end of the line Alice's voice became a faint crackle. 'Is everything OK? I can't hear you very clearly?'

'I'm in the lift, I'm on my way to pick up the car. I've been trying to get a free moment all day to call you.' He took hold of the phone again, lifting it away from the crease of his neck but keeping it close to his ear. 'Will you be in all evening?'

'Sure. Are you coming over?' She sounded hesitant, and added something that may have been important, but which sounded to him like a hiss of static on the line.

'I'll be there in about twenty minutes. I have a couple of things to do first. Is that OK?'

'Yes.' She still sounded uncertain. 'I'll see you then.'

There was something in her voice, in her hesitation, that sounded like mistrust, and he felt suddenly ashamed. 'I'm sorry it's so late.' Ashamed or not, he had no choice.

'It's OK. We can talk when you get here.'

The conversation was over by the time the lift reached the basement of the apartment building, and he slid the phone into his pocket. His other hand was holding a heavy, leather holdall and he stepped out of the lift with an awkward, tilting movement, swinging the bag as he went. As the lift doors closed behind him he dropped the bag to the floor and glanced around him.

The basement car park of his apartment building was cool and quiet, and only half full. He flexed the fingers of his right hand to loosen them, and then wrapped them around the handle of the bag and hoisted it up again. Slowly he picked his way between executive saloons and sporty coupes until he reached his Jaguar. He flicked the key fob at the car's rear end and the boot lid lifted smoothly and silently, and he heaved the heavy bag into the boot. He puffed out a breath, glad to be rid of the weight, and gently pushed the boot lid shut, turning on his heel towards the driver's door. He didn't hear the footsteps behind him, the noiseless padding of an uninvited guest, but he sensed a presence and spun back round to see a tall, lean figure emerge from behind a pillar.

'Planning a little trip, then, Luke?' The figure leaned back on the pillar, and a pale, unfamiliar face leered at him with uninvited familiarity.

'Do I know you?'

'Nah. But I know you.' The stranger smirked, and glanced over his shoulder. In the parking space behind him the engine of a black Lexus purred into life, and the car slid forward out of its space and turned across his path, until the rear door of the car's nearside was directly in front of Luke.

Luke, sensing danger all too late, felt a sudden rush of panic as the tinted glass of the window slid slowly down, and from somewhere inside the car's dark interior a familiar rasping voice echoed out to greet him. 'I hope we're not spoiling your plans for a quick getaway, Luke. We've been planning a little farewell party for you.' The disembodied voice gave a hoarse, hollow laugh. 'I hope you're not going to be ungrateful now we're here. We've put a lot of effort into this. I'd hate to think of you bunking off before we've had time to show you our party piece.'

18

'There ain't no great mystery, I was just tired last night.'
Michael focused his eyes on the bowl of breakfast cereal in
front of him, avoiding Vienna's gaze. He swirled his spoon
around absently in the milk, and hoped without much
conviction that she would stop asking questions about his
father sometime soon. He knew that she was worried
about him, but he wasn't ready to talk yet, still waiting for
his own abstract thoughts and fears to settle into some sort
of manageable pattern.

He looked up from his breakfast and watched as she
turned away from him with a grunt of displeasure, turning
her back to butter a slice of toast freshly wrested from the
toaster, her sense of hurt and grievance bristling in the
angry way she scraped the butter across the toasted bread.
He didn't like it when she was angry with him. It reminded
him of his mother, and the way she had of stealing his
wounds for her own use, rather than kissing them better.
He supposed he should be thankful that it was a trait
Vienna displayed only occasionally. Perhaps, he wondered,
she only displayed it when she was truly hurt herself.

His refusal to talk about his father had nothing to do
with Vienna's feelings, of course. More about his need to
keep her safe, to keep her close. She was precious, Vienna,
too precious to lose. But she was asking too many
questions. If she carried on asking them, he thought, he
might have to answer some of them. He watched as she

dropped her plate noisily onto the table and sank into the chair opposite him, and decided that attack was probably the best form of defence.

'My Dad's got himself a nice lady friend. Lucy, her name is.' He threw the information like a piece of bait to draw her off the scent. 'She seems a decent sort. Homely, like. And kind.' He tried to force a laugh. 'She ain't nothing like my mother. There's more for him to get hold of, for a start.'

Vienna lifted wounded eyes to look at him. 'So you met her?'

'Only briefly. I fink she wanted to stay and chat, but she took herself off shopping so we could have some time on our own.'

'And how was your Dad?'

He ignored the question. 'He wants us to look after Lucy. When he's gone, like.'

'Look after her?'

'Well, stay in touch with her, I fink. She ain't got no family, and I fink he's worried she'll be lonely.'

Vienna was watching him now, the dark intelligent eyes trying to read his expression. 'And how do you feel about that? I mean, he wasn't very good to your mother, was he?'

Michael shrugged. 'That ain't Lucy's fault. Mind, there ain't much I can do from up here in Yorkshire, is there? She lives two hundred miles away. And anyway, she might not want me to stay in touch.'

'And then again, she might.' Vienna's tone was becoming less brittle. 'Even a phone call now and again might be enough, and we can be there for her if there's an emergency.' She was beginning to soften. 'Maybe she could come and visit. Or we could visit her now and again. She'll be the nearest thing to family that you have, when your dad's gone.'

'You're my family, Vee. You, and Flo and the kids. I don't need no other family.'

'But you're pleased you went to see him?'

202

He dropped his spoon onto the table and pushed the cereal bowl away from him. 'You're just not going to let this rest, are you?'

'No.' A smile was growing in her eyes, the battle between them almost at an end, Michael on the verge of capitulation as usual.

He blew out a breath. 'You know how the letter said my Dad was really ill? Well, he is. I hardly recognised him.'

'Did you ask what was wrong with him?'

'No. I didn't like to ask. And to be honest, I didn't need the details. You only had to look at him.'

She stretched out a hand and placed it on top of his, and squeezed tightly. 'Are you going to see him again? Are you going to let me come with you?'

'No.'

'For heaven's sake, why not? Michael, he's your father. Don't you think you ought to make things up with him? Don't you think you ought to let me meet him?'

'It ain't that simple, Vee. My Dad … he ain't like a normal dad.'

She snatched back her hand, the gentleness gone, the hurt reappearing in her eyes. 'He's still your Dad. And you need to forgive him. If you don't forgive him, Michael, it will eat away at you. When he's gone, it will be too late.' She scooped up her breakfast plate, with its half-eaten toast, and scraped her chair away from the table. 'But what do I know? I'm just the one who's trying to make it better for you.'

He watched with a stubborn silence as she got to her feet and clattered the plate onto the kitchen worktop. She was beautiful when she was angry, the dark eyes flashing with self-righteous indignation, the raven curls shaking with a furious energy. Beautiful, he thought, but not always truthful.

He knew there was another reason she wanted to meet his father, and it was nothing to do with building bridges or making things better. It was for herself. It was to find out whether the stories he'd told her about his childhood were true. To see for herself what kind of man his father was, to discover just exactly how bad was "bad".

If only he could know that answer to that question himself. There had been something on his mind all the way back from Harlow, a troubling thought niggling away at him that he just couldn't persuade to go away. There were things in that house that his father kept hidden, things he didn't want Lucy to see, things he wanted Michael to dispose of when he was gone. And if that was the case, then Jack didn't want him to look after Lucy in the way most people meant. He didn't want his son to just hold her hand, to ease the pain of bereavement, to keep her company. He wanted Michael to be there for her if the truth came out. He wanted someone to stand beside her without judgment, to be there for her unconditionally, someone who knew that being close to Jack Canning was a perilous place to be.

Lucy, he reckoned, didn't know that his father was a bad lot, or if she did she probably thought he was a rogue, a half-baked chancer who took back-handers and did a few risky jobs that other men would turn away from. Lucy didn't know the half of it, but then it would seem that neither did Michael. Truth be told, he didn't want to know what was in that drawer in Jack Canning's desk. But he could take a guess, and be fairly confident that his guess was close to the mark. He knew how bad his father had been, and based on Jack's behaviour yesterday he could make a pretty shrewd guess that his father hadn't changed for the better.

The problem was, until the truth came out no one was really going to know just how bad Jack Canning could be.

In the privacy of a small meeting room, discretely tucked away behind the ENB's staff restaurant, Rose Bennett stared at the notepad in front of her, her eyes barely focusing on the hand-written notes she had made during the call. She had to admit that Alan Reeves had been thorough in his investigations, but she still wasn't quite sure where all the information he had passed to her was going to lead.

She tapped on the desk with the end of her pencil, undecided as to the next move. Strictly speaking she ought to consult with Clive first, but the information she had to impart could be critical to George Mulligan's investigation. Up until yesterday she wouldn't have harboured any doubts about speaking to Mulligan first, but she'd seen a different side of the usually easy-going policeman yesterday, not just less avuncular in his attitude, but quick to judge. He may be under pressure, but that was no reason in her book to ride roughshod over people who were trying to help him and clutch at a convenient conclusion.

Saddened by the thought, she leaned an elbow on the table in front of her and used the end of her pencil to dial a familiar number on the conference phone in front of her. The number answered almost immediately with a brisk bark.

'Clive Barden.'

'Clive, it's Rose. Do you have a minute to talk?'

'Ah, Rose. Yes, of course I do.' His tone relaxed. 'Have you spoken to the Saffron Walden branch?'

'Yes. I've spoken to the manager, Alan Reeves.' She leaned a little closer to the phone's receiver. 'It would appear that Saffron Walden branch have a rogue colleague.'

The elongated pause at Clive's end of the line signalled his concern. 'I'm not going to like this, am I?'

'No, not much.' She smiled, unseen, at his habitual pessimism. 'I had confirmation first thing this morning that Luke Kingsley's death was recorded on our system by a colleague called Karen Dimsdale. I asked Alan if she could join us on the conference call this morning, but she's done a runner.'

'A runner?' At the other end of the line Clive sounded disdainful. 'You mean she's disappeared?'

'Yes. According to Alan she was already on disciplinary for misconduct. She'd been under-performing … arriving late, leaving early, extending her lunch breaks, ignoring customer calls … you name it, she'd tried it. Anyway, she didn't respond to a verbal warning, so Alan began formal disciplinary proceedings last week.'

'How long had she been with us?'

'Less than a year, I think. Alan said she was personable enough, and her work – when she did any – was up to a good standard. But he said there was always something about her that didn't seem quite right. She often behaved as if the job was beneath her, somehow. And she didn't take kindly to authority.'

'And when exactly did she disappear?'

'Yesterday lunchtime. She took her lunch break as usual, and simply didn't come back to the branch. Alan has been very thorough. He spent yesterday afternoon trying to contact her, without much success. When he finally managed to speak to her boyfriend this morning, he learned that she's cleared out. The boyfriend came home last night to find all her belongings gone and her keys on the hall table. But not the rent money she owed him. The boyfriend has called round a couple of her friends, and one of them reckons Karen was flush with cash earlier in the week and boasting about booking a one way ticket to Alicante.'

Clive let out a heartfelt sigh. 'Another failure in our staff screening, by the sound of it. I suppose she took a bribe to load false data on the system to make it look as though Luke Kingsley was dead.' He cleared his throat. 'Have you checked the document imaging system, Rose?'

'Yes. The only document to support the notification of Luke's supposed death was the fake death certificate. There are no documents to support the identity of the informant. The whole thing looks like a set up. There's no evidence to show that Alice Blacklaws was actually involved.'

'And our system permitted the death to be recorded without all the necessary documents?' He clicked his teeth. 'We must clean that up.' He thought for a moment. 'Perhaps we could ask Stacy to look into it?' There was a longer pause. 'On the plus side, I suppose there are no legal implications for us. We can call it an administrative error. False information has been recorded to the ENB's systems, but we can easily rectify that. And if Luke Kingsley has incurred any financial losses as a result of the account closures, we can reimburse those and oil the wheels with a goodwill payment of compensation for the inconvenience.'

'And what about Alice Blacklaws?'

'She can't have incurred a loss due to this, surely?'

'No, not exactly. But Inspector Mulligan insisted yesterday that I provide him with the data we had on the system, and as you'd already told me to give him anything he asked for. I gave him the data. I told him that Alice had been named as the informant. But,' she added, 'I did explain that we needed to verify that, and that the ENB wouldn't be held responsible if he acted and the data was incorrect.'

'Then you had better speak to the Inspector as soon as possible and let him know what's happened. Arrange for him to have everything on Karen Dimsdale as a matter of urgency. I will call HR now and ask them to prepare copies of her employment records for you to hand over to him. And let him have Alan Reeves' number, there may be something Alan can do to help.'

'As you wish.' Rose paused, and thought for a moment, and then she asked 'Clive, are you still OK for me to have a chat with Alice Blacklaws today? I would like to spend a bit of time with her before I head off for home. Just to talk through her options regarding Nathan Kingsley's accounts.

I know it wasn't really our fault that she didn't receive the right information from the start, but I think it would be good customer service to give her some additional advice now.'

'Of course. As far as I'm concerned, Rose, your involvement in this will be over once you've passed Karen Dimsdale's details to George Mulligan. Speak to Alice Blacklaws by all means, but do it on an informal basis and please draw a line under the Kingsley affair after that.' He clicked his teeth again. 'I cannot deny that the sooner we are able to distance the ENB from this whole sorry mess the better I will like it.'

George Mulligan let out an expansive yawn, throwing back his head and casting his eyes up to the ceiling of his office. Out of the corner of his eye he saw Ian Scott watching him through the open doorway, and he pushed himself out of his chair and leaned across his desk to nudge the door shut. The last thing he needed right now was Scottie's remonstrative glances.

He sank back into his seat and swivelled gently to and fro, a comforting movement that usually helped him to think, but this morning both his intuition and his powers of deduction seemed to have abandoned him. He stifled another yawn, the result of last night's uncomfortable stretch of sleepless hours. Physically tired, he had gone to bed at midnight and found his brain still wired with adrenalin, the case teasing and torturing him into the worst kind of insomnia.

At one o'clock he was still staring through the darkness at the bedroom ceiling, worrying about fake death certificates, and Alice Blacklaws, and whether or not he had been right to listen to Scottie's advice to hold off questioning her until the morning. He'd pushed the thoughts to the back of his mind, but the vacant space created there had soon been filled by thoughts of Luke

Kingsley and the ins and outs of match fixing. There was fear there, in Kingsley's eyes, every time that Mulligan looked into them. Fear of something dark, something dangerous, more than a debt, more than a bit of gambling that had got out of hand. The sort of fear that might arise if you put yourself in the way of dangerous and organised criminals.

By three o'clock, and much to Mulligan's dismay, the contagion of his insomnia had spread to the long-suffering Mrs Mulligan, a woman who liked her sleep and was usually happy to take any opportunity to berate him for keeping her awake. On this occasion, though, she had shown an unexpected sympathy and risen to make tea for them both. For yet another hour they had lain awake in the near-darkness, propped up on pillows, sipping on their brew and muttering to each other about the case, and whether or not it was beyond his ageing capabilities.

There was no turning back. Before long what had begun as a conversation about old-school policing and trusting your intuition had developed into a one-sided debate about husbands, and particularly those husbands who didn't have the sense to know when it was time to retire and leave a job to a younger man. Something he hadn't wanted to hear. Perhaps, he wondered, that was why he couldn't bring himself to face Ian Scott this morning. Because even a younger man in a rank below him seemed to have a better grasp of what was going on here than he did himself.

He puffed out a sigh full of resignation and pulled a ballpoint pen from his shirt pocket, and flipping open the notepad on his desk he began to scribble with a broad, untidy hand. We need, he thought, to touch base with Rose about the Saffron Walden episode. And we need to lean on Luke Kingsley to name the beggars who are threatening him. He put the pen to his lips and chewed thoughtfully on the end. And if I'm not going to surrender this case, he thought, I need to know more about football matches and gambling.

He dropped the pen onto his desk and picked up the receiver of his desk phone, and jabbed at the keypad with a mischievous finger. Outside his office door he heard a phone begin to ring, and then Ian Scott's irritated Welsh lilt echoed in his ear from both the phone's earpiece and through the flimsy office door.

'For heaven's sake, George, I'm only outside the door. Couldn't you just come outside to speak to me?'

Mulligan grinned to himself. 'If I came out to talk to you I might have to look contrite, and then people would see. What good would that do for my image as a hard-nosed bastard?'

Scott ignored the question and ventured one of his own, his tone reproachful. 'Have you called Rose yet?'

'No. I was going to ask you to do it.'

There was a pause and then a click on the line as Ian Scott hung up, followed by the squeak of a hinge as he pushed open the door of Mulligan's office. 'You've got a nerve.'

'She'll speak to you.'

'She wasn't damn well speaking to me last night. You knew I was planning to ask her out for supper, but it didn't stop you from poking her in the eye, did it?'

'That sounds to me like cold feet, Scottie. Did you bottle it?'

'I didn't get the chance to ask her. After you pushed her into naming Alice Blacklaws she made herself scarce.'

Mulligan forced his face into a sheepish smile. 'So now I'm giving you an official excuse to give her a call and see if she can meet you for lunch. Ask her if she's found the missing documents that confirm Alice Blacklaws reported Luke Kingsley's death to the ENB, and then offer to take her to Umberto's by way of thanks.'

'Umberto's? On my salary?' Ian Scott thought for a moment. 'Supposing I do follow up with Rose, what will you be doing while I'm smoothing over your troubled waters?'

'I'm going over to Market Melbourne for a chat with Benny Bradman about match fixing. And then this afternoon, we're going to pay a visit to Luke Kingsley and talk to him about what it's like to take a bribe.'

'So you don't believe it was Nathan who agreed to throw the game?'

'No Scottie, I don't. I think Nathan knew about it, and I think he was threatened. But I don't believe he was responsible.' Mulligan folded his arms across his chest and scowled. 'I've dropped the ball on this one. We're going to have to hustle today for any chance of getting it back on track.'

Scott shook his head and leaned against the door frame. 'You're being too hard on yourself, George. This isn't your average provincial case, is it? We're both out of our depth here. But I think we can pull it back. When I've spoken to Rose I'll make a start on Luke and Nathan Kingsley's mobile phone records. I'll see if I can dig anything up before we see Luke Kingsley this afternoon.'

'Thanks Scottie. I owe you one.' Some of the pressure lifting, Mulligan felt his good humour slowly beginning to return. 'I'm sorry if I spoiled your plans yesterday. When you speak to Rose, tell her I'm sorry I lost my temper.'

Ian Scott raised an eyebrow. 'I think that's better coming from you, George. Rose deserves something better than a second hand apology.'

Mulligan watched as the detective sergeant turned away and drifted out of the office doorway, and waited for him to be out of earshot before mumbling his reply under his breath. 'And she deserves something better than a sandwich and a packet of crisps for lunch, Scottie. I hope you're not going to be too disappointed if she passes you over for a better offer.'

19

Luke eased himself down onto the sofa, lowering himself into its soft, velvet cushions as gently as he could. Soft or not, it would make no difference. The bruises from the beating he had taken last night were still tender this morning, the flesh around his abdomen still inflamed from punch after punch, the muscles of his right thigh still burning from the impact of one too many kicks while he was down.

'I thought you were coming to see me last night.' Alice perched on the edge of an armchair at the other side of the coffee table. She looked different today, fresh-faced somehow, scrubbed of the make-up and false nails and synthetic glamour that were expected of Nathan Kingsley's fiancée. She was wearing faded jeans and a blue t-shirt that clung to her slim, gently-curving frame. Stripped of the false glamour, she was beautiful in her authenticity, and now he was under no illusion just what it was that Nathan saw in her. She was *real*.

He lowered his eyes, momentarily afraid to look at her. 'I was beaten up, Alice. Last night, in the car park under my apartment.' He waited for her to respond, to make some sort of exclamation or expression of sympathy, but it didn't come. 'I've been hiding out in the flat all night.' He lifted his eyes to look at her face. She was regarding him with an inscrutable half-smile, not unkindly but rather disbelieving, as she might look at a child who had come up with one implausible story too many. 'I know what you're thinking.'

'Do you?'

He nodded, and pushed himself to his feet. 'You think I'm lying.' He tugged at the side of his shirt, pulling the cotton fabric up out of the waistband of his trousers. 'Does this look like a lie?' He lifted the fabric to reveal dark purple welts across his abdomen, and turned a little to the left so that she could see the unmistakable outline of a steel-toed boot where it had come into contact with his bare skin. 'You have to help me now, Alice. I took this beating for Nathan. You have to help me, if you don't they're going to kill me.' He let go of his shirt, and sank back onto the sofa. 'I can't believe that you didn't even try to transfer that money to me yesterday. Don't you care what happens to me?'

Alice frowned. 'Of course I care. And I'm so sorry they did this to you, Luke. But I don't believe you.'

'Believe me?'

'Oh, I believe that you were beaten up. And I believe that your life is at risk. But I don't believe that it's Nathan's fault. I think it's your fault, but I don't think you're strong enough to admit it. And now that Nathan isn't here to look after you, you need someone else to rescue you.' Her frown became a smile. 'But we all have a different opinion of what it means to rescue someone. You think I'm going to rescue you by giving you the money to pay off whoever bribed you to fix that match. But I'm not.'

'So you won't help me?'

'I didn't say that. Of course I'm going to help you. But I'm not going to give you the money to hand over to the people who are hounding you.' She stood up and rounded the coffee table, and sank down onto the sofa next to him, her slight frame perched at an angle so that she could look at him as she spoke. 'I'm going to help you to confess to Inspector Mulligan.'

He drew back, and looked at her through disbelieving

eyes. 'You're mad.'

'I'm going to help you to confess to Inspector Mulligan, so that you can clear Nathan's name. I won't have you telling everyone that this is Nathan's fault. Because it isn't.'

'You can't possibly know that.'

'Of course I can. Because I knew Nathan. And he would never have done anything so dishonest. He loved the team, and he loved the game. And he was an honest man.'

The game was over, then. Luke leaned forward again and rested his elbows on his knees, lowering his head into his hands. 'You'll get us all killed. They won't stop at me, you know. They'll kill me, and then they'll come after you. They won't stop until they've got their money. What about Olivia? Don't you care what happens to her?'

'Of course I care. Which is another reason why you have to tell the police. Tell them who bribed you, who murdered Nathan, and who gave you a beating.'

'They were waiting for me in the car park last night. I can't tell the police. I can't take another beating like that.'

'And you won't have to.' She stretched out a hand and rested it gently on his thigh. 'We're going to tell Inspector Mulligan that it was you, not Nathan, who took the bribe. And then you're going to tell him who bribed you. And when it's all over …'

'It's over now.'

'And when it's all over, I will sell the house, liquidate Nathan's estate, and I'll give you half of everything. To start again. A new life. An honest life. With me as your sister. I'll take Nathan's place, Luke, and I'll be there for you.'

'Don't you understand? Even if I tell Inspector Mulligan, they'll take me down with them. Do you think I'm just going to walk away from this? Don't you understand that whatever happens I'm facing a prison sentence anyway? If you give me the money now, today, I can pay them off and go abroad.'

Alice gave a gentle shake of the head. 'It stops now, Luke.' Her eyes were fixed on his face, her stare burning into his cheek. 'If you don't speak to Inspector Mulligan, then I will. I'll tell him that you took the bribe, that you've been beaten up, and that you're trying to extort money out of me to pay off your debts.'

'You wouldn't.'

'I'm not angry at you for blaming Nathan, Luke. I know that you don't have his strength or courage to do the right thing. But it stops *now*.'

'I can't.'

'Then start with me. Tell me who these people are, and exactly what happened. And then we'll talk again about how to make it stop. You're going to have to trust me like you trusted Nathan. You have no one else. There is no other way.'

Luke lifted his head and turned to look into her face. She was still calm, serene almost, a placid smile playing around her lips. He didn't know that anything so delicate could prove to be so strong. 'I owed them money.' The sound of his own voice surprised him, but he seemed suddenly incapable of silence. 'I owed them a lot of money. I'd gambled with them, and I didn't know when to stop.' He lowered his eyes again. 'They came up with a suggestion that I could do something for them, something that would wipe out my debts and leave me with more money on top. And I needed it. So I thought, why not? Nobody needed to know what happened.'

'They wanted you to fix the game.'

He nodded. 'But I didn't realise at first that I couldn't do it alone. And when I told Nathan what I'd done, what I'd agreed to do, he wouldn't help me.'

'And so they killed him.'

'They tried to screw the money out of him too, but he wouldn't pay them.' Luke swallowed back a sob. 'They killed him before the wedding so that I would inherit, so that I would have the means to pay them back using Nathan's money.'

'Who were these people, Luke?'

'I can't tell you.'

'You can. Who were these people?'

He turned his gaze back to her. 'It's no use, Alice. They're coming for us now. I had a text this morning. They want their money today. If I can't persuade you to sign everything over to me, they're going to come here. To the house.'

'I don't believe you.'

'If we go to the bank now it might not be too late. If I can show them that you've started to transfer the cash to me …'

Alice shook her head. 'It's not going to happen, Luke. And I'm not going to let you frighten me. You can run, if you have to. But I'm not going anywhere.'

'Well this is an unexpected pleasure, George. Two trips out to Market Melbourne in one week?' Benny Bradman eyed the policeman with a broad grin. 'Come to ask me about match fixin'?'

They were in the office above Bradman's betting shop, seated either side of Benny's large mahogany desk. Mulligan, his elbows resting on the polished wood, was trying not to look too weary. 'I was awake at four o'clock this morning, thinking about it. I'm out of my depth here, Benny. And I don't mind admitting it.'

'Nah, you probably just need a holiday. Anyway, this ain't your every-day provincial crime, is it? And it ain't just on your patch.'

'Now how did you know that?'

Benny tapped the side of his nose with a finger. 'All will become clear, George.' He chuckled to himself. 'Have you got time to watch the critical points of that Kirkby match again? There's somethin' I think you need to see. I've got the recordin' set up. Just bevel your chair around, and take a look at that screen.' He pointed to the wall behind Mulligan, where the widescreen TV was crackling into action. 'Now if we suppose that Luke was bribed to throw the last game of the season, he's got to have been feelin' a bit anxious by the time that game rolled around. There are only so many ways you can throw a game, and the stronger your team is playin', the harder it's going to be. I think Luke underestimated his team's enthusiasm for the idea of promotion. Mid-way through the season Kirkby weren't playin' that well. But they got a second wind after a couple of easy wins, and by the time of that last critical match promotion was lookin' like a certainty.'

'So the odds were stacked against him?'

'It looks like it. He could play badly, but one player draggin' his heels ain't goin' to swing the result if the rest of the team are playin' their socks off. He could score an own goal, but again it might not be enough. Foulin' another player, gettin' himself booked, all the usual tricks weren't necessarily goin' to guarantee the game would go to the opposition. But if he could get Nathan to play along with him, now that's a different matter altogether. Two of them playin' badly, well that might have possibilities.' He pointed at the television screen. 'Now watch this.'

He flicked the remote control at the screen. 'Look how Luke is pleadin' with Nathan about somethin' and Nathan is refusin'. Suppose he's askin' Nathan to help him to throw the game. Nathan doesn't want to know. He's a clean player, and he wants promotion for his team. It means a lot to him, to the supporters, even to the town in terms of commercial opportunity. There's a lot more ridin' on this game than his brother's gamblin' debts.'

He flicked at the remote control again, fast forwarding the recording, and then flicked yet again to start the replay. 'Now watch this, George. They argue, the ref comes over. Nathan backs off. And look at Luke. He's lookin' up at someone in the crowd, and he's petrified.' Benny paused the recording and zoomed up the image on the screen. 'Look at his face.' He rolled the recording further on. 'Now look at this, this is when Luke was taken off the pitch. He's beside himself, just look at him. They're barely twenty minutes into the game. And he's bein' taken off.'

At the other side of the desk George Mulligan was beginning to catch up. 'So you think he's distraught because if they take him off the pitch he loses the opportunity to throw the match. He wasn't trying to stop Nathan, was he? He was trying to get Nathan to work with him.'

'That's what I think.' Benny flicked off the recording and tossed the remote control onto the desk. 'And if you want a bit more to back that up, you can have this lot with my very best compliments.' He pulled a set of papers from a tray at the edge of the desk and pushed them towards Mulligan. 'I have a contact in the data industry, a specialist who monitors gamblin' data to help the industry identify where rigged bettin' is takin' place. Those documents are as good as evidence that there was a fix goin' on around that Kirkby game, and that the fix originated in Essex.'

'Essex?'

Benny's grin broadened. 'The beautiful county of my birth, George. I won't baffle you with science, but my contact reckons there were bets placed on Kirkby to lose in a number of locations in Essex.'

Mulligan frowned. 'That's not evidence. Surely the whole point of gambling is that it's a game of chance? People are apt to bet both ways, aren't they? Am I supposed to be surprised that a bunch of southerners bet against a northern team on its way up?'

Benny leaned forward. 'You're not pickin' up the subtlety there, George. They didn't bet for the other side to win. They bet for Kirkby to lose. That was the wager. Kirkby to lose.'

'Doesn't it amount to the same thing?'

'Not really.' Benny shook his head. 'Look, if someone

comes into my shop and says they want to place a bet on Kirkby to win a game, that's straightforward. If they favour the other side to win, that's straightforward too. But a specific stake on a side to lose? They're not fancyin' the other side to be stronger, George. They're fancyin' Kirkby to be weak, to not last the distance. A serious gambler doesn't just bet on the outcome of a fixture. They're tryin' to show their skill, their flair for predictin' the outcome.'

'Would you accept a bet like that?'

'I might. As a small scale business I can afford to indulge in a bit of fun now and again. You wouldn't believe what people ask me to take bets on. But I don't just agree to it willy nilly, do I? I bring a bit of nous into it. If someone asked me to take a bet on Kirkby to lose, I'd look at the form. I'd look at how they were playin', who was in the team, and I'd have a bloody good think about the odds of them losin'.' He leaned across the desk and fixed Mulligan with an earnest stare. 'If someone had asked me to take a punt on Kirkby to lose that Saturday, I wouldn't have touched it with a bargepole.' He sat back again and shook his head. 'Nah, someone knew they were on to lose that match.'

He watched Mulligan's suspicious look, the air of the unconvinced, and laughed. 'Alright then, if you don't want to take my word for it based on the local data, what about this?' He pulled two more sheets of paper from the in-tray and slid them over the desk. 'That's the overseas data. It takes longer to pull together, so I didn't get my hands on it until this mornin'.'

Mulligan ran his eyes over the numbers, but his face remained a blank. 'It's all Greek to me, Benny.'

Benny grinned. 'That's alright, George. I don't mind summarisin' for an old mate. How about you think of puttin' these few words together in a sentence, and see what you come up with? "Eastern Europe", "Kirkby to lose", and "individual stakes of well into five figures"? Is that makin' it any clearer for you?'

It took a moment for the implications of Benny's words to register. 'Overseas punters placing big money on a game rigged in the UK?'

'Don't sound so surprised, mate. It happens all the time.'

Mulligan was serious now. 'But you said there were bets placed in Essex. Does that mean you think the fix was run from there, rather than overseas?'

'It means it's likely. The main fix was for the benefit of the big players overseas, but news like that leaks. There's always some numpty in the gang who thinks he can have a flutter on the side himself, and make a bit of easy cash. That's where the local bets come in.'

'And these "local" bets, as you call them. Were any of those taken around the Saffron Walden area?'

Benny's grin broadened, and he settled back into his seat. 'I thought that would interest you, George. I had dinner with Rose last night. Who would have thought we'd end up talkin' about counterfeit death certificates?'

It was just after one o'clock when Rose left the ENB's head office building and set off walking in the general direction of Haverland Street. The morning had been a difficult one, and the opportunity to spend some time away from her desk was welcome. She paused at the pedestrian crossing that would lead her across the town's ring road and into the old city centre, and lifted her face to feel the warm breeze created by passing traffic, closing her eyes against the sun and savouring the opportunity to be outdoors.

It was a fleeting moment of peace. As the passing traffic slowed she felt a nudge from behind, an impatient shopper with money to spend, and she opened her eyes and stepped forward to be carried along by the general flow of pedestrians. She paused on the opposite pavement to get her bearings. Haverland Street was east of the office, and she turned on her heel and headed right, towards the Georgian end of town.

It was a walk that took her past the now-familiar restaurant of Umberto's, and she felt a twinge of guilt as she passed. Detective Sergeant Scott's visit to the ENB's office that morning had been unexpected, and not necessarily welcome. It had saved her the trouble of walking over to George Mulligan's office to deliver the news of Karen Dimsdale's indiscretion and disappearance, but at the same time it had robbed her of the opportunity to smooth things over with the Inspector. She didn't like the tension that had flared between them yesterday, and she hadn't wanted to leave Kirkby without the opportunity to smooth things over and offer a friendly farewell.

Worse still, Ian Scott's appearance had brought with it another embarrassment, in the shape of an unexpected invitation to lunch. She had tried to make light of the situation, teasing him that Inspector Mulligan had claimed Umberto's was too expensive for the police expense budget to cover. But the joke had fallen flat. Unlike Mulligan's, his invitation was a personal one, and he hadn't been impressed when she declined. She knew that her appointment to visit Alice Blacklaws early that afternoon, however true the fact may be, had sounded like a lame excuse. He had taken the rebuff with his usual display of good humour, but she could see the disappointment in his eyes.

But at least the morning had had its warming moments. A long chat with Stacy over more than one coffee had been a pleasant way to spend a working hour. Rose liked Stacy. There was an honesty about her, about the way that she faced up to her mistakes, that was refreshing. Honesty, willingness to learn, and those astonishing long, glossy legs … little wonder that Clive Barden had earmarked the girl for special treatment. Sometimes, she mused, Clive ran the risk of being his own worst enemy. A pretty face might one day be the undoing of him. He had a weakness for a pretty face looking up to him, especially if it masked a desire to learn and a hint of ambition. Still, she thought, it really was none of her business. The frisson between Clive and Stacy was probably harmless enough, the sort of thing that makes the working day go with more of a bang than a whimper.

Rose was almost at her destination now, the end of a row of Georgian houses coming into view, and she lifted a hand to her eyes to shield them from the sun. She could just make out the name plate affixed to a set of wrought iron railings at the end of the row. Another few minutes and she would be with Alice Blacklaws. She paused at the corner of the street and looked about her. To her left, a steady stream of noisy traffic was ploughing its way towards the town's outer edges. To her right, Haverland Street made a short, discreet cut through to what appeared to be the town's Victorian park. She turned towards the park and began to look for Alice Blacklaws' house. Number Twelve was the last house in the block, on the other side of the road, and Rose turned to step off the pavement to cross to the other side. As she did so, the front door of the house opened and a familiar figure stepped out onto the small run of steps that led down from the house to the pavement, slamming the door angrily behind him.

Luke Kingsley looked unwell. He paused at the top of the steps and swayed, uncertain on his feet, and then slowly eased himself, crab-like, down the steps and onto the pavement. Rose stepped back and turned away, and began to walk briskly towards the park end of the street. She didn't think he had seen her. At the edge of the park she turned to look back towards Number Twelve. Luke was manoeuvring himself awkwardly into a dark blue Jaguar, his hawk-like features flinching with obvious pain. Unsure for a moment, she stepped into the park and stopped at a vacant wooden bench. She rested her bag on the seat and searched for her mobile phone, and finding it quickly she flicked through her list of contacts, only stopping when she reached "M" for Mulligan.

20

Jack Canning pulled the Lexus slowly through the narrow alleyway and turned cautiously through a dilapidated gateway leading to a small private car park. He reversed the car into the only remaining vacant space, next to Hector Campling's Volvo, and turned off the ignition. 'What now?'

Beside him in the passenger seat, Larry pulled a small packet of chewing gum from his pocket and selected a strip, and then set about divesting it of its silver paper without offering a piece to Jack. Jack watched as he put the thin sliver of minty gum into his mouth and began silently to chew. It would never occur to him, Jack thought, to offer a piece to anyone. He knew well enough that what belonged to Larry was for Larry's exclusive use.

Eventually, Larry turned to him. 'There's no rush. We know he's in there.' He nodded towards the rear of the building. 'And it looks like he's with a client.' They had watched Hector Campling through the front windows of his office for almost fifteen minutes, the Lexus secreted down a side-street directly opposite the building. Larry glanced at his watch. 'These solicitors like to earn their keep. My money's on a thirty minute appointment. He won't let the bloke leave until two thirty.'

'Then what?'

'We have a little word with Mr Campling. If Kingsley is telling the truth, and there is a will leaving everything to that girl, it needs burying.'

'How do we know it hasn't already gone to her? Kingsley reckons she knows about it.'

'Just because she knows about it doesn't mean she's got her fingers on it. Kingsley spoke to her this morning. She's refused to hand over the money, but he reckons she still hasn't seen the will. He also reckons that this Campling bloke is sitting on the will, waiting for her to contact him.' Larry lifted his arm and rested his elbow on the door sill. He looked out of the window with a disdainful frown. 'Christ, this place is a dump. Why would anybody want to live around here?'

'Beats me.' Jack gave a shrug. The trouble was, he thought, people *did* live around here. They came here to live, and to work, and to run businesses. And to make a fresh start when their home turf was getting a bit too hot to be comfortable. He cast a sideways glance at Larry, and wondered if his boss really hadn't noticed that Benny Bradman's name was plastered in letters two feet high above the door of a shop diagonally across the road from Hector Campling's office.

The sight of Bradman's name had only added to the anxiety Jack was already feeling. When Larry had called him yesterday morning, sounding him out about a little trip north to deal with Luke Kingsley, the deal had been to drive to Kirkby. To put the screws on Luke Kingsley. To make sure Larry got his money back with the minimum amount of fuss. No one said anything about going to Market Melbourne.

No one said anything about staking out a solicitor's office across the road from the betting shop that employed his son.

He shrugged his neck into the collar of his shirt, as if shrinking in his seat would make him somehow invisible. This was all too painfully close to home now, and the risks of being spotted were making him twitchy. He didn't want Michael to see him, to know what he was doing, to know how he was earning that last wedge of cash that he was planning to leave for Michael and for Lucy after he was gone. And he couldn't risk Larry knowing that Michael was in the neighbourhood, a risk to Larry's plans, a witness who could finger him if their visit to Hector Campling blew somehow out of hand and attracted the attention of the law.

He turned his head and peered out of the car's tinted windows in the direction of the back door of the building. 'Are you sure we can get in through the back?'

Larry frowned. 'Kingsley reckons there's only Campling in there, and a woman who does the typing. I can't imagine she'll be a problem.' The frown morphed into a smile. 'I can't imagine either of them will be a problem, when we've had the chance to impress upon them how serious their predicament is.' He rolled the chewing gum around in his mouth. 'We can slip in through the back. I'll keep her talking, and you can lock the front door from the inside.'

'What happens if Luke Kingsley is wrong, and the will's already been passed on?'

Larry turned to look at Jack with a withering look. 'Then we get him to draft another will leaving everything to Luke, dated later than the original will.' He sniffed his contempt for the legal profession. 'I've heard that this Campling bloke isn't exactly straight, and he has all the details of Nathan Kingsley's estate. It shouldn't be difficult for him to draft a will to order. We can get the copy across to one of our boys, get Nathan Kingsley's signature forged onto it, and forward the final version to Campling. He can confirm it's legit, and that the original will is invalidated.'

'So once the money goes to Luke, he hands it over to you, and we're done?'

'Yup.'

'And what about Luke?'

'I haven't decided yet.' Larry lifted a manicured finger up to his mouth and pulled at a piece of gum stuck between two gold fillings. 'I might have another use for him. And then again, I might not.' He glanced down at his watch. 'It's nearly two thirty, Jack. Let's try the back door.'

Outside the car the afternoon sun was beating down fiercely and they walked briskly, heads down and hands in pockets, to the shabby wooden door at the rear of Hector Campling's office. The door was locked. Larry turned to Jack and muttered his exasperation under his breath. 'Can you force it?'

Jack bent his head and squinted at the lock, and gently pressed against the door with his hand to test the strength of the hinges. 'Not without being heard.'

'Then we'll have to go round the front.'

They moved silently along the back of the building, heads still lowered, and down a small pathway to the front of the block. Without a word they skirted the corner of the building and trotted swiftly up the few steps leading to the front door of Campling's office. Once inside they paused, silent, listening for voices. The air in the hallway was stuffily stale, and eerily silent. Jack turned and closed the door behind them, quietly knocking the lock off its latch. He turned to Larry. 'That should keep any nosy parkers out while you have a chat with Mr Campling.'

'I'm not too worried, Jack. It's not like anyone round here knows us.' Larry turned and looked about him, sizing up the doors leading from the hallway. 'Now, which one shall we start with?'

Behind him Jack felt a sudden surge of nausea in his stomach. Larry hadn't seen Benny Bradman's shop, then. But he was bound to see it on the way out. It wasn't directly across the road, but they would have to turn right to walk back round to the car. There was no way anyone could walk out of Hector Campling's premises, turn right, and miss it. And if Larry knew that Benny Bradman was across the road, he might also guess that someone else from the past was hanging out there with him. Either way, if Larry found out that Jack had failed to point out that someone who knew them very well indeed was barely sixty feet across the road …

He leaned his head towards Larry's ear and made the only move his tiring brain could think of. 'You look for Hector Campling, Larry. I'll find the back door and make sure it's unlocked so we can slip out the back when you've finished.'

Rose balanced the china cup and saucer on her lap and smiled at Alice. 'I can't remember the last time someone served me tea in a bone china cup. It makes such a difference to the taste.'

'Nathan thought it was old fashioned. But it's what I was brought up with.' Alice returned the smile with a wistful curl of the lips. 'Old fashioned china, fish on Friday, roast beef on a Sunday, never let your grass grow longer than next door's.' She blinked, as if dismissing a past she'd tried to forget. 'I was brought up on the Barnfield estate, just along from Vienna and Florence. All of this,' she looked up and around her, her eyes skimming the period furnishings and the room's high, ornate ceiling, 'is so alien to me.'

'But you'll stay, now that it all belongs to you?'

'I doubt it. It doesn't feel the same without Nathan. And I think I prefer a simple life.' So much, Rose thought, was evident in her appearance today. She looked tired, but it didn't mar her genuine, ethereal beauty. Her skin was pallid, her blonde hair swept up into an untidy coil at the back of her head, but her eyes were warm and intelligent, and somehow they were at peace.

'Is there anything else I can tell you about Nathan's accounts? Strictly speaking you will still need to go into the bank and speak to Stacy Singleton. Now that we know you're Nathan's beneficiary, Stacy can give you the official position on everything he held with the ENB.'

'I don't think there's anything, Rose. But it was kind of

you to come.'

'It was Benny's idea, to be honest. He thought you might have some questions, and want to be prepared before the solicitors start pouring over the terms of the will.'

'Benny's been so kind. He's been a good friend.'

'He tells me that you haven't actually seen the will yet.'

'It should be with us today. Richard Fleming – that's Nathan's solicitor – he's busy with another client this morning, but I understand that he's sent a request to Hector Campling for the will to be sent directly to him.' A smile appeared in Alice's eyes and she turned to look out of the French windows, to where Vienna was attending Olivia's latest tea party for Pooh, Tigger and Piglet. 'Vienna says that Hector Campling is a worm of the highest order, and that he could have given the will to Benny yesterday. She says he's keeping his hands on it for as long as he can.'

'He was probably hoping you would engage him to administer the estate.'

'Vienna would have seven fits if I did that. She's never forgiven him for trying to frame Michael for murder.'

'Well I don't suppose anyone could blame her for that.' Rose thought for a moment, and then asked 'what *will* you do, Alice? Now the estate is yours?'

'I'm going to sell the house, and the investment properties. And I'm going to look for a much smaller place for myself and Olivia, somewhere for us to make a real home. A home that can't be taken away from us. We've had too much uncertainty, and too many disappointments.' Alice turned back from the window and stared into her own cup. 'I'll probably look for somewhere near the coast. It would be good for Olivia. And I'm going to give some of the sale proceeds to Luke. It's what Nathan would have wanted.'

'Is it? If that's what Nathan wanted, why did he take steps to put everything in your name?'

'Because I think he wanted me to keep the money safe for Luke. He didn't want it to …' Alice's voice trailed away. She seemed to realise that she was on the verge of saying too much. 'Anyway, Nathan left a pension as well as the cash he transferred to me. Half of the estate is all I need to put a roof over our heads and meet the bills. And I have every intention of going back to work when Olivia is old enough to go to school. I might not be able to pay for a fancy education now, but to be honest, Rose, I don't think I want that for her. I want her to stay amongst friends, amongst her own kind.'

Rose inclined her head, and stared down into her own cup. Nathan Kingsley knew what he was doing when he fell in love with Alice Blacklaws. There was a simple honesty to her ethos, a quiet confidence that – no longer tempted by the glamour of Nathan's way of life – her own chosen way of life was the best. Rose wondered that Alice had ever been tempted by that glamour in the first place. Or perhaps that was just the price that Alice had been prepared to pay to spend her life with Nathan.

So where, Rose wondered, did Luke Kingsley fit into this simple, honest life that Alice was planning for herself and Olivia? Barely thirty minutes ago she had seen him leave the house, his head bowed, his posture contorted and awkward, his features pinched with the misery of some unseen pain. He didn't look to Rose like a man who had just heard he stood to inherit fifty percent of his brother's estate. Or had Rose misread the signals? Was his head bowed not because of some unseen pain, but with the shame of knowing that the woman he had tried to defraud out of her inheritance had just willingly gifted him half of what he'd tried to embezzle?

Whatever the answer, Rose decided, it wasn't any of her business to interfere. Alice was Stacy's problem now. And Luke was Inspector Mulligan's. She lifted her cup from its saucer and sipped back the last dregs of lukewarm tea, and then turned vague yet kindly eyes towards her hostess. 'I'd better be going. I have to pop back to the office and deal with a couple of queries before I head for my train.'

'Oh, please stay for another cup, Rose.' Alice glanced back to the French windows. 'Vienna was hoping to say hello, she'll be so cross with me if I don't keep you here a little longer.' She turned back. 'I'll warn you now, she heard that you had dinner with Benny last night.'

'Did she?'

'She was so pleased about it. He's been so lonely without Catriona.'

Rose narrowed her eyes, and adopted her best inscrutable expression. 'It was only two old friends having a bite to eat, Alice. Nothing to get excited about. And certainly not grounds for match-making.'

'But Vienna thinks you'd be so good for him.'

A faint, enigmatic smile made its way to Rose's lips. 'And so I might be. But that doesn't necessarily mean that he's done anything yet to deserve me.'

Michael Spivey pushed the door of Benny's office open, and leaned against the doorway. Benny looked up, disgruntled at the unexpected disturbance, but something in Michael's face betrayed that this was no ordinary interruption. He watched as Michael approached his desk, his face ashen, his eyes wide, the beat of his pulse visible in the vein throbbing at his temple.

Michael rested his hands on the edge of the desk, and leaned towards him. 'Charlie Oscar Delta Delta.' The words came out in a hoarse whisper.

Benny felt the contents of his stomach somersault. 'I hope this is a joke, Michael. Because I'm really not in the mood for ...'

'I've just seen him.' Michael's eyes were beginning to moisten. He swallowed hard and blinked. 'Going into Hector Campling's office.'

Benny closed his eyes and shook his head. There had been no question in his mind about who was responsible for trying to fix the Kirkby game. No question who was responsible for bribing Luke, for putting the screws on when it all went wrong, for coming up with the fake news boards, and the dodgy death certificate. He'd known yesterday at the first mention of Essex that Larry Codd was going to be at the back of all this. He felt a tear of anger stab at the back of his eyes. He'd known, however hard he'd tried to deny it to himself, that Larry would be the lowlife behind Nathan Kingsley's murder.

Larry Codd.

Larry Codd, with his affected ways, and his lisping speech. He could see him now, effete handshake extended, his head, bird-like, tilted to one side as he spoke. *Larry Codd, Mr Bradman. Codd, as in "Charlie Oscar Delta Delta".* Years of bile began to churn in Benny's stomach. *I hear there was a fire at your Chelmsford premises, Mr Bradman. I do hope no one was hurt?* He could see the girls now, lined up on the pavement outside the burnt out shop, dismay etched on their faces, relieved that no one was hurt, saddened to know that Benny was letting himself be driven out of town.

He thought it was all behind him. Larry Codd responsible for the Kirkby fix, that he could deal with. Even the notion that Larry was responsible for Nathan's death. So long as it was at a distance. But Larry in Market Melbourne? He opened his eyes and turned them onto Michael's face. 'Tell me you're not certain.'

'He was with my Dad.'

He was with Jack Canning? Benny lunged forward and grabbed at Michael's shirt, pulling him down across the desk. 'Is that where you were yesterday? Visitin' Jack?'

'I don't know anyfing about this Benny, I swear.' Beads of perspiration were running down Michael's face, or maybe it was tears. 'My Dad wrote to me. He wrote because he's dying. He said he wanted to see me. I … I had to see him. Vienna agreed with me. If he's dying, I had to …' Michael began to sink under the strain of Benny's grip. 'I didn't know he was still working for Larry. It's not the sort of fing you discuss when somebody's dying.'

Benny was perspiring himself now. He could feel his heart thumping in his chest, the fear of the past catching up with him, the dread of having to move on again. He squeezed his eyes tight shut and shook his head, his fingers still clutching Michael's collar, but when he opened them again, his rage subsiding, he saw only the misery on Michael's face. He relaxed his grip, letting go of the shirt, and slid his hand along to hold Michael gently by the shoulder. 'It's alright, Michael. We'll sort it.' He sucked in a breath. 'What the hell could they be doin' with Hector? Is this about the will?' He glanced down at the photograph of Catriona on his desk, and then looked back at Michael. 'You know what this means, don't you?'

Michael nodded, his face a mask of wretched despair. 'It was my Dad who murdered Nathan.' His mouth was twisted with impotent rage. 'We came up here to get away from all this. You said they wouldn't bother us again.'

'They ain't botherin' us, Michael. It's not us they're after. It's Luke. And Camplin's caught up in it.' Benny pushed himself to his feet. 'We'll have to go round there. Hector's so far out of his depth he'll be drownin' as we speak.'

'Benny, I can't. My Dad … I can't face him. Not like this.'

'Then I'll have to go round there on my own. You stay here and try to get hold of Mulligan. Tell him that Larry and Jack are here. Tell him who they are, and that we don't know when they arrived, but they've been seen in Market Melbourne.'

'You can't go over there, it ain't safe.'

'I know it ain't safe. But if I don't put a stop to Larry Codd, we'll have to move on from Market Melbourne and start over again. Is that what you want Michael? To keep havin' to move on? To give up what you've found here? To leave Vienna behind?'

'What does it matter now? She's going to find out about my Dad anyway.' Michael swayed under the weight of the thought, and placed his hands on the desk to steady himself. 'And when she does, when she finds out who my Dad is and what he's done, she'll pack her bags and she'll leave me.'

21

George Mulligan leaned against the wall with his right shoulder and nodded to Ian Scott. Scott, some eight feet in front of him and leaning against the wall with his left shoulder, nodded back with a smile. From the other side of the wall, the inside of Luke Kingsley's apartment, came the muffled sounds of cupboard doors opening and closing, and drawers being slid open and shut on their runners.

Mulligan pulled a crumpled packet of mints from his pocket, took one, and tossed the packet noiselessly to Scott. 'Mint?'

Scott took one and tossed the packet back. 'Do you think he'll be long?'

'I shouldn't think so. It sounds like he's packing. When Rose called she said it looked as though he was in pain. And he looked angry. It sounds to me like someone's put the screws on, he's tried one more time to force the money out of Alice, and she's refused. He hasn't got many options left now. Face the music, or pack his bags and scarper. I know which one I'd go for if I was in his shoes.'

'Shall we?' Scott jerked his head towards the apartment's front door.

'I suppose we'd better. We don't want to make a scene out here in the hallway.' Mulligan rolled off the wall and hammered on the door with his fist. The muffled noises from the other side of the wall suddenly stopped. Mulligan waited long enough to be sure that Luke had no intention of opening the door, and then bent down and pushed the letterbox flap open with his finger. 'Luke? It's DI Mulligan and DS Scott. We need to talk to you, please. It would be much better if you could just open up and let us in.'

For a moment it seemed as though Luke would ignore the request. And then the silence was broken by the sound of a bolt being slid back. The door opened a few inches and Luke Kingsley's face appeared in the gap. 'I'm busy.'

Mulligan put his hand on the door and pushed gently. 'Let us in, son. We need to speak to you.'

There was a moment's hesitation, and then Luke let go of the door and it swung open under the pressure of George Mulligan's hand. 'It will have to be quick. I'm … I have to … I have to be somewhere. In the next half hour.' Luke sounded vague, anxious. He led them into the lounge and turned to look at them. His face was grey, the hawk-like eyes sunken into their sockets. 'What do you want to talk to me about?'

Mulligan held his gaze. 'We've come to arrest you, Luke.'

The sunken eyes blinked. 'You can't. You have no reason to arrest me.'

'Oh, I think we do. In fact, I think we're spoiled for choice.' Mulligan lifted his hand and counted through his fingers. 'There's match fixing, for a start. Conspiracy to defraud. Withholding evidence. Perverting the course of justice.' The policeman paused and sucked in his cheeks. 'Accessory to murder.' He turned to DS Scott with a jaded look. 'I'm exhausted just thinking about it. Which one shall we go for?' He turned back to Luke. 'Or shall we go for the whole lot?'

Luke was trembling now. 'You can't arrest me now. They're coming for me.'

'Are they?' Mulligan's tone was sounding less sympathetic. 'And who are "they"?'

'It doesn't matter. I just … I have to get away.'

'Luke, son, you've tried my patience to the limit these last few days. And I'm telling you now, you're not going anywhere until you've answered my questions. I know all about the match-fixing. Oh, not the nitty gritty detail. There'll be plenty of time for you to tell me about that later. But I know that you were involved in the attempt to fix Kirkby's last game. And I know that Nathan wouldn't help you.' Mulligan paused, and thought for a moment. He didn't have any hard evidence yet to back any of this up, but it sounded plausible and so far Luke wasn't objecting to it. 'Stop me if you have anything to add to the story.'

Mulligan moved towards an armchair and perched down on the arm. 'I think you took a bribe to fix Kirkby's last game of the season and prevent them from getting a promotion. But I think you soon realised that it wasn't going to be as easy as you thought. And so you tried to get Nathan to help you. But Nathan wasn't on the same page, was he? Nathan wanted to play a fair game, he wasn't interested in your grubby little scheme. That's why you argued on the pitch, isn't it?'

Luke didn't answer. He turned his face away and lowered his eyes, and the redness of a guilty blush began to seep across his sallow cheeks.

'The people you took the bribe from, they had too much riding on that game to let it go, didn't they? You failed to throw the match, and they wanted their money back. And not just the bribe, they wanted their stake money back on top. And you didn't have it.' Mulligan narrowed his eyes. 'Did you set Nathan up, Luke? Did you arrange for the contract killing? Did you think that if Nathan wouldn't give you the money to pay them off, the only other way you could get it was to have him wiped out so that you could inherit? Wiped out before he married Alice, before she became his legal beneficiary?'

'It wasn't like that.' Luke's voice was low, almost inaudible.

'Wasn't it? Then how was it? I've heard that there's a will, a proper, valid will that leaves everything to Alice. That messed up your plans, didn't it? Is that why you've been leaning on her, trying to persuade her to hand over the money?'

'She doesn't care about me. She could have helped me now, helped me to pay them off, get them off my back. I told her they would kill me if they didn't get their money back. Even then she wouldn't help me.'

Mulligan stood up, his face solemn now. 'You disgust me. You know who murdered your own brother, and you've done nothing since the day he died but cover your own tracks and snivel about yourself. You wanted him dead, didn't you, Luke? You wanted him dead and out of the way so that you could inherit his money, pay off your persecutors, and save your own miserable, scrawny neck. Did you tell them where they could find him? Was it your idea for the hit to take place at the hotel? On the way to the wedding? Was that your final piece of revenge on Alice for taking him away from you?'

'You think I arranged for Nathan to be murdered? You think I could do that to my own brother?' Luke was animated now, breathing heavily, his eyes wide with self-righteous indignation. 'Nathan was everything to me. Everything.'

'Then help me nail his killer, Luke. Tell me what really happened. If Nathan really was everything to you, then for God's sake tell us now who murdered him.'

Hector Campling was slumped against the skirting board behind his desk. A dark, purple bruise was beginning to spread across the curve of his right cheek, and blood from his nose had left a tell-tale trail of drips between the buttons of his blue polyester shirt. He peered up from behind the desk and regarded Benny through stoical eyes. 'You're right, Bradman. I am out of my depth.' His right hand was clutching a large cotton handkerchief, and he dabbed at his nostrils, and then examined the spots of blood across the white fabric with a look of mild consternation.

'Look on the bright side, Hector. At least you're still alive.' Benny skirted the desk and put out a hand, offering to pull the solicitor to his feet.

Campling shook his head. 'I'm fine here for the moment.' His expression became wary. 'I take it you're acquainted with Mr Codd?'

'You could put it like that.'

Campling nodded to himself. 'My father always said there were unpleasant things lurking in your past. Did you run with that pack?'

'No. I left Essex to get away from them. Gettin' involved with Larry Codd was never on my agenda.' Benny reached behind him and dragged the visitor's chair away from the front of Campling's desk. He settled it next to the solicitor against the wall and sat down. 'Have you called the police?'

'Mr Codd informed me that if I call the police, he will ask his associate to come back and "finish the job". I'm assuming by "the job" he means me. It's not a chance I want to take.' He looked up at Benny. 'As far as I'm concerned, they were never here.'

'They murdered Nathan, Hector. Don't you want them brought to justice?'

The solicitor sneered. 'An unfounded accusation without evidence to substantiate it.' He turned his eyes towards the doorway of his office, and the tall, steely blonde now standing framed within it. 'Ah Linda, is that my coffee? Just on the desk, please.'

The blonde hardly seemed to register that her employer was sitting on the floor nursing his injuries. She placed the coffee gently within his reach and turned on her heel without a word, barely acknowledging Benny with a dismissive glance. Benny smiled at her back as she left the room. 'And what about Linda? Will she deny they were here?'

'Linda,' Campling smiled, 'didn't see or hear anything

either.' He pointed to a bookcase behind Benny. 'Would you mind, Bradman? There's a bottle of cognac on the middle shelf.'

Benny leaned over and retrieved the bottle, and watched as Campling poured a generous amount into his coffee, and drank deeply from the mug. 'I take it they wanted the will?'

'They did. Along with assurances that the will hadn't been seen by anyone other than myself and Luke Kingsley.'

'And has it?'

'Not yet, no. I still haven't heard from Richard Fleming. You, of course, know that the will exists and that it's in Alice Blacklaws' favour, as does Miss Blacklaws herself. In fact, I'm sure many people know by now. But "knowing" and "seeing evidence of" are not the same thing, Bradman. Without the physical document it just becomes hearsay, and I would argue as much if questioned on the point.'

'Did you give them the original will?'

'Of course I did. How else do you think I persuaded them to leave?' Campling drank again from his mug and then cast his eyes back to the doorway, distracted by the appearance of another visitor. 'Ah Michael, can we help you?'

Benny turned to look at Michael, and found him peering nervously around the doorframe. 'Hector's alright. He's had a visit from some old friends of ours. But he's not in bad shape, all things considered.' He turned back to Campling. 'Did it occur to you that they're probably on their way now to find Luke Kingsley?' He pulled his mobile phone from his pocket and began to dial George Mulligan's number.

Campling scowled into his coffee. 'If you're dialling the police, Bradman, I will deny everything that happened today.'

Benny pressed the phone to his ear, and frowned as he

heard the call divert straight to George Mulligan's voicemail. He cancelled the call and pushed the phone back into his pocket. 'If Luke Kingsley dies today, it will be on your conscience.'

'Perhaps. Perhaps not.' Campling swirled the coffee dregs around in the bottom of the mug, and drank them down. 'I think their primary concern at the moment is the recovery of their losses. They're not going to get that by murdering Luke Kingsley, are they? If they can suppress the will, then Luke will inherit. There are ways of making sure that he does. It wouldn't take much to draw up a second fraudulent will to supersede the one in favour of Alice Blacklaws. Of course, they will have to persuade her to return the house in Haverland Street to Nathan's estate. And the cash that was settled on her. No,' he shook his head, 'they're not on their way to see Luke Kingsley. Quite another person, I should have thought.'

'Another person?' For a moment Benny looked perplexed, and then the penny dropped. 'Oh, you're kiddin' me?' He turned to Michael. 'We've got to get to Haverland Street. Now.' He pushed himself up from the chair and strode over to Michael, and began to push him out of the office door.

But Michael wasn't ready to leave. He wriggled free of Benny's grasp and turned to look again at Hector Campling. 'Did Larry Codd do that to you, Mr Campling?'

Campling snorted a quiet laugh. 'Of course not. Mr Codd doesn't seem the type to get his own hands dirty. He had a trained monkey with him, a nasty, weasely-looking little devil with shifty eyes and a Roman nose.' He stared into his empty mug thoughtfully, and then started with some realisation, and lifted his eyes to look questioningly at Michael.

Michael opened his mouth to say something, thought better of it, and turned to follow Benny out of the room. Out in the hallway Benny began to chuckle to himself. 'Look on the bright side, Michael. Jack might not have done much for you over the years, but now that he's given Hector Camplin' a pastin' at least you'll be able to look back and say he settled one score for you before he checked out.'

Rose walked over to the French windows, and looked out into the garden. Vienna and Olivia were at the far side of the lawn, and from where Rose stood it appeared that Pooh, Tigger and Piglet's afternoon tea party was very much in full swing. It seemed a shame to spoil the proceedings, but Alice had insisted that Rose should wait until Vienna had returned to the house to say her farewells. It seemed a shame, too, that Alice had decided to give up this house, with its understated elegance and its beautiful, floriferous garden. The scene outside was making Rose feel wistful and for a moment, lost in her thoughts, she became distracted. She didn't hear the doorbell ring, nor did she hear Alice answer the door and usher two unexpected visitors into the lounge.

'Rose?' There was uncertainty in Alice's voice. 'These gentlemen have come to see me about Luke.'

Rose started, and turned her attention back to the room. Alice was hovering by the sofa, flanked by a short, dapper man in a sharply-cut suit and an unpleasant, sullen-looking individual in flannel trousers and a dark grey shirt. She looked uneasy, her eyes signalling caution. Rose beamed her best vacuous smile. 'Nice to meet you both.' To Alice, she said 'I'd better be on my way and leave you to it. Let me know if there's anything else I can do to help.' She tried to sound casual.

Before Alice could reply, the dapper man stepped forward and flashed a smile full of expensive porcelain and gold fillings. 'There's no need to rush off on our account, Rose. Please, won't you join us?' He pointed towards an arm chair. 'Alice might be grateful to have a friend with her while we have our little chat.' The subtext of his speech wasn't difficult for Rose to interpret. She wasn't going anywhere.

She lowered herself into the armchair, her expression still vacant, and turned her eyes to the man standing at his side. He looked surly, thin and wiry with a greying stubble of hair, and there was something vaguely familiar about him which she couldn't quite place. She nodded to him with a smile. He didn't smile back. She watched as he slid his hand into his trouser pocket and left it there, and couldn't help wondering what was in the pocket. Perhaps, she thought, it might be best not to think too much about it.

Alice, standing by the fireplace now, was beginning to regain some of her composure. She turned to the dapper man and motioned towards the Chesterfield sofa. 'Won't you sit down?'

He grinned and lowered himself onto the seat. 'Thank you.' He pointed to his accomplice. 'Don't worry about my friend here, he's quite happy to stand.'

Alice sank sideways onto the sofa beside him, and studied his face. 'Are you a friend of Luke's?'

He bowed his head. 'You could say that. You see, Alice – you don't mind if I call you Alice? – Luke and I have been engaged in a little business venture, but regrettably he's let me down very badly.' His voice was surprisingly effete, with the hint of a lisp. 'We've come up to Kirkby to have a word with him, and remind him of his business obligations, if you like. He owes us money, quite a lot of money as it happens. And we don't take kindly to being let down.'

'Are you the people who've been threatening him?' It was a simple, direct question, and it took all four of them, even Alice herself, by surprise.

The dapper man looked irritated. 'Did he tell you that he'd been threatened?'

'Yes. He told me that he'd taken a bribe to fix Kirkby's last game, but he couldn't manage it alone, and Nathan wouldn't help him. He told me that the person who bribed him, the person who wanted his money back, murdered Nathan because he wouldn't pay off Luke's debts.'

The man pursed his lips and took in a sharp breath, and then his cheeks relaxed and he gave a sinister smile. 'You're telling the story very badly, Alice. Nathan had the opportunity to pay back what his brother owed, and he chose not to. So we had to make sure that Luke inherited Nathan's money. That's why he had to die before he married you.' He made it sound like an everyday occurrence. 'Of course, Nathan spoiled that little plan by making a will leaving everything to you.'

'Luke didn't tell me your name.'

'You don't need to know my name, Alice.'

'Are you admitting that you murdered Nathan?' Alice's voice had dropped to a whisper.

'Of course not. Do I look like a murderer?' He smiled to himself. 'You know, Luke and Nathan were joined at the hip, Alice. Or at least they were until you and your little poppet came alone. We hoped that Luke would inherit everything, and I have to tell you that as things stand, he will. You see, Nathan made a second will leaving everything to Luke.' He leaned closer to Alice until his face was almost touching hers. 'He disinherited you, Alice. He left a will leaving his whole estate to Luke.'

'I don't believe you.' She sounded calm. 'But it doesn't really matter. Because Nathan gave most of his estate to me before he died.'

'Ah yes, indeed he did. And that's exactly why we're here. To appeal to your better nature.' He turned his head and broadened his smile to include Rose, and she returned it with an enigmatic one of her own. He looked suddenly a little uncertain. He turned back to Alice, and when he spoke again his tone was brusque. 'Luke needs that money, the money that Nathan gave to you. And he needs this house. So we've come to appeal to you on his behalf. To persuade you to hand it over to him.'

'And if I don't?'

He pursed his lips and tilted his head to one side, and then heaved himself up from the sofa and walked across to the French windows. 'Is that your little girl out there, Alice, your Olivia? She's a pretty little thing, isn't she?'

'Olivia is my daughter. She's nothing to do with Nathan.'

He was smiling to himself again, an inane crease of the mouth that made him look slightly unhinged. He lifted his right hand and rapped loudly on the window. 'I think your other friend out there has seen me, Alice.' He crooked his index finger and beckoned through the glass. 'Oops, yes, there we go. She's bringing the little girl in with her.' He turned back to Alice with an affected frown. 'I do hope I haven't startled her.' He gestured to his accomplice to open the lounge door. 'Let the lady in, will you? She may as well join in with our little chat.'

The tension in the room was palpable now, and Rose could sense that danger was coming ever nearer. She had been watching the dapper man quietly, thinking about her last conversation with Benny, wondering about the man's lisp, his style of dress, his general affectations. She had a suspicion she knew who he was. And a need to let someone know that he was here, that they were trapped in the house with him. She knew that any attempt to retrieve her mobile phone from the handbag down beside her chair was likely to meet with opposition, any effort to alert the outside world to their situation was going to increase the danger. But there had to be some way of throwing this intruder off his game, some way of distracting him from his purpose, if only to buy more time. There was one thing she could try, but it was risky, acting only on a hunch. Then again, it was probably a bigger risk not to try.

She licked her lips to moisten them, and coughed to clear her throat. And then in a low, discreet voice she said 'forgive me, I know this Luke business is nothing to do with me. But is your name Larry Codd?'

Larry turned the full force of his gaze towards her, and for a fleeting moment he looked like a cornered animal. And then he hissed at her with undisguised venom. 'What did you say?'

'Larry Codd. Codd, as in *Charlie Oscar Delta Delta*.'

Her words were met with a deafening silence, and then an ominous click which seemed to come from the surly man's trouser pocket. No doubt now, then, that there was something more menacing in that pocket than a wallet and a mobile phone. Larry took a slow and single step towards her, but as he did so the young woman he had summoned from the garden walked into the lounge. She was balancing Olivia on her hip, and her face was drawn with consternation at the sight of strangers in the house. She glanced at Alice, and saw apprehension in her eyes, and then turned to look at Rose. 'Is everything alright?'

Rose gave a reassuring nod, and when she spoke her voice was as calm as she could make it. 'This is Larry Codd, Vienna. He's a friend of Luke's and he's come to speak to Alice about the will.'

Larry's face was contorting now, and pointing at Rose he turned to his accomplice. 'Keep this one quiet, will you?'

But Jack Canning was no longer listening to him. He was staring at Vienna with a look of unmistakable dismay, and she had turned to look at him, and was staring back with total, absolute bewilderment.

22

Michael gripped the steering wheel, his arms and shoulders rigid, his face frozen with concentration as he sped Benny's Mercedes along the Market Melbourne bypass in the direction of Kirkby. Beside him in the passenger seat Benny, ashen-faced, was repeatedly dialling Rose Bennett's number.

'She's not answering.' Benny jabbed at the recall button one last time. 'Or else she's got the damn thing on silent again. What the hell is the point of having a mobile phone if you keep puttin' the damn thing on silent?' Exasperation was getting the better of him.

'She might have left already, Boss. Alice and Vienna might be on their own.' Michael didn't want to think about what that might mean. He didn't really mean "on their own". He meant "with Larry and Jack". And with no one there to protect them.

'I'll try George Mulligan again.' Benny flicked his fingers at the phone's keypad, but there was no answer from Mulligan either. 'I'll have to send a text.'

'Jesus, Benny, why can't you just call 999?' Michael was becoming agitated now. 'If Larry's gone for Alice, and he's taken my Dad with him …'

'I know. I know what you're thinkin'. But they won't hurt Alice. It wouldn't pay them to. Alice has the money, and they can't access it if she's dead, can they?'

'Dead? No. But they can hurt her. They can hurt little

Olivia, or Rose. Or …' he couldn't bring himself to say 'they can hurt Vienna.' He glanced at Benny again. 'Call 999.'

'I can't do that Michael. You know what Larry is like, and you know what Jack is like. If I call 999 they'll send uniformed officers. If Jack and Larry are still at the house, there'll be a stand-off. Do you want another death on Jack's conscience?'

'My Dad ain't got a conscience.'

'What was his state of mind like, Michael? Yesterday, when you saw him?'

'State of mind?'

'Was he rational?'

'He was never rational.'

'Is he still capable? Of killing?'

Michael banged his fist on the steering wheel. 'Jesus, Benny, how the hell am I supposed to answer that? I ain't seen the bloke for twenty years, I hardly recognised him. He's dying. You only have to look at him.' He pursed his lips. They both knew that he didn't really need to answer the question. As long as Jack Canning had the ability to hold a gun in his hand, he would be capable of killing. But Michael couldn't say that to Benny. 'I know he ain't scared of dying. Maybe that makes him even more dangerous. If he ain't scared of dying, then he's got nuffing to lose, has he?'

They travelled several miles in uncomfortable silence, fields and villages and passing traffic whizzing past them, the world at large going about its business, oblivious to the looming crisis in Haverland Street, impervious to the possible consequences. Eventually Michael asked a question that had been troubling him for some time. 'Do you care about Rose, Boss?'

Benny winced, and turned his head away to look out of the window.

'She wouldn't mind.' Michael wasn't minded to let it go. 'Mrs Bradman, I mean. She'd like Rose. And she wouldn't want you to be on your own.'

Benny turned and scowled at him. 'What the hell does it have to do with you?'

Michael shook his head, determined to have his say. 'You've done a lot for me, Boss. But you're always telling me what to do. You never want to know what I have to say.' He gave a deprecating sniff. 'Vienna means everyfing to me. I never knew what that meant, to have someone care about you like that.' He cast a knowing glance at Benny. 'If you like Rose, you ought to tell her.'

Benny growled under his breath. 'Keep your nose out, Michael.'

'She's alright, Rose. She's done right by me and Vienna when we needed her. And by Alice.'

'Drop it.'

A strained silence hung between them for another mile and a half, and then Michael opened his mouth to speak again, but seeing Benny's forbidding expression out of the corner of his eye, he thought better of it.

Benny, sensing there was more to come, turned to him with a bark. 'What? What is it now?'

'Nuffing.' Michael shook his head. 'Only … if my Dad's laid a finger on just one of those girls, I swear to God, Benny, I'm gonna kill him myself.'

Jack Canning was gazing at Vienna Fielding, his face blank. Somewhere to the right of him Larry Codd was shouting instructions. He turned his head. 'What? What are you talking about?'

Larry blew out an exasperated sigh and pointed at Olivia, the child safely cradled in Vienna's arms. 'We'll take the kid. Maybe then Miss Blacklaws,' he turned to Alice with a sneer, 'will understand that we mean business.'

Jack followed his gaze and looked at Alice with reluctant eyes. She was looking back at him, but she wasn't afraid. Her composure made him feel uncomfortable. She knows, he thought, that I murdered the man she was going to marry. But she isn't afraid of me. He turned his head further and looked at the other girl, the smart-looking redhead that Larry wanted him to keep quiet. She was smiling at him vacantly, taking it all in, saying nothing. She wasn't afraid either.

He pulled his eyes back to Alice and held her gaze. 'I'm sorry for your loss.'

There was a moment's silence, and then Larry's face contorted into a snarl. 'Pull yourself together, Jack. And keep your mouth shut.'

'Did one of you murder Nathan?' Vienna's voice, when she spoke, was so low that Jack could hardly hear her. He wanted to look at her, but he was afraid to. She was so pretty, just like the photograph Michael had sent to him. That lovely creature, with her raven black curls and her dark, intelligent eyes ... that girl, he thought, cares for Michael. She cares for my son. And if she's recognised me, she knows now that Michael is the son of a murderer. He opened his mouth to speak, but no sound would come out.

He could feel her eyes upon him now, questioning, searching for an answer she didn't really want to hear. Despite his illness, despite the distance between himself and his son, he knew there was a resemblance, a likeness in their height, their build, their posture, the height of the forehead, the angle of the nose. It was something that couldn't be hidden.

Somewhere beside him Larry had begun to speak again. '*I* have never murdered anyone.' He looked meaningfully at Jack. 'What the hell is the matter with you? Take the kid, and let's get out of here.'

Jack heard the words, but he wasn't really listening. He was thinking, thinking about Alice, and Nathan, thinking about Michael, and about Vienna, and suddenly about Lucy. This could have been Lucy standing here. This could have been Lucy facing the man who murdered her lover.

Worse still, this could have been Lucy facing the murderer who fathered her lover. He would do anything to protect Lucy. Just as Michael would do anything to protect Vienna. Just as Nathan had tried to protect Alice.

He felt a sharp, intense stab behind his eyes, and he flinched with the intensity of the pain. They'd told him that it would get worse towards the end. It might not be long now. He looked again at Larry. There were going to be consequences. There had to be consequences. Whatever he did, it was too late to save Lucy from the fallout, to protect her from what was to come. He could only do what he had to do.

Larry was beginning to lose patience now, and Jack watched as he stepped forward towards Vienna. She instinctively moved backwards, Olivia still cradled in her arms. 'You're not taking her.' Jack straightened, and pulled the small revolver from his pocket and looked at it, and then he turned to Larry with a smile.

Fury lit up Larry's face. 'Put that bloody thing away,' he hissed. 'I told you to keep it out of sight. We don't need it. Not yet.'

But Jack still wasn't listening. He turned again to Alice, the gun resting gently in his hand. 'I'm sorry for what I did.' He was mumbling now, his voice low and indistinct. 'But it stops now. I promise you that this is the end.'

'What the hell are you talking about?' Larry was pointing at him with a furious finger. 'It's not the end until I get my money.'

Jack shook his head. 'It's the end now, Larry. It stops here. For these girls, for me, and even for you.' And, he thinks, for Lucy. He stepped forward towards Vienna. 'Look at me.' It was a simple appeal. 'You know who I am. You can give the girl to me.'

Vienna took another step backwards. 'I can't.'

'You can.' He gave a gentle nod of the head. 'I promise you, *on my son's life*, that she'll be safe with me.'

'Vienna, no ...' There was sudden panic in Alice's

voice.

'It's OK, Alice. It's going to be OK.' Vienna nodded gently back to Jack, and he knew that she had understood. She whispered to Olivia. 'Go to Jack, sweetheart. It's OK. He won't hurt you.'

Olivia hesitated, and then held out her arms to him, and he slipped his free arm around her waist and balanced the warm, delicate body for a moment on his hip. A moment he never thought he would see. A child holding on to him for safety. He smiled at Vienna, and then turned and smiled at Alice.

Beside him, Larry had begun to shout. 'About bloody time. Now let's get out of here before the kid starts screaming.'

But Jack wasn't interested in what Larry had to say. He crossed the room until he was face to face with Alice, and then he gently leaned forward and delivered Olivia safely into her mother's arms. Alice, bemused, slowly took the child from him, and he nodded to her. 'Thank you for letting me hold her.'

'Have you completely lost it?' Larry was gibbering now, his face contorted with a vicious rage. 'I swear by all that's holy, Jack, you'll be sorry for this. You're ruining everything. This wasn't the plan.'

'It might not be your plan,' Jack said quietly, 'but maybe your plan wasn't the best way. Maybe there's a much better way for this whole, damn mess to be dealt with.' He looked down at the gun resting gently in his hand, and then lifted it up and pointed it directly at Larry's chest.

23

Rose wrapped her hands around the brandy glass and tried to hold it steady. The twitching in her muscles was involuntary, though whether it stemmed from the fear of captivity or the relief of liberation she still hadn't managed to work out. Benny had pulled his chair closer and was looking into her face with a quiet concern.

She managed a weak smile. 'I think I've missed my train.'

'I wouldn't bother tryin' to claim compensation. I don't think they have a refund policy for "delayed by a gun-totin' psychopath".' He picked up the brandy bottle and topped up her glass. 'Did you really front him out?'

'Who, Larry? No, of course not. I recognised him, from the story you told me last night. And it rattled him when he realised that someone knew his name. But I was just trying to play for time. If anything, it was Alice who stood up to him. And Vienna.' She laughed. 'He couldn't cope with all three of us. He must have thought it was an audition for Macbeth. The three witches of Haverland Street.' They were sitting at the table in Alice's dining room, a quiet retreat away from the commotion that filled the rest of the house. 'Is Mr Mulligan here?'

'He's on his way. They arrested Luke this afternoon. He finally squealed and told them about Larry and Jack.' He jerked his head towards the door. 'There's a house full of uniforms out there. Anna Hill's with Alice and Olivia. Michael's looking after Vienna.'

Rose lifted troubled eyes to look at him. 'Jack Canning.

Is he really Michael's father?'

Benny pouted. 'He is. But that ain't Michael's fault.'

'Poor Michael.'

'Oh, he'll be alright. He's got Vienna.'

'It was Jack who saved us, Benny. He turned ... I don't know. He turned sort of odd, and he turned the gun on Larry.'

'Jack's dyin', Rose. Michael only found out this week.'

'Perhaps his own mortality helped him to find his conscience.'

'Maybe.' Benny stretched out a hand to the brandy bottle and topped up his own glass. 'Well, now you know everythin' about us, Rose. Everythin' there is to know about me and Michael. Not just why we left Essex, but what drove us out. And you haven't just heard about it, you've seen it for yourself.'

'Will you stay in Market Melbourne now?'

'I hope so. It depends what happens when they finally track Larry down. He doesn't work alone. And stickin' him in prison for a stretch won't stop him. He's got too many puppets on the outside.' He swigged on the brandy. 'I'm more worried about Michael and Vienna. They need a break, and I thought I had the answer. A mate of mine has a nice little business, just on the main road as you're headin' in to Scarborough. He's sellin' up and he's given me first refusal. I thought I might put Michael in to manage it, start to build the business up again.' He looked uncertain. 'But this stunt of Larry's ... I don't know, Rose. I don't want to go back to the days of lookin' over my shoulder, worryin' about my people.'

'You don't like difficult decisions, do you?'

'Not really.' He gave a self-deprecating laugh. 'It's funny, ain't it? I don't usually find the big decisions difficult. It's the small things that keep me awake at night.'

Rose smiled into her brandy. 'Any small thing in particular?'

'You know that Lu comes back from Naples the day

after tomorrow.'

'And that small, white, four-legged thing that's been keeping you company for a few days has got to pack his blanket and his squeaky bone, and go back home to where he belongs?' She turned to him with a sympathetic smile. 'Where is Mac now? Please tell me you haven't brought him with you.'

'Nah, I left him at the shop. You know what he's like when he turns nasty. I couldn't take the risk of him savagin' Jack Cannin'. It wouldn't have been fair on Jack. I told Sal to keep an eye on him. She'll have taken him home for his tea.' He heaved a sigh. 'I'm goin' to miss him, Rose.' He gave a self-pitying sniff. 'Do you think he'll miss me, when Lu takes him back?'

Rose leaned back in her seat and swirled the brandy around in her glass. 'There does seem to be a fundamental point that you're missing here. You seem to be forgetting that the decision might not be down to you or to Lu. The way you're talking, anyone would think that Mac wasn't capable of barking for himself.'

The phone was ringing with a persistence that couldn't be ignored. George Mulligan stretched out a hand and grasped for the bedside clock. It was twenty minutes past two. He fumbled in the dark for the phone, and snatched it up to his ear. 'Mulligan.' He hissed into the mouthpiece, anxious not to disturb Mrs Mulligan, and keen to avoid another lecture.

Ian Scott's voice at the other end of the line was sombre. 'They've found them, George. In a lay-by off the Great North Road.'

'Alive?'

'Both dead. It looks as though Jack Canning shot Larry Codd and then turned the gun on himself.'

'Is the car there?'

'As I understand it. And the gun.'

'Has anyone spoken to Michael Spivey?'

'Not yet.' There was hesitation in Scott's voice. 'Jack Canning left a note. He pinned it to his shirt to keep it secure.'

'A note for Michael Spivey?'

'No. We don't know what to make of it. It's a note for someone called Lucy ...'

ABOUT THE AUTHOR

Mariah Kingdom was born in Hull and grew up in the East Riding of Yorkshire. After taking a degree in History at Edinburgh University, she wandered into a career in information technology and business change, and worked for almost thirty years as a consultant in the British retail and banking sectors.

She began writing crime fiction during the banking crisis of 2008, drawing on past experience to create Rose Bennett, a private investigator engaged by a fictional British bank.

Death Duties is the third Rose Bennett Mystery.

www.mariahkingdom.co.uk

Printed in Great Britain
by Amazon

12294686R00150